HOLDING OUT

RETURNING HOME BOOK 4

SERENA BELL

JMG
JELSBA
MEDIA
GROUP

For Romancelandia and its generous denizens,
especially Rachel Grant.

1

Torture.

The universe clearly had it out for Griff Ambrose. A room full of beautiful women, all of whom were completely off limits. And, as if it weren't bad enough to be the only bachelor at a dinner party with his happily attached friends, Becca Drake had just walked in. She wasn't dating anyone as far as Griff knew, but she was a firm no-go all the same.

Their hostess, Alia, jumped up from the dining room table to greet her sister with a big hug. "Becca! What the hell are you doing here? I thought you had a date tonight."

Becca waved a hand airily. "Didn't happen. And then I saw on Facebook that you guys were doing Indian tonight, so I booked it down here."

"You drove almost five hours to have Indian?"

"I drove almost five hours to see some of my favorite people in the world," Becca corrected.

Griff's other friends leapt in, telling Becca how glad they were to see her, and how she had to have some of the *amazing* chicken. Becca greeted them all with smiles and big hugs, but she wasn't fooling Griff with the "no biggie" hand wave or the claim that she'd made the drive just to see them. She was bummed about the date that had fallen through. What was that all about?

Becca was twenty-four and had been single for as long as Griff had known her, which made no sense, because *reasons*.

Guys should be falling all over themselves to date her. She was tall with pale blond hair, big blue eyes, and a sweet, wide smile. Also, she had big, perky tits, a curvy ass, and a Betty Boop–tiny waist. Despite the screaming sexiness of the package, she gave off a young, fresh, innocent vibe that slayed him.

Of course, that was also the reason he wouldn't touch her with a ten-foot pole. He had a weakness for that type, and he knew from past, painful experience where that road led. Not that he ever planned to venture into serious relationship territory again, but if he did, it would be with someone well-seasoned.

Besides, Becca was Alia's little sister, and Alia was married to Griff's best friend. Nate and Alia were extra protective of Becca because she'd been hurt badly before.

If that wasn't a flashing neon warning sign, he didn't know what was.

As the greetings concluded, everyone returned to the dinner table. Griff had stood up when everyone else did—it would have been rude not to—but he hadn't rushed in for the hug. For, well, *reasons*.

"Hey, Griff. Good to see you."

"You, too, Bex."

As they embraced, Griff kept himself at a respectful

distance and did his best to ignore the softness of her breasts and the way her hair smelled.

Nate dragged an extra chair into the dining room and set a plate and silverware in front of Becca.

"Hit me," Becca said, extending her plate.

Alia filled Becca's plate to heaping with chicken tikka masala and rice. That was something else Griff appreciated about Becca: her willingness to eat. *Eat*-eat, not just a few nibbles here and there like she didn't need food to sustain her.

"A beer wouldn't go to waste, either," Becca said, eyeing Griff's with enough lust that he wrapped his fingers around his glass protectively. That made Becca laugh.

Nate went to the kitchen and came back with a frosted mug, which he set in front of Becca. She took a good slug, then licked her lips. A tiny speck of foam remained on her upper lip, and Griff contemplated all the ways he'd like to remove it.

Clearly, if he was paying this much attention to a woman he'd already crossed off the list, he needed to get his head in a different place. It had definitely been a while since he'd gotten laid—shit, a couple of months, maybe?—which was probably why he was such a horndog tonight. He would drive into town after everyone else went to bed, spend a couple of hours drinking and flirting, and blow off some steam afterward.

For now, though, he intended to get every last drop of pleasure out of the meal in front of him. He considered himself a simple man. Give him a plate full of home-cooked food, a decent beer, and plenty of good friends and conversation, and he'd call an evening a success.

"More bread?" Alia asked. She had her infant son, Robbie, neatly bound to her front in one of those cotton knit wrap things, and she cupped his head as she leaned over to pass Griff the basket.

"Hell yes." Griff took another piece of the tender, buttery flatbread. So damn good.

"You guys ever think about opening a restaurant?"

That was Jake, Griff and Nate's good friend who ran the veterans' retreat where they all worked.

"And quit working for you? No way," Alia said, laughing.

Her words were light, but Griff knew she meant it: Jake was a great boss, and they all had a shit-ton of respect for him. He and his wife, Mira, were regulars at Friday Night Dinner, a tradition that Nate and Alia had started after Robbie was born to make sure they still saw their friends regularly. Babies—Griff was learning from observation—fucked up your social life.

The baby in question cried out and squirmed under Alia's wrap. "Uh-oh," she said, touching her lips to his fuzzy head. "You were supposed to sleep till dinner was done."

Griff eyed the fussy lump on Alia's chest. He was Robbie's number one fan, and not at all ashamed to admit it. "I could take Robbie," he offered, reaching his arms out. He loved holding the kid, with his warm heaviness and clean baby scent—except when Robbie had one of those not-so-fresh moments. Then Griff was more than happy to return him to his parents.

Alia began unwrapping the baby from her chest. "I think I need to feed him first or he's not going to be a whole lot of fun."

"I could hold him till you finish eating?"

She laughed at the eagerness in Griff's voice. "Are you sure you want to be a bachelor?" Untangling Robbie, she handed him to Griff. Robbie's fat face was creased with lines from Alia's shirt. He looked up at Griff, then broke out beaming.

"Well, hello to you, too, little dude. You and me, bro. We're the last single guys on the planet." He lifted Robbie up so their faces were level. "Batching it with Uncle Griff," he told the baby, who gave him another big, open-mouthed smile, then farted. Griff grinned. "That's right, that's how it's done, Robbie boy. What are you *doing*?" he demanded of Alia, who was photographing him.

"I'm taking a picture of you and Robbie in case you want it for your online dating profile."

"I don't have an online dating profile," Griff said. He preferred the old-school techniques. Buy a girl a drink. Make a lot of eye contact. Say the right things.

Tell her up front you don't do relationships.

One thing that had surprised him was how many women were just fine and dandy with that. Maybe even preferred it that way. That had been a pleasant revelation after his marriage had ended.

Every once in a while, though, you could see the disappointment on a woman's face, and that was the best reason to steer *wide* clear.

"Well. If you ever decide to, you would clean up with this profile pic." Alia held out her phone.

Griff winced. "God! Do I really look that goofy?"

"You look like a happy uncle," Becca said, taking the phone from her sister and studying the picture.

"That's right. I'm happy. As an uncle. No need for the rest

of it."

Alia and Mira exchanged an eye roll.

"Speaking of dating, I've been meaning to ask you—" began Mira.

Griff eyed Mira suspiciously. He was pretty sure he knew where this was going. His female friends were determined to matchmake.

"I have a friend—"

Alia broke in. "It's hopeless, Mir. He's not fixable." She shot Griff an apologetic glance. "I didn't mean that the way it sounded."

He shrugged. It took more than that to hurt his feelings. "I didn't take it that way. And I'm not opposed to being fixed up, it just never works out."

Alia gave him a sharp look. "Because you dump anyone who starts to get serious."

He shrugged. "Guilty as charged."

The truth was, he hadn't met anyone he wanted to get serious with. Not since Marina. And he really, really didn't want to think about Marina right now.

Or ever.

Alia took the last few bites of her dinner, then reached for Robbie. "I'll feed him—oh, for Christ's sake, Griff, I'm going to give him back! You are *so* full of it. You are *so* daddy material."

"Nope."

Once upon a time, he'd thought he was daddy material. It was just that a lot of shit had gone down since then.

He handed Robbie back to Alia, ignoring the ache of that particular memory. That was the good thing about other people's babies. You could return them when you were done.

"Hey, you guys," Becca said. "What do you say we clean up and play a game of Taboo? My roommate Jenina and I have been playing it with our friends in Seattle and it's super fun. I brought my set."

Griff raised an eyebrow. "Taboo?" he leered.

Becca gave him a look. "Not like *that*. You pick a word and then try to get your teammate to say it, but there are lots of 'taboo' words you can't say. Like—for 'Easter,' Jenina did, 'when an oversized long-eared rodent puts oval baby-makers in woven bowls.' Because she couldn't say 'holiday' or 'bunny' or 'egg.'"

"Wow," said Griff. "I'm going to *suck* at that game." He cast a glance in Becca's direction.

Her lips curved. "Sorry it's not dirty. Guess that would be more up your alley, huh?"

A flash of heat knocked into him. The half-smile, maybe. Or the tease she'd packed into the question. Or just the word, *dirty*, on her full lips. For whatever reason, it caught him off guard. Becca wasn't supposed to be able to get that reaction out of him. Becca was—well, she was just *Becca*.

But there she was, giving him a quizzical look, like he'd held her gaze too long, so he turned away and shook it off.

"I think it sounds like a blast," Mira said, and jumped up to clear the table. They all chipped in, and when the kitchen was mostly clean, Becca brought out the game. She pulled out cards, two card holders, and a buzzer.

She looked around the table. "Um, Griff, you'll be my teammate, I guess?"

They were the only non-couple in the room. He shrugged. "Sure."

"Jake, you go first. Griff, you can buzz for them," Becca instructed.

He took the pink and purple buzzer from her. "What do I do?"

"You stand behind Jake, and if he says any of the words on the card, you hit the buzzer."

Griff jammed the buzzer threateningly up against Jake's neck like he was the thug in a stickup.

Jake took a card from the deck. "Um, so, um, this is when you make a really super big deal out of something in order to get all the potential buyers or fans excited about it ahead of time."

"Advertising."

"More general, and bigger," Jake said.

"Billboard. TV commercial."

"No, *more* general. Not just that first thing you said, but it could be on social media, like if a movie's coming out and everyone's super jazzed up about it . . ."

"Star Wars," Mira hazarded.

"No, like any movie, not a specific movie, and if you do too much of this then everyone's expectations are way up and people get super disappointed and say it was 'over—'"

Mira clapped. "Hyped!"

"Ding, ding, ding!" Jake said, pulling another card. "This is a thing that you put in your mouth . . . it's oval-shaped and really small and you swallow it to kill the things growing in your body that you don't want—"

"Antibiotic!" cried Mira, just as time ran out.

On Nate and Alia's turn, Alia sailed through *jingle, fortune cookie, Rollerblade,* and *gremlin.*

"We're going to get *clobbered,*" Griff told Becca.

She shook her head. "Have some faith, Griff. I had trouble reading all the way through school. You get really good at slinging the BS when you take all your tests orally."

Heh. Heh. She said orally.

Grow up, Griff.

She pulled a card. "This is something you eat."

Dirty Taboo would be a really fun game, Griff thought suddenly, and then had trouble putting the idea away so he could concentrate on what Becca was saying.

"It's a miniature of something that you would have at a party . . . you can put twelve of them in one baking tin."

"Cupcake."

"Yes!" Becca said, grinning like mad. It was a lot like having Robbie beam at him—he instantly felt like a champ. It wasn't like he'd never seen her smile, but it was different to be on the receiving end. Like stepping into the sun out of shadow. She had a great smile—straight white teeth brilliant in contrast to her red lips.

She pulled another card. "You ride in this on the water to get from one place to another, and you can put a car in it, on the bottom deck—"

"Ferry," Griff said, stupidly pleased with himself and rewarded with another Becca smile.

"All green growing things start out as one of these—"

"Seed."

They were on a roll. He was totally tuned in to her. He grinned at her, not consciously trying to eke another smile out of her, but getting one anyway.

"This is a baby version of the thing that gives us beef."

"Calf."

"No, the baby version of the actual beef. Animal rights

activists hate this—"

"Veal."

"Yup. Okay, um, let's see . . . this is the opposite of rigid, it's like—"

Her face got pink.

"—when something is, um, just hanging down instead of being stiff."

Griff's mind had veered way off track, as had, apparently, Becca's. Which was . . .

Fucking hot.

She peeked up from the card and caught him staring at her, probably open-mouthed, and the flush in her cheeks deepened. And—

Damn. His *something* was not so much hanging down any more. More . . . well, not quite *stiff,* not quite *yet,* but well on its way.

"Time!" Jake cried.

Griff's jeans were too tight.

"What was the word?"

"Floppy," Jake announced, waggling his eyebrows.

Griff snuck another look at Becca. She was biting her lower lip. White tooth, plump red flesh.

Not. At. All. Floppy.

Mira grabbed a card, and the game sailed on. Thankfully.

But he couldn't help himself; he chanced another look at Becca.

She returned his glance. Raised an eyebrow. And *smirked.*

Well, fuck.

It was good that he had a solid plan to de-frustrate himself after this dinner, otherwise he'd be tempted to initiate some taboo of his own.

2

"So, what happened to your date?" Alia asked Becca, hanging the dishcloth over the oven handle.

They had just finished the end-of-evening straightening up—putting the last of the dishes away, wiping down the counters, washing out the sink. Mira and Jake had gone home, and Griff was making a beer run. He said it was poor form to leave your hosts beer-less after such a great evening, and since he'd been responsible for a good quarter of the beer consumed, it was his God-given duty to remedy the situation. Nate stayed behind to put Robbie down.

"Whatever. The guy was just an asshole." Becca pulled out the stool from the kitchen island and sat. Alia took a seat next to her.

Becca knew if she told her sister the story, she'd end up feeling sorry for herself, and New Becca didn't feel sorry for herself. New Becca was brave and bold and believed in herself. New Becca went after what she wanted and if someone else didn't like it, that someone could fuck himself. She had watched her sister come out of her shell, and it had inspired Becca to do the same. She was still a work in progress, but she was proud of how far she'd come.

"*Becca.*"

Unfortunately, Alia was the best bullshit detector—or at least the best detector of Becca's specific brand of bullshit— on earth. There was really no getting around it. Becca sighed. "We were sexting before the date we were supposed to have tonight. He said some stuff—"

"What kind of stuff?" Alia demanded, sisterly antennae obviously on high alert.

"Rough-ish stuff he wanted to do to me. Not *bad* rough, just..."

"Not first-timer stuff." Alia sighed. She obviously could feel the punchline coming.

Becca shook her head. "Not first-timer stuff. So, I figured I'd better tell him. And he said he didn't do virgins."

"He—he said *what*?"

Alia might have been surprised, shocked even, but Becca hadn't been. Not at all. She shook her head. "There are two categories of guys—the ones who are falling all over themselves to pop my cherry because it's some kind of virgin fetish thing or they think I'll be extra tight or whatever, and the ones who can't put enough distance between themselves and me because of the stupid myth that no woman can ever get over her first time."

It was Alia's turn to shake her head. "There are guys who aren't like that."

Becca raised her eyebrows. "Really? You should introduce me to them, because I can't figure out where they live."

Alia snaked an arm around her sister's shoulders and squeezed. "You've just had a run of super bad luck with men."

That was true for sure. So many jerks and losers, bad blind dates, non-starters, and all-around assholes who'd said hurtful things without a second thought. Not to mention the awkward situation with Nate before he and Alia had gotten together, which was now just a humorous footnote. But none of that had hurt like what Todd had done.

Probably nothing ever would hurt like what Todd had done.

"You know what, hon? Those guys don't deserve your virginity."

That made Becca smile. "Well, I'm not sure it's such a cherry on top at this point, but I like the way you think."

Upstairs, they could hear Nate singing Robbie a lullaby. Nate was a great guy, even if he could get a little too into the big brother role at times. She was so damn happy for her sister. Now, if only she could find someone like Nate for herself.

She had a flashback to the ovary-busting sight of Griff grinning stupidly at Robbie. She was half tempted to ask Alia if she could have that photo, just to take it out and look at it on shitty days. But that would probably be a bad idea. She had a half-crush on Griff already, and he was a terrible choice for her. He didn't even try to hide the fact that he was a player and a commitment-phobe. She couldn't guess which of the two categories he'd fall into—virgin fetishist or run-screaming-in-the-other-direction—but either way, she wasn't going to find out.

"Did you ever read Mom's ratty old copy of *Valley of Horses*?"

Becca's mouth fell open. All these years, she'd thought she was the only Drake sister to have discovered the dog-eared book—which had originally been their grandmother's —and read it by flashlight in a closet. Even though she'd been what teachers referred to as a reluctant reader, she'd devoured every page of that big, fat saga with wide-eyed delight (and damp panties).

"Oh my *God*. I *loved* that book. Jondalar and his mighty wang. It was like a magic wand, devirginizing women everywhere. First Rites of Pleasure. You're right! That's exactly what I need. I need my own personal Jondalar."

Alia laughed. "Totally. Do they have guys like him anymore?"

"Yeah, they call them escorts. And don't think I haven't considered that."

Alia's eyes got big. "You wouldn't actually *do* anything like that, would you?"

She sounded genuinely concerned, which made Becca roll her eyes internally. Her sister had so little faith in her judgment. "No, of course not! No hiring people to take my virginity. As tempting as it is." She bit her lip. "Somehow, I don't think the reality would match my fantasy of Jondalar laying me down on a bed of furs."

"Nothing's *that* good," Alia said, a faraway look in her eyes.

They observed a reverent moment of silence, remembering Jondalar's skill. Or Becca did, anyway. She suspected that Alia's mind had roamed elsewhere, probably to Nate.

The front door opened, and Griff came into the kitchen, brown bag in hand. "Hello, ladies," he said, *Princess Bride*–style.

"Hello, Fezzik," Becca said.

"You got my reference," he said, pleased.

"It's my favorite movie."

"Who's your favorite character?"

"Inigo Montoya," she said without hesitation.

"Good answer." He grinned at her.

Maybe because she'd written him off as a sexual partner, Griff was one of those guys who she found attractive but not intimidating. He had rumpled brown hair and gray eyes, and a kick-ass body that rocked his usual uniform of T-shirt and battered jeans. He came across calm. Steady. Easygoing.

Although she thought she'd caught something else in his eyes right after the Taboo blushing fiasco. Something she would have called predatory.

It had made heat flush all over her body.

She was still feeling self-conscious about falling apart over the word floppy. She *hated* how easily she blushed. And unfortunately, even New Becca couldn't control that reaction.

She peeked in Griff's direction, but his attention was on the paper bag in his hands. He pulled out a six pack of beer and opened the fridge.

"You want this in here in the cardboard? Or I can put the bottles in individually."

"Either way." Alia shrugged. "I seriously cannot bring myself to care about shit like that since Robbie was born. Thanks for getting more beer, though. That's something I can firmly stand behind."

He loaded the six pack into the fridge and closed the door. "I should head out. This was really fun." He hugged Alia. "Thanks for loaning me Robbie."

"You big softie." She turned to Becca. "Wasn't that the cutest stinkin' thing?"

"It was pretty damn cute," Becca said, figuring if she

owned it, it wouldn't seem like she was crushing on him.

"Yeah. So. I'm outta here," Griff said, grinning. He hesitated, and there was an awkward moment when Becca wasn't sure if he was going to hug her or not. Then he said, "Hug it out, sister," and drew her into his arms.

It was a different kind of hug than the awkward A-frame one he'd greeted her with. He felt *ah-mazing*. Like no kidding. He was head-to-toe muscle, not a soft spot on this guy. Also, he smelled *good*. Like . . . she tried to figure it out. Something musky. Something leathery. Something piney. Had some deodorant manufacturer actually managed to cram every appealing male scent into one stick that dispensed *Griff*?

She realized she was still hugging him and stepped back.

"Yeah. Um. Bye, guys," he said.

She watched him go, thinking, *That is a guy who can make going look as good as coming.* Those jeans were the universe's gift to women everywhere.

Too bad Griff didn't offer a First Rites of Pleasure service.

An idea formed itself in the back of her mind, and then she squashed it dead, dead, dead. The door shut behind him, sealing out the dangerous notion.

Alia leaned on the counter.

"How's the job search coming?"

"It's coming."

The salon where Becca worked was closing soon, and she had been on the hunt for a new gig. She tried not to talk to Alia about stuff like that too much, though, because Alia got way up in her business about it.

"If you need help with anything—"

Aaand, here she goes.

"I could read your cover letters? Proof your resumes?"

"Jenina's great with that," Becca said, referring to her roommate, who worked in marketing.

"If you need help with choosing clothes for intervie—"

"I can choose my own clothes," Becca said tightly.

Alia looked unconvinced. "Just make sure you don't wear anything too revealing, right?"

"A-*li*-a," Becca said.

"Sorry. Sorry! You know I worry."

"Have a little faith in me."

"I do. You know I do. And you know I love you like crazy." She pulled Becca into a hug.

Becca hugged back, hard, but she wasn't so sure about the rest. About Alia having faith in her. Alia had done more to support her than anyone else in the world, but she'd also known Becca at her worst, seen her struggle and flail and fall apart more than anyone else ever had. She was pretty sure that in Alia's eyes, Becca was still closer to twelve years old than twenty-four.

"Hey."

Alia's expression was serious, and Becca wondered if she, too, had been thinking about their childhood.

"Robbie and I drove to Portland and saw Mom on Tuesday."

That would be a yes.

"She looked good. She said her medications were still making her really tired—"

"Li—"

"Okay," Alia said. "I'll shut up. But—she asked about you. She'd love to see you, you know."

Becca shook her head.

"I guess it's just nice to see her doing better, and it's

helpful for me to, I don't know, start fresh with her. I thought maybe if you saw her now, some of your anger—"

"I'm not mad at her. None of it was her fault—she couldn't help being sick. I just don't want to put myself in a position to be—" Becca stopped.

Alia's eyes were sympathetic. "Hurt. Disappointed."

"Exactly. Can we not talk about this?"

Alia sighed. "I just think—"

Becca raised an eyebrow. "You said you'd shut up."

That made Alia smile. "I did, didn't I?" She gave Becca another hug, then leaned heavily on the kitchen counter. "God, I'm so stinking tired. I feel like that kid is sucking my life force out of me. Bex, you're sleeping on the pull-out. I'll help you make it up."

"Is everything in the linen closet? I'll take care of it myself."

Alia gave her a grateful look. "Oh my God, would you? I swear when you get pregnant and have a baby, I will wait on you hand and foot."

"Ha!" Becca said. "I would like to see that."

Alia went upstairs, her footsteps heavy.

"First," Becca said aloud, "I would need to have sex."

She sighed.

She got the bedding and stepped into the dark living room, colliding with someone. A short, terrified shriek escaped her. The someone felt like a wall of muscle and smelled of *Griff*, and he grabbed her arms to steady her.

"Sorry," he said. "I left my phone on the kitchen island."

"Oh, it's you." Her heart was pounding, two-thirds from being scared into an early grave, and one-third from the effects of Griff up-close-and-personal.

He was still holding onto her arms. His hands were warm. And strong. She obeyed an impulse that came from nowhere. "I was just going to watch *The Princess Bride* before bed. You want to stay and watch with me?"

"What, like now?" He let go of her arms and stepped back.

Damn, she thought. The offer had just popped out, but he wasn't into it, which made her—weird and pathetic?

He tilted his head and looked at her curiously. Not like he thought she was weird and pathetic. More like . . . like he'd never quite seen her before, but she was coming into focus. It was a nice feeling.

He shrugged. "I mean, I don't have anywhere to be. If you aren't too tired."

"Nah." She shrugged. "I'm wired to the gills, to be honest."

A little bubble of excitement, which had no right to be there at all, formed in her chest. Probably better to pop that sucker before it exploded in her face. She shouldn't have made the *Princess Bride* overture, but now that she had, she should definitely keep two feet of couch space between them, send him home, and go to sleep.

That would happen anyway, because she and Griff had known each other for two years and if he'd had the *slightest* interest in making a move on her, he would have done it ages ago. Instead, he'd always treated her like Alia's little sister, and she was sure that her PG movie selection was going to firmly root her in that territory.

Even so, the dangerous, NC-17 idea she'd had earlier raised its snaky little head and hissed enticingly at her.

Shut up, she told it.

But it didn't.

3

The woman on the couch next to him smelled so good it was *killing* him. Some girly scent like vanilla. He didn't think it was fair that women used food scents on their bodies. It made him think about licking them even when he knew better.

And he definitely knew better than to lick Becca, even if she did smell like a cupcake. The thought made him remember their winning streak in Taboo and he smiled.

His other problem was that she was just far enough away that they weren't touching, but close enough that he could feel her warmth, which meant the skin all down the side of his arm was lit up with awareness. And not just his arm, if he was being honest. Pretty much his whole body.

He had no idea how this had happened. How watching *The Princess Bride* had somehow morphed into a sexual minefield.

He'd been on his way to get laid. He had a plan. Buy himself a drink. Survey the bar. Buy the prettiest girl there a drink, or two. Ask her about herself. Listen. Tell her how beautiful she was. Ask if she wanted to go somewhere else. And so on.

Instead he was watching Inigo Montoya cross swords with the six-fingered man and thinking about a little swordplay of his own.

He told himself that as soon as the credits rolled, he was going to jump to his feet and get the hell out of there.

But then the credits rolled, and he didn't move. Becca got up, turned on a lamp, and sat down a little farther from him on the couch. It was theoretically a safe distance. It did stop the buzz that had been leaping between her skin and his, but now he could see her, and she was extra pretty in the low light.

And he still didn't get up. Instead, he sought around for small talk.

"Hey. You still working at that salon place?"

"Yeah. Well, sort of. Julia's Salon and Day Spa."

"Sort of?" He raised an eyebrow.

"The building got bought and they raised the rent. The owner can't afford to stay there, so she's going to close that business and semi-retire to Bainbridge Island, open a smaller salon there. So—" She sighed. "I've got to find a new job."

"Will you stay in Seattle?" Alia always talked about how much she wished Becca would move closer. She said she worried about her living and working on her own way up there—that Becca would forget to pay rent or get in some kind of trouble. The way Alia talked about Becca made her out to be, well, *dumb* was the wrong word, but maybe *flaky*, and since Griff knew Becca only a little, from family get-togethers over the last couple of years, he'd never questioned that impression. But now that he was paying attention, she seemed pretty damn competent. "How come you don't live closer to Alia and Nate? In Portland or something?"

"We all needed a little space."

"Oh, yeah, right." He always forgot that there was a story there. Becca and Nate had dated before he and Alia got together.

"No, not that," Becca said, reading his mind. "We're all over that. Nate and I were never anything except a bad idea. But Alia was like my mom growing up, and I didn't want her to feel like she had to keep taking care of me. For both our sakes, I wanted to be on my own for a while."

"And that's been good?"

"It's been great," Becca said. She pushed her beer mug away from her on the coffee table.

"So, what kind of job are you trying to get?"

She shrugged. "Just another reception desk job. There are plenty of salons, and there's a lot of turnover. Me being in this position for two years was crazy long."

That was a pretty long time—more evidence that whatever Becca was, she wasn't flaky. She was dependable and responsible, loyal even. "Do you like it?"

She shrugged again. "It's fine."

"Just fine?"

"Yeah. I mean, it's a good job for a high school grad, pays decently, consistent daytime hours, I get treated pretty well." She hesitated.

"What?"

"It's just—sometimes I feel like I don't know what I want to be when I grow up, you know?"

"Yeah," he said quietly. "I do. For me, it's that I'm still here."

"Still at R&R, you mean?"

He nodded. "I've tried to leave a couple times, but I always end up back in the same place."

She tilted her head. "And that's a bad thing?"

"Nah. Just—you look at guys like Jake, Nate, Hunter—they know what they're doing. And I'm the odd jobs guy. Which—Look, I'm not complaining. Jake's a great boss. But I hear you on the 'what are you going to be when you grow up' thing."

"Maybe no one knows," Becca said. "Maybe the trick is just to act like you know. That's what I'm working on now."

"Faking it?"

She laughed. "That sounds horrible, doesn't it? I'm not faking it, but—I've sucked at the self-confidence thing until recently. Now I'm turning over a new leaf. Meet 'New Becca.' Just like the old Becca, but doesn't take any shit from anyone, including the voice in her head saying, 'You can't do this.'"

Her body language changed as soon as she said, "Meet New Becca," her shoulders straightening, her chest rising, even her chin coming up a notch. And her eyes met his, dead on.

Her eyes were very blue, and he had trouble looking away.

He *liked* New Becca. Possibly a little too much. And he didn't think it was just because when she rolled her shoulders back like that, her breasts tipped up appealingly and he could see the shape of her nipples through her bra and T-shirt.

Although that didn't hurt.

What he needed to say next was, "I'd better go. I gotta get up early tomorrow morning."

What he said instead was, "Hey. What happened with the date you were supposed to be on tonight?"

She didn't answer.

He held up his hands, palms out. "I'm sorry. It's none of my business." He looked around the room for a clock, failed to find one, bulled through anyway. "I'd better go. I gotta get up early tomorrow morning."

There. He'd done it. Even though he still didn't seem to be getting up on his feet.

"No, it's okay. I—it's just kind of embarrassing." The pink was back in her cheeks.

"You don't have to tell me."

She reached for one of the throw cushions on the couch, wrapped her arms around it, and held it tight to her chest. "The guy didn't like the fact that I didn't have a lot of experience."

He really needed to get up and leave. But once again, his mouth seemed to have disengaged from his brain, and it was saying something:

"How much is not a lot?"

Silence.

Right. Bad question for so many reasons. "You know what? You don't have to answer that. It's *really* none of my business."

"No, um, it's okay. I have lots of experience in lots of things but no experience in, um, one specific thing."

His brain got tangled there for a second over "lots of experience in lots of things." He wanted a detailed explanation of that. Then he caught up to the end of the sentence. "That one specific thing being . . . ?"

As soon as the prompt was out of his mouth, he regretted

it. How did he *think* she was going to finish that sentence? *Jesus, Ambrose, think before you talk.*

"Intercourse," Becca whispered.

The word occupied a lot of space in the dark, quiet living room. And then Griff got his brain unstuck on Becca's experience or lack thereof, and what exactly it entailed, and put the last pieces together.

"Wait, and *what*? He didn't want you because you're a *virgin*? What a *dick*." Not to mention an *idiot*, but Griff wasn't going to say that. "And an *idiot*! What kind of moron would turn down the chance to be a girl's first time?"

Okay, whoops, he *had* said it. He really needed to work on the coordination between his better judgment and his mouth.

"You wouldn't?" She sounded surprised. In a good way. Pleased.

Which—uh-oh. Had he sounded like he was volunteering?

Was he volunteering?

No. No, no, no, he was not. He'd had sex with a virgin once, and it had taken him to hell, by way of divorce. No way would he do that again, even if the woman in question did not already have a big *No Entry* sign tattooed across her chest.

Of course, she hadn't asked. Wasn't asking. He was just being a dope. And she was sitting there looking at him with a sad expression on her face, because *what kind of assholes had she been dating*? He had to at least reassure her that all men were not created equal in the douchebag department. And that there was nothing wrong with being a virgin, at any age.

"My ex-wife, Marina, was a virgin," he said.

Those were not the words he'd intended to say. He'd meant to say something neutral, like, *It would depend on the*

*circumstances, of course, but if I was with her and she wanted me
to be her first, I wouldn't walk away from that.*

Becca's eyebrows went up. "And that wasn't a problem for
you?"

"No. It was . . . For me, it was kind of a plus. It was, I don't
know. Nice."

Way to go, Ambrose. "Nice"?

"Griff? Can I ask you something?"

Every cell in his body screamed, *Danger.* "No," he said,
definitively.

She drew herself up. Straightened her shoulders. Squared
her chin. "But—you don't know what I'm going to ask."

Damn New Becca. He was guessing Old Becca would have
folded already. "No to whatever you are about to ask."

"You must have slept with, I don't know, a hundred
women? At least?"

That made him laugh. "Who told you that? Nate?" Nate
had an exaggerated idea of Griff's prowess, and Griff had,
admittedly, never tried to set him straight.

She crossed her arms, framing her gorgeous tits and
forcing him to make a conscious effort to keep his gaze on her
face. "My point being, it's not a big deal to you. Sex isn't."

"No," he admitted. After Marina, he'd gone out of his way
to make sure he never did that again—mistook sex for more
than it was.

"So . . . what if you agreed to, um, take my virginity?" Her
cheeks were pink, and her eyes were bright. It was a deadly
combination. Maybe looking at her face wasn't the safest
idea, either.

"No." He stood up. "Becca, no. It's a terrible idea."

"Because you're not attracted to me." Her full red mouth

formed a little pout.

Which shouldn't have been sexy at all, but was. Damn it. He *was* attracted to her. New Becca was a menace to society. A woman with the courage and confidence to ask a guy a question like that straight to his face—pink cheeks or no—was a turn-on.

"It's not that. It's more everything that goes with it. The fact that you're Alia's little sister. And that you dated Nate, so guy code—"

"Seriously, Griff, we *barely* dated. He could not be more like a brother to me."

"Well, exactly. He's almost your big brother at this point, and I'm his friend, and he would cut my balls off and stuff them down my throat if I went through with what you're proposing. That's if Alia didn't get to me first." He realized he'd taken several steps away from her toward the door, and forced himself to stand his ground.

"They don't need to know."

Those eyes, so eager, were going to do him in. He shook his head. "They would find out. Secrets like that don't keep. Anyway, I don't do complicated. And this situation is complicated. Inherently."

He should know.

"It wouldn't have to be complicated. One and done."

He shook his head again, at a loss for words. *One and done* was usually his favorite phrase, but . . . "What you have to understand is how low my threshold for complicated is. These days, I don't even stick around for donuts and coffee."

"Look," Becca said. "My virginity is a royal pain in the ass at this point. If I'm seeing a guy, I either have to lie about it by omission—which I won't do, because that shit always comes back to haunt you—or tell the truth. And if I tell the truth, guys are universally weird about it. *Like you're being*." It was her turn to get up from the couch. She crossed to the wall and flicked the overhead light on. Both of them blinked.

"I'm not being weird about your virginity. I'm being weird about taking the virginity of my closest friend's almost-sister. Plus, when you're someone's first, they get feelings even if they don't mean to."

She rolled her eyes. "You're arrogant, Ambrose. What about the possibility that you would get feelings for *me*?"

"Impossible. I don't do relationships."

She shook her head and gave him a disgusted look. "I wouldn't *get feelings*. I'd know up front what the terms were, and so would you. Plus, we don't cross paths that often, so we could easily avoid each other. I could stay away from Friday Night Dinners to dodge any awkwardness until things cool off. It would be fine."

He was still shaking his head, at a loss for any other words to describe what a bad idea this was.

"I like you, Becca. I think you're great. And I am sympathetic about your, um, situation. But I don't want to die. And Nate would *kill* me if I went through with what you're suggesting."

That got her. She sighed heavily. And bit her lip again.

Fuuuck. She needed to stop doing that.

She paced back and forth a few times, and he was afraid New Becca was steeling herself for another approach. But then she crossed her arms and gave him a dark look.

"Fine," she said. "If you won't help me, I'll find someone else. Let's just hope whoever it is won't do anything you wouldn't do."

4

Becca woke up as soon as Nate and Robbie came downstairs. She heard coffee being ground and brewed in the kitchen. Robbie babbled, and Nate answered him in earnest grownup sentences, as if he could understand everything Robbie had "said." It made her grin.

Nate and Robbie wandered into the living room.

"Hey," she said.

"Oh, hey—I forgot you were in here. Didn't mean to wake you up."

"I was awake before you came in. Is that coffee brewing?" She sat up.

"Stay there. I'll bring you a mug."

He came back with a steaming mug that had the logo of his new nonprofit emblazoned across it. Nate was part-time aquatic director at R&R, but most of his time was spent working on his nonprofit, KidsUp, which helped kids in low-income rural communities stay away from drugs and other kinds of trouble. He handed her the mug and eyed the two beer steins still sitting on the coffee table. "Were you double fisting it after we went to bed?"

Damn it; she hadn't rinsed out her and Griff's glasses. "No. Griff stuck around a while after the party."

Nate raised an eyebrow.

She shook her head. "Believe me, there is nothing going on. Griff wouldn't touch me with a ten-foot pole."

Even if I begged him.

Granted, she hadn't exactly *begged*, but in the cold (and sober) light of day, her behavior seemed totally outrageous and embarrassing. She would never be able to look him in the eye again. Luckily for her, she could probably mostly avoid him; she only saw him every few months for a couple of hours at a time, and if she skipped Friday Night Dinners, she probably wouldn't see him at all.

She didn't dwell on how she felt about *that.*

"Good," Nate said. "I love Griff, but he's *not* a good guy for you. You're not his type at all."

"What's that supposed to mean? That he's a player and I'm the Virgin Mary?"

"I'm just saying, he goes for women who know their way around."

She glared at him. "You better not be implying that that's a bad thing." She *hated* slut-shaming. It was the flip side of virgin-worshipping. You couldn't have one without the other. Madonna, whore: women lost either way.

He held up his hands, palms out. "It's not good or bad. No judgment. It's just what he does. The bottom line is, you and he want different things."

"And what *does* Griff want, in your opinion?"

"To bang enough women that he forgets his ex-wife.

Which, I might add, is a lost cause. He's totally not over her. I think he'd take her back in a heartbeat if she asked. Even though she is a cold-hearted—"

Nate looked down at Robbie, who was drooling and whapping his hands up and down happily.

"She's not a nice human being," Nate finished.

Robbie hooted, by way of punctuation. Nate smoothed his son's wispy baby hair back off his forehead. "Are you sticking around for the Memorial Day picnic on Monday?"

Becca shrugged. "Sure. The salon's closed till Tuesday, so if you guys are okay with having me here all weekend, I can stay and help out with this little goober." She scrunched her face in Robbie's direction.

"If you don't mind the couch. Trina and Hunter are coming with the girls for the picnic, and they have dibs on the guest room."

"Nah. It's fine. And it'll be great to see them." Hunter was the fourth guy in Nate, Griff, and Jake's group of friends. He and his wife and their girls lived a few hours away but often came down for picnics or other events.

Becca's coffee was finally cool enough to hazard a sip. It was terrific—dark and hot. Like Griff's eyes, the split second after she'd told him she was a virgin, *before* she'd propositioned him.

It was that brief look he'd given her, thick with longing, that had made her brave and stupid enough to ask the question. But she'd miscalculated. Or hallucinated.

"How's it going with KidsUp?" she asked Nate, before she could think about Griff any more.

"Mostly really good. But we're having a hell of a time getting enough homework helpers. You wouldn't believe the demand that's coming out of the woodwork. So many of these kids *want* to do well, but they're flailing. And their wealthier peers can afford tutors, so kids with money are killing it and kids without money are falling through the cracks."

"That sucks."

"I know, right? Griff's been taking on a few kids. He's really great with them."

"I can see it. He's so friggin' cute with Robbie."

Nate squinted at her. "Don't get any ideas. Just because he holds Robbie doesn't mean he's family man material."

She shook her head. "Believe me. I know exactly where I stand with Griff."

He'd made *that* abundantly clear.

"Becca?"

She raised her eyebrows. "Uh-huh?"

"Speaking of holding Robbie, if I hand him over to you right now, could you watch him for an hour while I, um, catch up on sleep?"

She gave him a dark look and took the proffered baby, whose diaper needed changing.

"Just keep it down up there, okay?" she said sternly, though she was secretly delighted, as always, by Nate and Alia's happiness. "When you guys go at it, they can hear you in China. You wouldn't want to scare the paying guests away."

He gave her the finger and booked it upstairs.

"Looks like it's just you and me, Robbie. But that's okay, because you're the only male I understand," she told her nephew, and was rewarded with a ginormous grin.

5

"Do you think he has a chance?"

Griff, Nate, Jake, and Hunter were sitting at a table in Bottoms Up, watching CJ—a newcomer to R&R—chat up a redhead at the bar. The bar was a dive on the surface—scarred tables, neon beer signs, a menu of rubbery burgers and limp fries—but it played a great selection of country and classic rock, the beer flowed freely, and, for reasons known only to God, twenty-something women seemed to love it.

Griff shook his head. "No way."

"Diagnosis?" Nate asked.

Griff watched CJ's moves for a second. "He's talking too much. I don't even know what he's saying, but I know whatever it is, she doesn't give a shit."

"Can you save his sorry ass?"

"What am I now, roving wingman?"

Nate laid his palms open. "I'm just saying, maybe take pity on the dude. He hasn't gotten laid since he got back."

As if on cue, CJ retreated to the table and slumped into the booth beside Hunter.

"No luck, huh?" Jake asked sympathetically.

"What were you planning to do if you scored, anyway?" Nate ribbed him. "Let her ride between us in my truck?"

As always, CJ had bummed a ride to the bar, even though he owned a lean, mean black Ford Mustang Shelby GT350 that none of them had ever seen him drive.

"Yeah, man," Griff said, leaning in. "What's that car for if not to get you laid? If I had a car like that, I'd drive it every chance I got."

"Fuck you," CJ said, and there was an unexpected bite to his voice that made Griff give him a second look. You could feel the other guys flinch back, too, like, *whoa*. The kid wasn't a hothead, so what was up with that?

The truth was, Griff had a soft spot for CJ. It had started one night, two weeks ago, when CJ had frozen and then bolted from the card table during Oh Hell when the guys rapped their fists on the table to place their bets. Griff had watched him go, exchanged nods with Jake, and then chased the kid down to the lake, where CJ stood, staring bleakly at the water.

Griff had joined him, standing shoulder to shoulder.

"Hey."

No response from CJ.

"We've all been there. Everyone's jumped a foot for no reason. Everyone's frozen in some situation where it doesn't make sense. Everyone's freaked out, run away, whatever."

Griff could have told CJ a whole lot more than that, but he kept his mouth shut. This wasn't about him; it was about CJ.

"You're just one of us now, that's all. You don't have to talk about it if you don't want to, but you should know that if you do want to talk about it, pretty much any guy here will listen. And understand."

CJ didn't move. He didn't acknowledge Griff's words in any outright way. But Griff could feel the tension leaving the kid's body, inch by inch. Shoulders dropping, jaw releasing, heart slowing.

CJ had no way to know that Griff was a total and complete hypocrite.

Now he reached across the table and clapped CJ on the arm. "You want a tip, kid?"

"I can get my own pussy."

Griff felt a growl form in the pit of his stomach, but made himself breathe slow. It was a trick he'd learned a long time ago. If you were calm, you made the people around you calm. "Not if you talk that way, you won't."

CJ's eyes flicked up from the table. "You telling me how to get laid?"

Okay, so maybe the kid *was* hotheaded. Not surprising in a twenty-something guy who'd been back from the Middle East for all of about ten minutes, but . . . Griff noted it.

"I'm telling you to have some respect," Griff said. "That's step one. Step two is, remember you're not convincing her. You're letting her convince you."

"The fuck?" CJ demanded.

"Listen to him," Jake said. "He has a one hundred percent success rate."

"Nah, that's bullshit. He's full of it," Griff told CJ. "Maybe ninety-eight percent max. But I'm right about this. Women— hell, everyone—want to be listened to. To feel like someone gives a shit about who they are. So, you go up to someone and you're really curious about who they are? They want to open up. Talk, fuck, whatever."

For some reason, that flashed him back to sitting on the couch with Becca. Which in turn made him think of her proposition. Basically, he hadn't been able to get it out of his head since she'd issued it. He'd had quite the restless night last night, asking himself the *entirely* hypothetical question of what he would do if he were in charge of taking Becca's V-card. Which was just more of the bullshit she wanted to avoid, right? She didn't want it to be flowers and candles and a big deal. It would just be sex. Clean, simple—

But he couldn't quite banish the idea that he could make it something special. Something memorable for her.

Damn it. *He* wasn't going to *make it* anything.

She was going to find someone else to do it.

And that . . . that fucking *rankled*.

"We call him Dr. Griff, the looooove doctor," Hunter said. "And this—" He gestured to the bar around them. "—is his office."

"Nah," Nate said. "Everyone knows Griff's office is the archery range."

CJ cocked his head. "How's that?"

"You ever been to the range with Griff? You'll end up pouring your guts out. It's way better than the therapist's couch. You think you're going out there to jab arrows in a big target, but what you're really doing is fessing up to all your crap."

"Look who's talking," Hunter said to Nate. "Speaking of guys who should open a head shrinking practice."

Griff didn't know the whole story of what had gone down

between Hunter and Trina, only that Hunter had come back from Afghanistan with a year missing from his memory, including his whole relationship with his girl. Now they were married, and soon their adoptions of each other's kids would be finalized. So whatever advice Nate had given him seemed to have worked.

"I'll leave the headshrinking to Nate," Griff said. "I'm not qualified. I've got enough of my own crap. But if you want a wingman?"

He addressed this last to CJ.

"I'm your guy."

6

"**C**an you believe how huge Sam is?" Alia asked Becca, inclining her head in the direction of Mira and Jake's son.

It was Monday afternoon and Mira and Jake's Memorial Day picnic was in full swing. Sam had organized the kids into a game of Ultimate Frisbee. The age range was huge, the skill range even wider, but Sam seemed unconcerned, corralling five-year-old girls in Wonder Woman dresses and pimpled teenaged boys with equal ease. He was a natural-born leader, like his dad.

"No," said Becca. "Is he *taller* than Jake?"

"I know, right?" Alia said. "That first picnic you and I came to, Sam was so skinny you could have snapped him like a toothpick."

"I love it," Becca said. "It's probably my favorite thing about these picnics. Seeing the kids grow up, and change." She sighed. Seeing the families warmed her heart—and also set off a wave of longing. She wanted a family, too, someday. If she could ever do some growing up and changing of her own, and stop exclusively dating self-involved pricks.

"Not the hunky servicemen?" Alia teased.

"That, too," Becca said, grinning.

She couldn't help it, her eyes sought one in particular, not for the first time that day.

She'd been trying *not* to watch Griff all afternoon, but wherever he went, she knew where he was. Chatting with Jake, throwing his head back as he roared with laughter or listening intently as Jake told a story. Tossing a football back and forth with Sam, thick biceps and triceps appearing where his T-shirt rode up his sculpted arm.

Nate came over with a fussy Robbie in his arms.

"I think this dude desperately needs a nap," he said.

"I got it," Becca said. "You guys go get some food."

Alia and Nate shot Becca looks of gratitude, but then Alia, ever the big sister, said, "What about you?"

"I'll jiggle him till he passes out and then—can I put him in the stroller?"

"Perfect," Alia said, sounding relieved. "*Thank* you. I can't even express how much having you here this weekend is helping. I feel eighty percent more like an actual human being."

Becca did what she'd said she would, bouncing and jiggling Robbie against her shoulder until he melted into a puddle of baby sleep. Then she found where Nate and Alia had parked the stroller under a tree and settled him in. He stirred and for a moment she thought he was going to wake and spoil her plan, but he sighed heavily and relaxed his fat little body into the curve of the bucket seat.

She looked up and her eye caught Griff, leaning against a

tree not too far away, watching the Frisbee game, a half-smile on his face. She knew she should look away, but she couldn't take her eyes off his broad chest and narrow hips, the way his jeans outlined his solid thighs, the scruff clinging to his jawline.

It didn't make any sense. If anything, his rejection of her the other night should have made him *less* appealing. She didn't want to be the kind of woman who wanted a guy just because he didn't want her. But the truth was, that might have been part of it.

What had he said?

What kind of idiot would turn down the chance to be a girl's first time?

But then he had.

She knew what he'd meant. He'd meant, *What kind of guy would turn down the chance to be the first* for the woman he's dating. He hadn't meant guys should be lining up to take V-cards from random women in need of deflowering.

He wasn't *Jondalar*.

He didn't have the giant schlong of wonder and he wouldn't ride her the way the stallion had ridden the mare as Ayla watched—

Okay, enough with *The Valley of Horses*. One reason she was still a virgin was because she harbored these unrealistic fantasies around sex. She had to let them go, along with her childish expectations that her own Westley was going to rush in and give her life meaning. New Becca was a realist, and she would make things happen for herself.

She couldn't quite forget, though, that something hot had flared in Griff's eyes when she'd thrown down her gauntlet. *Fine. I'll find someone else.*

She hadn't *really* meant it. She wasn't on some kind of mission. She'd just had that impulsive and probably ill-advised idea that Griff could pocket her V-card and simplify her dating life. When she'd said she'd find someone else, she'd mostly just been needling Griff because she was, well, a tiny bit hurt that he hadn't found the proposition appealing.

But Griff hadn't liked that. His eyes had told her so, clearly.

7

Griff watched as Becca wound her way toward him at the food table. She heaped her plate with egg salad, macaroni salad, green salad, corn on the cob, buttered bread—

Any woman who could eat like that had to have a good appetite in other arenas, too.

See, this was the thing. Ever since she'd made him think about what she had and hadn't done with that curvy body of hers, he'd been seeing her in a whole new and extremely inconvenient light.

Food. Food was what they were doing right now. He looked down at his own plate, heaped to overflowing, then at Becca's. "If we had a scale, who do you think would win?"

She looked up at him, eyes wide, then smiled in a way that made him feel like she was genuinely happy to see him. Which—okay, he liked that. No crime there.

She assessed the two plates. "It only counts if you eat it all, though."

"Is that a challenge?"

Her eyes met his. "Sure, why not? As you may have noticed, I am a fan of throwing down a good challenge."

He let that comment slide as he led her to a spot on the grass, where they sat side by side.

"What've you been up to since Friday night?" She was wearing a flowy tank that shouldn't have been sexy but was, partly because it was made of some gauzy fabric that revealed a lacy shadow, and partly because it was loose around the arms and he could see the peekaboo of her bra and the sweet, generous curve underneath.

What he most wanted to ask was whether she'd had any success finding a willing participant for her virginity project, but he kept his mouth firmly shut. Returning to that topic was pure danger, since he didn't trust himself not to lose his resolve and volunteer.

She paused with a forkful of potato salad en route to her mouth. "Playing with Robbie, mostly. Trying to give Alia and Nate as much of a break as possible. He's so stinkin' cute. Have you gotten kisses from him yet? If you hold him up to your face, he does this little open-mouth thing. It's adorable." She wrinkled her nose, which was also, well, adorable. "What've you been up to all weekend? Other than out with Nate last night, which I know for obvious reasons."

She ate the bite she'd lifted to her lips. He watched her mouth, the way she tugged the food off the fork, then made himself look away. "Yeah, out last night with the guys. That was fun."

Even as he said it, he heard how lukewarm he sounded, which was strange because he'd had a good time. CJ hadn't turned his drought around, but he'd worked his new skills for phone numbers and pocketed two.

Griff, however, hadn't been in the mood to do the same. He hadn't seen anyone who made him want to bother. Which was rare for him. Not because he would stalk anything that twitched, but because he could always find something to like in anyone he talked to.

He shrugged. "Otherwise, it's just been the usual. I did some odd jobs Saturday, took a long bike ride and then lazed around like a slug on Sunday—oh, and spent a couple of hours on the archery range."

"I've never done archery," Becca mused.

Impulse had the words out before he could think better of it. "I'll teach you."

"Yeah?" Her face lit.

"Any time. Actually, I could teach you when we're done gorging ourselves sick."

Now why had he said that? Standing behind her, tweaking her stance, looking over her shoulder as she lined up shots? While knowing that no one had ever gone where his dick suddenly and inconveniently wanted to go? Pure torture.

"Sure! I'd love that."

And damned if he wasn't glad to hear it. Because obviously he was a total masochist.

"Hey," said a voice behind them.

Griff turned to find CJ there and instantly wished for him to go far, far away, possibly to another time and place entirely. But he forced himself not to be a tool. "Oh, hey, CJ."

Becca turned, too, and gave CJ the same smile she'd given Griff a few minutes ago. The one that made him feel like he was the only man who could ever bring it out of her—except unfortunately, that appeared not to be true. "Hey." She balanced her plate carefully on one hand and extended the other. "I'm Becca."

"Oh, sorry, my bad." Griff had dropped the ball on intros because—truth was—he didn't actually *want* CJ to meet Becca.

Damn.

"I'm CJ," the kid said. "It's really nice to meet you."

He held onto Becca's hand a beat too long and prolonged eye contact with her exactly the way Griff had advised him last night.

Grrrrr.

"So, what brings you to R&R?" CJ asked. "I haven't seen you around before. I'd remember."

Oh, *Jesus.* Griff had to grudgingly admit, it was a nice touch. Not too over-the-top, but setting the tone. And judging by Becca's blush and smile, she liked it. "Just visiting. My sister, Alia, is a PT here."

CJ lit up. "Oh, right, Alia. She's great. I busted up my knee and she knew exactly what to do to fix it."

Becca sent Griff a sideways look. It seemed to be asking a question. Griff was afraid the question was, "What about him?"

If he cock-blocked CJ and Becca when he knew they were both legit on the market, he was definitely an asshole. He bit down on his own frustration and managed a smile and a non-committal shrug.

"Have you had the potato salad yet?" CJ asked.

"God, yes, Mira's potato salad," Becca said. She'd demolished the whole scoopful he'd seen on her plate earlier.

She would *be greedy in bed.*

Griff shut his eyes. When he opened them again, CJ and

Becca were smiling at each other. "It's so good, right? This is my third helping," CJ said, gesturing to the potato salad on his plate.

Even though Griff had been using The Force to keep CJ from sitting, the kid lowered himself to the patch of grass on Becca's other side. "So, are you hanging with your sister for the weekend or something?"

"Yeah. I try to come down here whenever I can to see her and Nate and their baby. I don't visit as often as I wish I could, though. I usually have to work Saturdays."

"Yeah? What do you do?"

"I'm a receptionist at a day spa. Like a salon—hair, nails, all that."

"Wow. That's neat. How long you been doing that?"

He was using Griff's patented technique of drawing out the subject, getting her to talk about herself, making her feel as though he was interested in her.

The thing was, Griff never did it as a technique. He always *was* interested. And if he'd been the one asking Becca questions, he would have asked way better ones. Like did she really like her job, or was she just doing it until she could figure out the what-she-wanted-to-do-when-she-grew-up thing? And what, when she was really, really honest with herself, *did* she want to do when she grew up?

"I need a beer," he said abruptly. "Anyone else?"

CJ looked at Griff as if he'd just remembered he existed. "No thanks, man."

Griff didn't wait for Becca's response as he rose to his feet and headed to the drinks table. He wasn't thirsty, but he didn't think he could stand to watch anymore.

He scrubbed his hand over his forehead, the other one a fist at his side.

Becca would never let CJ take her V-card, would she?

Because Griff was positive: That guy wouldn't be careful with her. He wouldn't take his time.

He wouldn't insist, no matter how much she protested, that her first time could and did matter and that it wasn't something to just throw away.

He would never treat her the way that Griff would, if he could.

8

Becca's fingers slowly formed into a fist in her lap. CJ was asking her his ten millionth question. It was like he was interviewing her for a job, and while at first it had been kind of flattering to be the subject of all that interest, she was . . .

Well, she was bored.

Her attention had started wandering. She kept catching herself *not* looking at CJ and instead searching for Griff.

She took the last bite of food on her plate—not because Griff had laid down the challenge, but because she was desperate for an excuse to leave the interrogation. "Hey. I'm going to get myself another lemonade. And then I think I'll probably check up on Alia and see if she needs any more help with Robbie."

"Are you headed home tonight?"

"Yeah."

"Will you be back any time soon?"

She hesitated. "Uh, not sure."

"Could I convince you to let me take you out to dinner next time?"

She should be thrilled about the invitation. CJ had green eyes and dimples and he seemed to actually give a shit about who she was as a person. "Um, sure," she said.

"Here, you have your phone? I'll give you my number, and you can text me if you're planning to be in town."

"Um . . ." She'd left her purse, including her phone, in Alia's office. "No, sorry. But if you give it to Alia, she'll text it to me."

He nodded.

"Nice meeting you," she said, rising to her feet.

He rose, too, and reached out his hand. When she put hers out to shake, he took it in both of his and said, "Great meeting you."

Something about the gesture felt—rehearsed. She took her hand back, relieved to walk away from him.

She was hoping Griff had been serious about his offer to teach her archery. She'd never had much interest in bows and arrows, or any form of weaponry, before, but she wanted to know more about what made Griff tick, and she knew archery was something that mattered to him.

She scanned the picnic-goers, looking for his rumpled hair and gray eyes, for the T-shirt that clung to his sculpted pecs, but she didn't see him. She started a slow roam around the periphery of the picnic, stopping to greet people she knew, but she completed a circuit without finding him.

"Who are you looking for?" Alia had materialized from nowhere at her side. Or, probably not from nowhere. Becca's attention had just been focused on her search.

She hesitated, and that split second was long enough to

arouse Alia's suspicions. Her eyes narrowed. "Who?" she demanded.

"Griff told me he'd teach me archery," Becca said.

Alia's expression relaxed. "Oh, yeah, Griff will take any opportunity to evangelize."

"Did you see where he went?"

"If you can't find him, try the range."

Becca wandered in the direction Alia pointed her. As she approached the range, she saw him with the big bow in his arms, slinging arrow after arrow into the center of the target so they stuck out like bristling porcupine quills.

She hung back, watching. He wore a plastic chest guard and a leather arm guard, which made him look a little bit like some medieval hero. And she wasn't sure which was more mesmerizing: the clutch of muscle in his back and shoulders, the cords in his forearm, or his absolute laser focus.

She imagined what it would be like to have all that intensity and concentration turned toward her. That *precision*. That *devotion* to his task.

Her body warmed and softened in appreciation. Which was unusual for her. She didn't get turned on *looking*. She didn't get turned on that easily, period. She usually needed a lot of warming up.

Except, apparently, when it came to Griff Ambrose.

He reached into the quiver hanging across his body and came up empty.

"Hey," she called.

He jumped. When he turned, the expression on his face was dark. Angry, she thought.

"Sorry—I didn't mean to startle you."

He crossed his arms. "I'll do it."

"What?"

She'd heard the words but couldn't make sense of them.

"If you still want me to. If you haven't already enlisted CJ or some other *boy*. I'll—take your V-card."

She felt a huge smile threaten to break out all over her face, but her gut told her to play it cool. She shrugged. "CJ wants to take me out for dinner. He was actually quite the gentleman about asking me on a date."

His expression darkened further. "No. No dates with CJ. That's the deal. If I'm going to do this—"

She raised her eyebrows at his grim tone. God, he was making it sound like a household chore. "It's not like you *have* to. I told you, I'll find someone else—"

"God. No. I'll do it. I said I'd do it. I don't want you to pick some random guy. Then Nate would *really* kill me."

"It's sex with a virgin—a friend, even—not a *death march*," she snapped.

She was aware of an ache in the center of her chest. For a minute there, she'd thought—

But he was just doing her a favor, of course.

He shook his head. Closed his eyes. Then opened them again. "You're right. I'm sorry, I didn't mean for it to sound like that. It's not a hardship," he said, then gave a short dark laugh. He took a step forward, touched his hand to her cheek, his thumb moving over her mouth without touching it. An unfamiliar stab of heat shot through her. She wanted to lean forward and take his thumb between her teeth.

That wasn't her, either.

He took a step back, dropping his hand. "I know you don't want to make a big deal of it. So I'll just say this. It's an honor, okay?"

For some stupid reason, that made her eyes fill up with tears. She blinked, and luckily none of them fell, though he blurred in her vision.

"I guess we have to figure out when?" she said. "And, um, *where*?"

"Does this Saturday work for you? I can come to Seattle." She nodded.

"In the meantime, until then, *no dates*. Especially with CJ."

"What do you have against him, anyway?"

"I just don't think—he's not the right guy for this job."

That made her smile. "And you are?"

"You obviously thought so when you asked me."

His eyes were dark, his gaze intense. She felt that same deep pulling sensation, like something opening and flowering low in her belly. If he thought he was Jondalar material, she sure as hell wasn't going to argue the point. "If you must know, I was trying to figure out how to get out of the CJ thing anyway. He seemed nice but—he asks too many questions."

One corner of Griff's mouth lifted, which dug a dimple in his cheek and made her own mouth go dry.

"What are you going to tell him?"

She hid her own smile. "I was thinking of the truth. That I have a date to lose my virginity and the guy who's in charge of that wants an exclusive till the deed's done."

Griff hooted with laughter. "That should go over well."

"Truth is stranger than fiction. No, seriously, I'll just say I'm not interested."

"Okay, then." He shifted from one foot to the other. "So, um—We should have some ground rules."

"Okay."

"The first rule of Operation V-Card is, there is no Operation V-Card."

"My lips are sealed." That didn't bother her. She already knew Nate wouldn't like the idea of her messing around with Griff—or vice versa—and telling Alia would be as good as telling Nate. She could mention the situation to her roommate, though, without getting into details. Jenina didn't know her family or Griff and wouldn't mention it to anyone else who mattered.

"And it's one and done. Just to keep things simple. And clean."

"Well, yeah," she repeated. "Don't flatter yourself, Ambrose."

That made him laugh. "Oh, honey. Just you wait."

"Arrogant bastard."

But the truth was, his teasing had licked under her skin, like so much else about him.

The moment stretched to awkwardness, and she looked away. When she turned back, he was examining the string of his bow.

"You still offering that archery lesson?

"Hell, yeah. Walk with me. We'll collect the arrows."

She fell in beside him.

"When you approach the targets, you always need to make sure no one's shooting. It's easy right now because we're the only ones here, but sometimes it gets a little more complicated."

He tapped the target at the base of one of the bristling arrows. "You want to grab the arrow close to the target face, down low on the shaft," he said.

She wasn't someone who heard double entendres everywhere. Or at least she *hadn't* been, before playing Taboo the other night with Griff. Something about him wrapped everything up in sex. Add to that the fact that he'd actually agreed to have sex with her—

Yeah. She was thinking about shafts. And grabbing them down low. She could *feel* her cheeks getting pink, and she cursed the fact that she blushed so damn easily.

Were words supposed to do that? Creep under your skin, down your spine, along your nerve endings? Were they supposed to light you up like a Christmas tree?

While she'd been getting wet over skinny sticks with feathers on the end, Griff had pulled the arrows from the target, collected them in a fist, and turned back up-range.

She followed him back, suddenly wishing she'd said something. Some brilliant sexy teaser about how she always liked to grab low on the shaft. Something provocative enough to make him drop the arrows, take her in his arms, and kiss her until she couldn't breathe.

She'd never been kissed till she couldn't breathe, but she suspected Griff could have that effect on her.

"Stand here," he said, toeing a sandy spot on the ground. "This is the foot marker."

He gave her an arm guard and showed her how to strap it on. "You don't really need a chest guard. It's just to make sure the string doesn't catch on your clothes. If you were hunting or fighting it would be a bigger deal."

He stood behind her. "Is this okay?"

"Is what—?"

He wrapped his arms around her so that the bow was in front of her and lifted her left hand to the grip. She was hyperaware of his body behind hers, solid and hot.

He showed her how to nock the bowstring into the cleft at the end of the arrow shaft.

Cleft.

Not a word she'd ever heard used. Or used herself. Or contemplated. Not a word she would have said was sexy. But with him standing just behind her, his breath against her ear, his hands guiding hers, it was a word that could lick itself right into every last *cleft* on her body.

If she turned around right now—

But she couldn't. The way they were standing, and the bow in her arms, froze her in place.

"And then you draw it back, tight—"

He wrapped his hand around hers, drawing her fist back, and the string with it. Now she made herself focus on the bow and arrow, because it was taut in her arms, and it didn't feel like something to mess around with. Its contained energy was fierce.

Like the man behind her.

"See this?" he said, and he drew the arrow back a little further, until his fingers brushed her mouth.

It was difficult to breathe.

"This is called the kisser button. For obvious reasons. You use it to get alignment with your mouth at full draw. You line up on the gold—that's what we call the center of the target. You sight it over the top of the grip. Right where the arrow head is aimed, see? And then you let it fly. Release it. Okay. I'm going to let go. You keep the tension on."

He unfurled his fingers from around hers and stepped back, taking his body heat with him and leaving the full strength of the bowstring in her fist. Her arm muscles trembled—maybe from the pull of the string, or maybe not.

"Let go," he said.

She released it. The arrow flew and lodged itself with a hiss in the target. Not anywhere near the center, but still.

She stood there a moment. Her hands and arms still felt shaky. Hell, her whole body felt shaky.

"Nice," Griff said. When she turned to look at him, his gaze was steady on her face. His eyes seemed to bore into hers.

"Now you just need practice."

9

"What is *up* with you, man?" Nate asked him.

He and Griff were replacing cracked boards in the jumping dock down at the lake. They'd cut them ahead of time, so all they had to do now was pry up the old ones and nail down the new, which was easier said than done. After two hours of work, Griff's splinters had splinters.

He set a rotted board aside, grabbed a fresh one, and knelt to pound in the bright new nails from the tub Nate had set between them. "What do you mean, what's up?"

Nate shrugged. "You're a million miles away."

"Nothing's up."

He bent a nail, swore, and tossed it into the discard pile.

"You can tell Uncle Nate."

"Seriously, nothing's up." That was the biggest, most bald-faced lie Griff had probably ever told. He *was* a million miles away, or at least a couple hundred, his mind constantly jumping ahead to this weekend. He hadn't looked forward to anything this much since . . .

Since he'd been waiting for Marina's parents to head out of town so the two of them could be alone in her childhood bedroom.

Ugh, he didn't want to think about that. Not about Marina or her virginity or where all that happiness and anticipation had landed him in the end.

He apparently was bad at learning from his own mistakes. He should not have let Becca talk him into taking her virginity, rules or no rules.

And yet? The truth was, he was glad she had. Because bottom line?

He wanted to do it.

He wanted to do *her*.

He'd spent several very restless nights imagining *exactly* what he'd do, from the moment he'd finally tease his tongue along the seam of her barely-there secret smile to the moment he'd—

In fact, he was so enthusiastic about his role that he was starting to wonder if he'd missed his calling as a sexy escort. Maybe he could do this for a living: hang out his shingle as a hired dick.

"Well, when you're ready to fess up, I'm here," Nate said.

"There's nothing to confess."

Nate rolled his eyes. "Suuuuure."

But he dropped the subject. Griff was grateful for the reprieve, but he figured he'd have to do a better job of covering his distraction, or Nate—and all the guys—would be on him.

They worked on the dock until they put down all the new planks, then hauled the materials back to the main toolshed behind the central building.

Griff went back to his room. He had a couple of phone calls to make.

He dialed.

"This is Becca."

"If we're going to do this, we're going to do it right."

She laughed, a fat, round, lovely sound. "What does that mean, exactly?"

"Dinner, a hotel room." One of the things he'd decided last night—between bouts of abusing himself, which only barely took the edge off—was that he wanted Becca to remember her first time for the rest of her life.

"We said *simple*. That's not simple. That sounds—over the top. I wouldn't want you to get any ideas."

He chuckled, then instantly sobered up. "I am *not* going to take your virginity in my dumpy little room. Or your sister's guest room."

"Oh, hell *no*," Becca said. "God. That's—awful. But what about my place up here?"

"Do you have a roommate?"

"Yeah."

"Does she have somewhere to go for three or four hours?"

"Three or four hours?" her voice rose, incredulous.

"Look, sweetheart. If you hire Griff Ambrose for a job, he's going to do it right."

She giggled.

"Dinner and a hotel it is," he said.

"It's just—aren't you worried one of us will get the wrong idea?"

"I don't have the wrong idea," he said. "Do you?"

"No," she said quickly.

"Then we're good."

He hung up feeling ridiculously cheerful. Also, he was hard. It seemed to go with the territory lately where Becca was concerned.

"Soon," he said aloud to his dick, and then rolled his eyes at himself and tapped his phone to wake it up again.

He had a lot of money saved up. Jake paid him well and he got free room and board. Plus, aside from burgers and beers, he bought almost nothing.

The Edgewater Hotel it was.

And no fucking "cityside" room for Becca, either. Bay view.

He almost swallowed his tongue when he saw the price, but he clicked, entered his credit card number, added a bunch of notes in the "special requests" field, and made it so.

You only lost your virginity once. And unless he did go into escorting, he wasn't going to get another chance to do this in style.

Next up, dinner reservations.

The Met. Best steaks in Seattle. He ran his eyes down the menu, spent a moment contemplating the idea of Becca eating oysters, and then got a grip on himself.

He hung up with the restaurant and stared out the window of his room, which overlooked the lake. One of the perks of his job.

A guy he didn't know walked out to the end of the dock, jumped off, and set out across the lake with strong strokes. He was wearing two swim prostheses, one on an arm and one on a leg.

Griff had the satisfaction of knowing that his work on the dock that morning was for a damn good purpose. Another perk of the job.

He looked down at the notes he'd scribbled on a piece of scrap paper about the coming weekend.

It felt like something was missing.

Today was technically his day off, and since he'd spent a good portion of it fixing the dock, no one would fault him for going on a shopping trip. So he did.

First stop, North Coast Candle Company.

The women who ran the shop gave him a funny look, but he didn't give a shit. He picked up candle after candle, sniffing them. Patchouli? No. Lemon? No. Chocolate? No, that would make them hungry and there were other things he wanted to put in his mouth.

He chose a combination of vanilla and cinnamon candles, the squat ones that wouldn't tip over and light the hotel room on fire. He and Becca would do that without any help, thank you very much. He flashed back on the way she'd felt in his arms and found himself instantly hard again.

If he hadn't pulled away—

If he'd stepped in closer—

Would she have turned in his arms and let him have his way with her?

He wanted to find out what would happen when the chemistry between them had a chance to play itself out.

It could be epic.

When he was suitable again for human interaction, he carried his candle purchases up to the front of the shop and checked out.

"Big weekend?"

There was a smirk on the face of the twenty-something blonde behind the checkout.

"Nah," he said. "Power got turned off yesterday for non-payment."

"Oh, geez, I'm sorry—"

"I'm just kidding."

She laughed. "Well. Have fun, whatever the candles are for."

"I plan to," he said, and winked at her.

She blushed. He waited for his body to react, but nada. Apparently, it was only Becca's blushes that had the power to drop him to his knees.

Next stop, the lingerie shop nestled into the back corner of Tierney Bay. For, um, party favors.

The middle-aged proprietor, a slim gray haired woman, greeted him cheerfully. It seemed she was accustomed to male visitors. "Buying a gift?" she asked.

"What if I said for myself?" he teased.

She grinned. "I'd say, let's look at some of the larger sizes."

Damn, he hated to disappoint her. "Gift, yes."

"Something practical? Or impractical?"

"As impractical as you've got."

"Ah," she said, with a huge smile. "Right this way."

She wrapped his purchase in a pink gift bag stuffed with pink tissue paper.

"Sorry about the packaging—" she said.

Griff shrugged. "Real men don't mind pink tissue paper."

Her laughter followed him out of the store.

His last stop was Ocean Front Market, where he grabbed a large box of condoms. He had some in his room, but—

Well, he felt like she deserved a freshly opened box. No need to make her think about the women who'd come before her.

The truth was, none of the women who'd come before Becca had been noteworthy, with the exception of Marina. And definitely no one since then. He hadn't wanted anyone to be noteworthy, because—

Well, because it still hurt. Not just the night he had come home to find Marina gone, but the other memories. The good ones. The first night after they'd bought the house, when they'd picnicked on the kitchen floor, sharing a pizza and passing a bottle of wine back and forth, laughing and kissing. Making love right there on the floor, and declaring the new house christened.

He had felt so damn *lucky*. Like a guy who'd woken up from a childhood dream to find the dream was *real*—he wasn't just playing house, but living it. He had a place to call his own, a beautiful wife who reached for him at night, fucking bacon and eggs on Sunday mornings. He'd done nothing to deserve any of it, but it was his to keep.

And then it wasn't.

He realized he was standing stock still in the middle of the grocery aisle, staring at the condom display. And goddammit, why did Marina have the power to do that to him?

He realized his free hand was wrapped in a fist and made himself unclench it.

This thing with Becca had *nothing* to do with what had happened with Marina. This was just *fun*. After all, they'd agreed on the rules so it couldn't get messy, couldn't get serious.

He put the big box back on the shelf and took a pack of three instead.

Just in case he needed a reminder.

10

"What do you think?"

Becca stepped out of the dressing room to show Jenina the dress she was trying on. It was cornflower blue with a halter neckline that cut away from her shoulders. It fell barely to mid-thigh in gauzy layers. Becca twirled, then quickly dropped her hands to push the dress back down over her ass.

"Wow," Jenina said. "That is beautiful. And really hot on you." She narrowed her eyes. "What are you wearing under it?"

"A bra? And panties?"

"Which bra and panties?"

"Does it matter? He's a sure thing."

"Oh, it matters. He's only a sure thing until he lifts that hem up to reveal your favorite cat-print cotton boy shorts. You need to make sure he wants seconds."

"He won't want seconds. We made a deal. Rules. One and done. And shit—the first rule of Operation V-Card is, there is no Operation V-Card, so total cone of silence, Jenina. I shouldn't have even told you."

Jenina zipped her lips. Then promptly unzipped them. "Honey. If it's even remotely decent sex, it's not going to be one and done. And believe me, even if you don't want seconds, you want him to want seconds. You want all the power to be in your hands. You want him begging for more. Then you can turn on your stiletto heel and walk out."

Becca squinted at that. She'd never worn a stiletto heel in her life. "That's not going to happen. Griff can have any woman he wants, and he doesn't want Nate to know there's anything going on between us, so he's going to stick to the rules."

"Unless you make it impossible for him."

"How would I do that?"

The words had spilled out of her mouth without her meaning to say them aloud. She didn't want to leave him begging for more.

Did she?

"Let's buy the dress," Jenina said. "Then we're going shoe shopping and lingerie shopping."

Ten minutes later they were in the shoe store, and Jenina had three pairs of stiletto sandals hanging over her fingers.

"Can I help you with those?" the saleswoman asked.

"They're for her," Jenina said. "She needs to make a guy beg."

The saleswoman's mouth opened, then closed, then opened again. She was a dark-haired woman with white roots —Becca guessed she was pushing sixty. "Um, what size?" she asked.

"Eight," Becca said.

The saleswoman brought out all three pairs and began opening boxes and pulling cardboard and tissue paper out of the sandals. The first pair Becca tried on were made up of a million spaghetti-thin silver straps, crisscrossed back and forth over each other. She admired her foot in the sandal, then stood and fell right back into her seat.

"I'm not going to be able to walk in these," she said.

"You're not going to be walking," Jenina said. "You're going to be hooking your ankles around his back."

The saleswoman coughed and looked away.

"You're evil," Becca mouthed at Jenina.

"I'm pragmatic."

Becca was pragmatic, too, or at least she'd always *thought* she was. But even though she needed to unfasten the sandals, take them off, and return them to the box so she could try on something more practical, she couldn't make herself do it. She kept thinking of what Jenina had said, and the thought of Griff between her thighs and the sandals digging into Griff's ass—

New Becca, among other things, was apparently a lot more good-to-go than Old Becca. She was all *hooray* about the stiletto sex.

The other thing she couldn't stop thinking about was the look on Griff's face when he saw the sandals. Saw *her* in the sandals. Saw the length of her legs, her ankles crisscrossed with those impossibly slim straps.

She wanted him to give her that look again, the one he'd given her just briefly when he'd found out she was a virgin. Like she was a meal he was about to ravage—with gusto.

"I'll take these," she told the saleswoman.

Lingerie was easier, mainly because she didn't have to show it to Jenina, who was trying on practical panties—her phrase—in the next dressing room.

The panties Becca had on were not practical. Not at all. They were shimmery silver and barely there. If she weren't wearing the obligatory underwear-under-the-underwear, she would be able to see herself through them. The thought made her extra glad she'd indulged in some ladyscaping earlier this morning—something she did *not* feel the need to share with Jenina, who would have put too much weight on it. She wasn't *trying* to impress Griff or anything. She just liked things trim and tidy.

There was a matching bra. Her nipples stood at attention beneath it. She stared at herself in the mirror. He'd seen a *lot* of breasts. There was no reason hers should impress him. And Jenina's assertions aside, this wasn't about impressing him.

Jondalar would tell her that her breasts were the most beautiful breasts he'd ever seen, and he'd *mean* it.

It was a damn good thing she was going to lose her virginity so she could stop having Jondalar fantasies and move on with her life.

Her hand rose, without her consciously deciding to do it, to brush over the sheer lace of her bra and the hard tip of her nipple. She shivered. And did it again. Then the other.

Wow. So, there was that.

It wasn't like she'd never engaged in a little ... self-love ... but it was usually the quick and efficient Hitachi Magic Wand kind of thing. This slow burn sensuality thing that Griff had started—

Whole different ball of hot melting wax.

Old Becca gave New Becca the side-eye. New Becca gave Old Becca the finger and pinched a nipple. Sensation rolled down her belly, arrowed to her clit.

She'd be ready for him by the time Saturday rolled around, that was for sure.

11

I'm on my way, Griff texted.

Holy shit, this did feel like Christmas. Like when you know you're the first one awake in the house, and there's all that *treasure* downstairs, just waiting for you to tear the shiny paper off.

Except in this case, the treasure was Becca's body and the shiny paper was her clothes. And the fantasies he was having were *definitely* not the stuff of a family-friendly Hallmark flick.

He drove up 101, past the tourist helicopter ride, surf shops, pizza parlors, pot dispensaries, dive bars. Nestled between the storefronts were small houses, some still impeccably maintained, others falling to shit. He passed his favorite sign of all time: I'd Crack That Chiropractic, with the illustration of a woman whose back was bent at a spine-endangering angle. Best advertisement ever for chiropractic services. Sign him right up.

Griff's phone buzzed. He broke all his own rules and peered down at the screen.

I'm ready for you.

Well, holy fuck, that had just taken him from *calmly puttering down the highway* to *primed to the teeth.*

He picked up the phone. Traffic wasn't too bad. "Send a message to Becca Drake," he instructed Siri.

"What do you want to say to Becca?"

She was so cooperative, that Siri. He wondered how many nerdy high school boys were in love with her.

"'You're going to need to explain what you mean by that,'" Griff dictated.

"Your message to Becca Drake says *You're going to need to explain what you mean by that.* Ready to send it?"

"Yes."

He set the phone down, jazzed to the gills. He couldn't wait to see what she'd text back.

Highway 101's flotsam gave way to estuary and farmland, then to a stretch of big box stores, the land all jagged geometries, and Griff stopped at the light in front of a Fred Meyers. Grabbed his phone. She'd texted back, which ratcheted his heart rate up.

You'll see when you get here.

Give me a hint, he tapped.

You'll like what I'm wearing.

Oh, now. He would. He was pretty sure of that, no matter what it was. *I still have four hours of driving, Becca.*

The light turned. Goddammit, that was the last light before the bridge, wasn't it? Grudgingly, he pulled forward and accelerated.

Buzz.

He wasn't going to look.

He wasn't going to look.

He grabbed his phone.

That will give you plenty of time to get ready, too.

The only body part he needed for the job crowed, *I'm ready!*

"Hey Siri, text Becca Drake, 'I don't need time to get ready for you, gorgeous.'"

Just past the last of the strip was one of the wildest and most beautiful sights Griff knew, the place where the Columbia River emptied itself into the Pacific, freshwater mingling with salt, flowing to the horizon in what felt like every direction. He crossed the bridge, circled the round-about, and came into Astoria.

A weight settled in his stomach. This—up on the hill to his right—was where he had once lived with Marina. He couldn't see it from here, but somewhere up there was the house that he had come home to, only to find it empty and her gone. She'd gotten that house in the divorce—he hadn't wanted it—and she lived there now with her boyfriend, Scott.

Griff's stuff was still in the basement of that house. Marina had asked him to come get it, but he hadn't been up to seeing her, or the house, or—most of all—her and fucking Scott living happily together. So she'd told him she'd keep his things there until he was ready to grab them.

Pretty decent of her, actually. His stuff had been sitting there ever since, although a couple of weeks ago he'd gotten an email from her asking him to finally get the job over with —she and Scott needed the basement back. His stomach had clenched in knots and he'd deleted the email.

He turned onto the Astoria-Megler Bridge. The water rolled out on either side of him, blue-gray and mottled with brown at the shallower spots. Fucking beautiful. That and the hills on the other side of the water, sprawling and nearly unspoiled. It always put him in a great mood. Screw Marina and her basement and his sad leftover shit, he was on his way to have a good time—and more to the point, give someone else a *really* good time—tonight.

He had to grin at that.

The *Entering Washington* sign reminded him of a child-hood ritual, and he hummed, "Roll on, Columbia, roll on," an old Arlo Guthrie song he and his family had always sung when they crossed the Columbia River.

He turned off the bridge and—

Buzz.

He pulled over at the Dismal Nitch rest area—no joke, that was really a place. And he was glad he'd done so, because she'd sent him an essay.

No pressure or anything, but you should know that when I was a teenager, I read this book called The Valley of Horses. It's set in prehistoric times, and the hero initiates the heroine into the First Rites of Pleasure. He was a total pro. Plus he had a schlong so big that all the women were afraid they wouldn't be able to fit it.

He laughed, then frowned. *You're not scared, are you?*

No!

He was about to text her back to say, *Good, you have nothing to be scared of,* when the three dots appeared again.

Okay, maybe a tiny bit. I did try to have sex with this one guy and it didn't, um, *work*.

He was instantly pissed at whoever that asshole was. Some noob like CJ, probably, more intent on notching a bedpost and claiming a conquest than making it good for his partner.

You should have told me that.

So you could have backed out?

She really had no idea who she was dealing with. *No, doofus, so I could plan on spending an extra-long time making you ready.*

Long, long silence. He almost started the truck, but just as he reached out his hand to turn the key in the ignition, his phone buzzed again.

I told you, I am ready.

Do me a favor, okay? Go online and find something really sexy.

Like porn?

Doesn't have to be porn. You have a Kindle?

Yeah.

Get that book. The one you used to read when you were a kid. Read the good parts, so when I get there, you can tell me if I'm forgetting anything. And feel free to warm up. I won't be angry. Just don't—

He became suddenly conscious that his dick was right-angled and ferociously hard. Not okay. He straightened himself inside his jeans, looking around first to make sure no one was in his line of sight. Last thing he needed was to get arrested for perving in Dismal Nitch.

—don't come.

No danger of that. I have to work at it. Hope you're okay with a challenge.

Griff would not have pegged himself as a man who got off on that particular challenge, but his dick disagreed. He'd be fine if it took hours to get her there, because he was going to love every last freaking minute of it.

Tonight it won't be work for you. I promise.

I like sexting with you.

I like sexting with you, too, honey. But I've got to put the phone down and drive now or I'll never get to the really good part.

Put the fucking phone down and fucking drive.

He laughed out loud.

He put the phone down. But it took him a few minutes before he felt like he was safe to pull back out on the road. And the drive to Seattle felt like it was a hundred fucking years long.

12

The doorbell rang. Jenina, thankfully, had agreed to make herself scarce, so Becca didn't have to try to figure out whether she should play coy and let Jenina answer or make a grand entrance.

She took a deep breath and pulled the door open.

The man standing there was so good-looking he took her breath away. He was wearing gray dress pants that clung to his thighs and revealed just enough about his size to suggest that he could give Jondalar a run for his money. He'd paired them with a white Oxford button-down—nothing fancy, but the way the shirt fit across his chest and shoulders made her want to yank it open and send buttons flying. Maybe she'd do that later. The nice thing about a one-and-done situation was that it didn't matter—despite what Jenina had said—if you did something outrageous or embarrassing.

She finished her appraisal and realized he was doing one of his own. She could feel his gaze as it traveled over her body, taking in her bare shoulders, the curve of her breasts, the short flippy hem of her dress, the long expanse of bare thigh and calf, and the sandals. When his eyes reached the sandals, they flicked back to her face.

"You are forbidden to take those shoes off until I tell you to," he said mildly.

Oh. That was sexy.

"You look unbelievably hot, Becca."

Even if he was saying it because she'd made him feel competitive with a fictional character, she didn't really care. It still felt like a caress, like he'd reached out and run an admiring hand down her body.

"You're not so bad yourself."

She was about to turn and reach for her clutch, which she'd set on a table in the hall, when he took a step forward, reached out, slid his hand up her neck, threaded his fingers into her hair, pulled her forward, and kissed her. She let out a gasp, half surprise and half pleasure, and he groaned and nipped her lip, then licked it. His mouth was warm and certain, the perfect amount of pressure. His tongue made another exploration of her lower lip, teased her open, and stroked her expertly, making her think about what else she'd like him to do with it. Her body, which had been primed from a week of anticipation and several hours of *Valley of Horses*—she was nothing if not obedient—tightened all the way down the front, a subtle but very real tug.

"That's it," he urged, pulling her closer so their bodies were lined up. The feel of his washboard abs against the curve of her belly intensified the tug. Maybe she'd done too much priming. Maybe she wasn't a challenge at all. Maybe she was going to start humping his leg.

As if he'd read her mind, he slid his thigh between hers and his tongue back into her mouth, and she squeezed her legs together, pressing her needy body against thick muscle. He made a sound that was stuck somewhere between groan and grunt and grabbed her ass with both hands. Then abruptly, he let her go and stepped away.

"I think we should probably go to dinner. Right now. The sooner we eat, the sooner we can have dessert."

She didn't think those exact words had ever come out of Jondalar's mouth, but she was okay with that. All she could do was nod mutely, however, which made him laugh.

She grabbed her shoulder bag—she'd shoved in a toothbrush and a change of undies just in case—and pulled the front door shut behind them, locking it. As soon as she dropped her house key back into her purse, he took her hand. His was big, warm, and rough with callouses as he walked her down the front path to his truck. He helped her up, his hand on hers, the other one at her back.

"Not a lot of guys do that," she said, when he'd walked around to the other side and slid into the driver's seat. "By which I mean, none."

"What's *wrong* with men?" he demanded.

"I think chivalry's dead," she said. "No one expects it anymore, so no one bothers."

"See, that's exactly the reason *to* bother. It's like when people say nobody bothers with details anymore. Be the person who bothers, that's what I say. If it's worth doing, it's worth doing right."

Becca made a small noise of appreciation, and he turned his head and narrowed his eyes darkly at her. "That's right," he said, low and growly. "If she's worth doing, she's worth doing right."

She couldn't help herself, she reached out and put a hand

on his forearm, gave a little tug, and he grabbed her wrists, pulled her toward him, and kissed her breathless.

"Dinner," he said firmly, breaking away. "That's part of the foreplay, too. Don't let anyone else tell you otherwise."

He kept his eyes on hers as he slid the key into the ignition—infinitely slowly and gently—and turned it. Heat suffused her face, and he raised his eyebrows and smirked.

When he finally let her off the hook, aiming his gaze on the road, she collapsed back against her seat, almost relieved.

Her whole body was screaming for more. And the thing was, her body didn't scream. It cooperated. Or maybe, if she was with someone really hot who was a good kisser, it gave a quiet little *yippee*. But there was no screaming and no begging.

Griff had leveled her up, and she was starting to think—to *fear*—that when he was done with her, she'd be spoiled for everything she'd *thought* sex was supposed to be.

Which was exactly what shouldn't be happening.

13

Her eyes got huge when they stepped into the Met, which made the whole thing worth it. Becca had fucking amazing eyes, a shade of blue that was like the clearest North Coast sky in July. She was wearing some smoky eye makeup—not cat eyeliner or anything, but something silvery that made her eyes even bluer and prettier. And whatever you called that stuff on the lashes, so they were a thousand miles long.

But he liked her the other way, too. Without makeup, the way she'd shown up the other night at Alia's. Lashes the same light blond as her hair and the skin around her eyes pale and delicate. That look made him want to peel her slowly out of her clothes. This one made him want to tear them off.

It might be tougher to go slow with her than he'd thought.

She tucked her hand into his, a trusting little gesture that made something slip in his chest. Her head was practically swiveling as she took in their surroundings.

He was awed by the Met, too, but for his own reasons. All

those photos—signed—of famous Seattle sports personalities. Like many of his North Coast friends, he was a Seattle sports fan, so he'd keep his eyes open in case any Grizzlies or Mariners or Storm players showed up.

They got seated in a quiet booth, like he'd requested.

"Is that the wine list?" Becca asked, pointing to a leather-covered tome. Her eyes were big again, and he realized she was panicking about how fancy things were. Maybe they would have been better off somewhere more casual. Or, you know, with Indian food. Maybe this whole *snow her* thing had been a bad idea.

"I know *shit* about wine," he told her.

The corners of her mouth turned up. "Me neither," she admitted, and he watched her shoulders drop and her lips soften.

It made him want to kiss her.

The waiter drifted back a moment later to see if they wanted wine. He must have correctly interpreted the glance that passed between Griff and Becca, because he asked, "May I recommend the Gramercy Cellars Cabernet? It's an excellent value." Actually, he didn't so much ask as *inquire*, because that's what guys like him did at restaurants like this one.

Griff was so grateful at being rescued from the price problem that he didn't even mind that the waiter obviously knew he was not a $300-a-bottle kind of guy. Or a $1,000-a-bottle kind of guy, because he was pretty sure that people who ate at the Met popped that kind of money regularly to show off for their friends.

"Sounds good," Griff said. "We'll take a bottle of that."

When the waiter had gone, Griff turned to Becca and said, "That was cool, how he did that. Said it wasn't expensive without saying it. When I grow up, I want to be that natural. The kind of guy who can make everyone feel comfortable and not like a schmoe because they have no idea what kind of wine to order. You know?"

"*Yes*," she said. Just that. But she reached across the table and took his hand. Which—well, fuck, it felt really good. Her hand was small and cool, her fingers were slim and—wow, there was apparently a direct line from his digits to his dick, because all she'd done was slide her hand into his and he was hard. She pulled her hand back again right away and bit her lip, like she thought she'd overstepped.

It didn't go with the vibe they were supposedly setting up here—this one night, one time, *I'm doing you a favor* setup— but it hadn't felt wrong.

It had felt right. Maybe a little *too* right.

"I guess we should figure out what we're having," he said.

They opened their menus and she made a small noise from the other side of the table.

"Forget the prices," he said. "I just wanted you to feel special." Because that was the thing. Losing her virginity was about *Becca*, and any guy who'd try to make it about himself was just a dick.

The look she gave him pretty much tore his chest open. Because it was so *surprised*. That feeling, of being ripped throat to gut, gave way to something way more familiar, a sense of anger at all the idiots—the CJs—who'd missed seeing that there was *way* more to her than met the eye.

"Get whatever you want," he said. It came out rough, almost abrupt, because he didn't necessarily want to spill out all the thoughts in his head, not to mention the crap crowding in his chest.

The waiter came back with their wine. He uncorked it, poured a little into a glass, and handed it to Griff. To taste, Griff was pretty sure, so he did. "It's, um, great," he said, and it was, though he had no real point of comparison. Now, set him up with a blindfold and a few brews and he would know his way around. But he wasn't going to fake it and do the wine-talk thing, *nose* or *finish* or whatever. He'd leave that to the rich guys at the tables all around him.

The waiter poured the wine and took their orders. Becca ordered a fancy salad and a filet with garlic mashed potatoes, and Griff ordered clam chowder and a boneless rib eye with a baked potato.

The waiter jotted their order down and melted away. More fancy restaurant waiter skills.

"So. Um. Tell me shit about you."

Becca laughed. "Is that always your small talk opener?"

"Something like that."

"Well, you know some of it. Alia and I grew up in Seattle. Our dad died of pancreatic cancer when I was six and Li was nine."

"I didn't know that. I'm sorry."

She made a *no big deal* gesture, the same one she'd made when she'd waved off the failed date the other night. He was about as convinced of her unconcern this time as he had been then.

"But you had Li and your mom."

"Well, I had Li."

He raised an eyebrow.

She looked down at the table and twisted one hand in the other. "My dad was retired FBI, and after he died, there was enough money from that and his life insurance that we were okay financially, but my mom fell apart. She just withdrew into herself. She didn't really have a diagnosis and we were too young to know it was depression. Li basically did everything. She had to grow up really fast. She was essentially full-time momming by the time she was ten. When a lot of kids still believed in Santa Claus, Li was buying her own Christmas presents."

She raised her gaze and caught him wincing. Her story explained a lot about Alia and her hyper capable schtick.

"And you? What was it like for you growing up?" She tilted her head.

"My dad wasn't around either. He left when I was eight. Married again, had a second family. Three adorable little girls—not so little anymore, obviously—who he dotes on. My mom never remarried. I think my dad was the love of her life —she just wasn't the love of his."

She winced. "No wonder you're not so interested in marriage and commitment."

He shrugged. "No—I thought I *wanted* to settle down, when I was a kid. I wanted what my dad had with his second wife. But you know, kids, they think they have it all figured out. It wasn't in the cards for me, and I'm good with that now."

"It sounds like there's a story there."

Griff shook his head. "Yeah, of course, there's always a story." The last thing he wanted was to tell it right now, cast a pall over things and let her know what a pathetic wreck he'd been when Marina had left. "Maybe some other time. The gist is, you're right about me. I'm not interested in that stuff. At least not anymore."

The waiter saved Griff by showing up with their soup and

salad. Becca's salad featured what he and Nate called "spiky" lettuce, plus candied nuts and goat cheese—definitely not his thing—but she dug into it and made a humming sound that found its way to his dick. She was so intent on the salad that he could watch her eat, which—damn. Neat, delicate, but fully invested, her eyes widening when she liked something, so he practically got a vicarious taste of all the flavors. She looked up and caught him staring, cocked her head to one side like she was asking a question.

He shrugged. "It's hot. The way you eat."

She laughed. "How do I eat?"

"You get into it. You enjoy it."

"Yeah. I freaking *love* food. It's probably my favorite thing." She dove back in, deftly spearing a pecan and humming again.

Yeah. Who didn't love food? But truth? Right now, Griff wanted to dig into the woman sitting across the table and savor every bite. If watching her eat a salad was making him drool, he couldn't imagine what would happen when she sank her teeth into a piece of meat.

14

O kay. Now she got it. The dinner-as-foreplay thing.

Griff took his credit card from the leather portfolio and tucked it into his wallet. He'd taken the bill from the waiter and relentlessly refused her offers to split it or chip in.

She wasn't opposed to paying her own way, but Griff made it easy—and sexy—for her to back down and let him handle it.

It was the same way he'd been about the wine. Zero bull-shit but also so, so competent. It was obvious he was ill-at-ease with the whole ridiculously expensive wine list thing. But he'd handled it perfectly. He hadn't starting posturing, but he also hadn't acted intimidated. What he'd said, about wanting to be a guy who made everyone comfortable when he grew up? That was already him, in a nutshell.

And it was unbelievably hot.

Then there was the way he'd been watching her eat, before she'd caught him. If it had been anyone else, it might have been creepy, but there was nothing creepy about having

Griff's attention on her mouth. Plus, she got it when she'd watched *him* with his clam chowder. He took the first bite and said, "God. Good," and made a rough noise of approval. Sort of like a hum or a groan. A noise she'd want to hear him make after he slid down her body and—

It had gone on like that through the main course, too. But what else could you expect from a guy who made turning the key in the ignition sexy?

Dinner hadn't been all dark looks and food flirting, either. They'd talked about her salon job and her relationship with Alia, then about his siblings and what had brought him to R&R. He said it had been pain from a serious knee injury— but she thought there was probably more to that story, too. Obviously, Griff didn't love to talk about himself. Which was actually way better than the alternative. She'd been out with mansplainers who couldn't shut up about their jobs, their cars, their doctoral dissertations, whatever. But Griff's restraint made her want to probe. Find out the whole story.

Except that was something you'd do if you were getting to know someone. If you were going to have a relationship with someone. And she was not. He'd made that abundantly clear: *You're right about me. I'm not interested in that stuff.* Meaning commitment, marriage, family, kids.

She'd made that one misstep, reaching for his hand after he'd been so great about the wine. She'd pulled back right away. Touching him like that had been too familiar, the kind of thing you'd do on a first date but wouldn't do on whatever this was. Foreplay for First Rites of Pleasure.

"You ready to go?" Griff asked.

"Sure," she said. Something wiggled in the pit of her stomach. Nerves. She hadn't been nervous up till now, but this was the rubber-meets-road portion of the program. If there was going to be any awkwardness, it was coming soon.

But he rested his hand at the small of her back and guided her out of the restaurant, and she felt herself relax into the sure touch.

Griff's truck was waiting, and he helped her up again.

She could get used to this treatment, but she wouldn't let herself. At least she wouldn't let herself expect it from him.

He drove them toward the waterfront and turned off into the Edgewater Hotel.

"What—"

"I wanted your first time to be someplace nice."

Oh, *God*. That made her throat tight. The fancy dinner had been way more than enough. "This place is—it must have cost you a fortune. I can't let you do that."

"Look." He faced her across the center console of the truck. "I don't have a lot to spend my money on, okay? I get room and board, and Jake pays well, with benefits, and—let me treat you. You asked me to do this, right? This is what you get when you ask Griff Ambrose to take a woman's V-card. The luxury *package*."

God help her, he smirked, and she was way beyond God's help because she felt it *all* the way down. She bit back a smile. "If she's worth doing . . ."

"Exactly. That book you were talking about. The one you were reading. Do you think he would have done her just any old where?"

"No way. Furs and firelight and all that."

He nodded, as if she'd just proved his very important point.

"Can I at least split it with you?"

He shook his head. "No."

"But—"

"No."

He turned away, dismissing the topic, threw his door open, and jumped down. He came around, helped her out, got a small bag out of the back of the truck—"supplies," he said, which made her low belly pull up tight with nerves and excitement—and ushered her into the lobby.

"Oh," she said. Under a vaulted ceiling, a wall of windows looked right out on the sound. "That's pretty."

The floor around the check-in desk was carpeted with plaid, and sculpted metal tree branches protruded from the front desk. In the main seating area, there was a stone fireplace with models of fish mounted over it, and a mammoth chandelier of antlers. If a hunting lodge, a cruise ship, and the Hilton had a love child, this lobby would be it.

"Have a seat. Relax. Wait here."

She sat in a comfy arm chair, and he set his bag beside her on the floor and went to check them in.

When he came back, he had a room key in his hand. "Key to the castle."

Various dirty jokes occurred to her, but she pressed her lips together. He took her hand, threading his fingers deliberately through hers and giving her a *look*. Several thousand volts of chemistry zinged the receptive parts of her. Her nipples tightened and her clit stood at attention and—

Those body parts were not usually nearly so—chatty.

"You ready?" he asked.

He was smirking again. The bastard. He knew. And the worst part was, there wasn't a damn thing she could do about it.

15

He kissed her in the elevator. Because, elevator. Because she was just so damn *cute*, all big-eyed and awed one minute, then a moment later flushed and flustered, her nipples visible through the lightweight cloth of her dress. Maybe the innocent thing was an act, maybe it wasn't, but he had to admit that it worked on him, like a ton of bricks.

But the kiss wasn't cute. It was—

She was—

Her mouth was soft. Warm. And the way she opened for him, it felt so personal. Like she was letting *him* in. And she didn't just take his tongue, which would have been sexy enough, she gave back. She tangled with him. She teased him. She edged into his mouth and took control for a hot second, which jacked him way up, fast. He took control back, pressing her against the wall and wedging his thigh between hers, and that pushed his buttons hard, too.

So did the little moan she let out when his thigh made contact with the vee of her legs, and the heat he could instantly feel through whatever she was wearing—not much —and his own pants.

Ding!

The doors opened. She clutched at his arms when he pulled away, trying to keep him close, and he laughed. She laughed, too, and let him go.

"You're hot, you know that?"

Again, that goddamn surprise on her face. Fuckers, all of them, whoever they were.

He led her out of the elevator and down the hall. To their room. He didn't look down because he knew his dick was making an undignified tent in his pants, and he didn't want to draw her eyes there. Not yet, anyway. Later, he'd want her looking plenty. The tent jumped at the thought of her, big-eyed, her mouth puffy from kisses, staring at him with the same awe she'd given the Met earlier tonight and the Edge-water lobby just now. Not that he deserved any particular awe —although he did okay for himself—but just because that was what he wanted, desperately, to put on her face.

He opened the door to the room and let her walk in ahead of him. It wasn't a brilliant act of chivalry or anything, it just let him ogle the sway of her hips under that teeny-tiny dress. The dress was so ridiculously short and so ridiculously loose that a stiff breeze would bare her ass to him. He wanted so badly to flip the edge up and look at what she was wearing underneath . . .

But he was a tour guide tonight, and he had responsibilities. He had to set the standard for all visitors to come, so she would know what she deserved and never settle for less.

"Oh my God, Griff, *look*. Furs!"

There was, in fact, a fat little fur-covered ottoman in the shape of a bear.

And a fireplace, with a fire in it. One of his requests. And a bottle of champagne on the table and a bowl of chocolate-covered strawberries.

She clapped a hand to her mouth. "Oh, Griff."

"First things first." He opened the champagne, poured two glasses, and toasted her.

Her eyes were not just big. They were shiny. His chest ached, hard. Well, damn. It was so easy to please her. Like no one had ever goddamn tried. And as mad as he was at all the other assholes who hadn't, he was way happier to be the first, which worried him.

He set the candles he'd brought around the room and lit them while she watched and sipped champagne. She'd kicked her shoes off, and he thought of telling her to put them back on, but he liked the way she was wiggling her toes against the plush of the carpet.

"It's so much," she whispered. "It's too much."

"That's what she said," he quipped, trying to lighten the mood a little. He didn't *want* her to cry. That hadn't been the point of any of this.

She giggled and came close as he lit the last candle. She put a hand on his chest and slid it slowly down his stomach to his belt, where he caught it and removed it before she could finish her exploration.

"Not yet."

"But I want to feel you."

The body part in question throbbed at the sentiment, but he shook his head. He felt wound up all over. Like his skin was too tight. Like his blood was rushing too fast. Like he was going to lose his mind if he didn't kiss her.

He touched her cheek. Eased his hand back to cup her head. Stepped forward at the same time as he drew her to him. And kissed her.

She whimpered into his mouth. *Fuck.* She dug her fingers, hard, into his biceps. Clutched him, her body alive against his. She was going to kill him.

He metered the kisses. Held them back, held her still, a hand on her head, then her arms, then her waist. He didn't want to lose control. He could taste the wine she'd drunk but mostly he could taste *her*, a pleasure with no name at all that he was pretty sure he was going to crave for months after this.

The length of her body pressed to his. Curves against chest, and then she tipped her hips against his dick, seeking him with her heat. The shamelessness of it, so at odds with the good-girl vibe, slayed him. He tipped back, rubbing against her, abandoning better judgment. He slid his hands under the front of her dress and found a triangle of lace that subsided to a sopping string before it dove between her ass cheeks. J*esus*. He made a noise he didn't mean to make and she bit him, hard.

This wasn't supposed to be like this. He was supposed to be in charge here.

He forced himself to man up. He crushed his lust, put an inch of space between his throbbing dick and her heat, slid his hand up the curve of her waist to the lace cup of her bra. He brushed the lace away. Her skin was softer than satin, and he wanted to apologize for the roughness of his palms, but he didn't think the sound she made when he circled in on her nipple was begging for an apology. It was begging for *something*, but not that.

Her nipple was the tightest knot. And when he brushed the tip, she whimpered again. And again. He tested her preferences. The flick. The pinch. The tease. The good news was, Becca liked it all. He knew that because his other hand was cupped over those practically non-existent panties, and he could feel her getting wetter against his palm.

He pushed her dress up. And drew back so he could look. She was—

"Becca, you are so fucking gorgeous."

Her eyes were huge, her lower lip slack and reddened—she was wrecked, and it looked good on her. So did the barely-there bra and panties. She was perfect. Generous but compact. Those tits—

"I fucking love this dress," he said, and sucked her nipple through the lace of her bra.

She cried out. Not a little whimper or moan. A full-on cry that arrowed straight through his erection. Her knees buckled, which gave him such a double surge of lust and satisfaction that it almost felled *him*. He was going to have to get them both horizontal.

Which—

He hadn't thought this all the way through. Her book fantasy man probably would have been twelve steps ahead of him, but apparently that guy hadn't been with anyone half as hot as Becca or he wouldn't have been thinking at all.

He walked her backward to the bed and gently tipped her back so she was sitting on the edge. When he tried to pull away, she protested and clutched at him again.

She was greedy, just like he'd been sure she'd be.

Why the fuck hadn't every guy on the West Coast wanted to give her the world?

Idiots, all of them.

He was going to have to compress the world into a single night, because that's all he could give her. Maybe he was no better than all the other douchebags in the long run, but at least he would show her what she deserved. Just this once.

16

N*o.*

That was about how well her brain was working at this point. She just knew she didn't want him to walk away. She wanted his body pressed against hers, she wanted as much of him as she could have, and she wanted it as soon as possible. The idea of him moving away, taking his warmth and the intense pull of chemistry that had pretty much blown all rational thought away—

No, no, no.

She grabbed his arms, but he evaded her grasp. He had a plan she couldn't understand, because she just *wanted*.

He was turning the covers down for her. Pushing them back. Making a space for her on the clean white sheets.

He came close again, stood between her legs, and she reached for his belt buckle. He batted her hands away.

"Patience," he said.

"I'm ready."

He laughed. "Not yet."

"You're a tease!"

"I'll tell you when you're ready. You wanted the job done right."

He stepped closer, which made her pussy cry out for contact, but all he was doing was reaching for the zipper of her dress. He maneuvered it down, and she let the dress fall away from her shoulders. "Yeah," he said. "Yeah, yeah, yeah. God. You are—"

She lifted her butt, pushed the dress to the floor, kicked it away. Reached for his buckle again and was rebuffed again. "I just want to touch," she whimpered. "I just want to *see*."

Apparently she wasn't above begging. She'd never actively longed to see or touch a penis before, let alone begged to. *This* was what people meant when they talked about sexual chemistry. It was some weird fucking magic.

"Scoot back," he said.

She obeyed.

"Lie back."

She did, and let her knees fall open, and he groaned. He traced a finger along the top edge of her panties, which sent heat surging to her core. Then along the edges of the vee, and she closed her thighs on his fingers. He cupped her, and she rubbed herself against his palm. And holy, holy, that was sweet friction.

He took his hand away.

"Nooo!"

He laughed at her.

"*Griff.*"

"Are you always like this?"

She was suddenly insanely self-conscious. She sat up, brought her legs together, crossed her arms.

"Oh, no, hell, no, don't do that. It's a good thing. It's the sexiest fucking thing I've ever seen. You, all—" He gestured at her. "Flushed and riled up and sprawled out and sopping wet. So fucking hot."

Ohhhhh. Well, hell yes, then. She uncrossed her arms. Lay back again and let him resume his work. Which he did, running a fingertip along the skinny little strip of damp fabric between her legs. Pausing to nudge it aside and find her clit. Just for a second, but her hips bucked. He knelt. Even that made her wetter. He kissed his way from one knee up her inner thigh and back down the other side.

He settled a kiss on her, through the lace, and she strained for contact. Putting a hand on each of her hips, he held her steady as he teased over the fabric with his lips, nipping and licking and blowing heat.

"Griff."

"What do you need?"

"More."

He tugged the ruined underwear down, knelt again, and touched his tongue to her clit. Circled it. Just the tip, then the flat, the tip again, his lips closing over her. She felt his teeth for an instant, and the almost-pain of that doubled her sensation. Then more caresses, his tongue so skilled she froze like she was listening to the feel of it. Besides, he was holding her down so she couldn't move, even if she'd wanted to.

She was going to come. She could feel it gathering. She was panting, the back of her throat dry with it. One of her hands had fisted the covers, and her heel was dug into the side of the bed.

And then he stopped.

"No! I was going to—"

"You were going to what?"

"Come. I was going to come."

"I know. That's why I stopped."

"No. Fair."

"I want you to come with me inside you. If you can."

She knew that wasn't easy for some women—she'd had enough conversations with friends and read enough books. And if it wasn't easy for most women, it would probably be even harder for her.

But she had confidence that if anyone could make it happen, it would be Griff.

She reached for his belt buckle again.

"Not yet."

"But—"

"But what?" he egged her on.

"I want it."

"You want *what*?" He was smirking again.

"I want you."

His eyes got darker. "What do you want me to do?"

"I want you to—" She faltered and pulled in a deep breath. "I want you inside me."

"That's not what you were going to say," he scolded. "Say it."

She didn't even care anymore. She was beyond feeling self-conscious. "I want you to fuck me."

"That's the way. But you know what? You're not ready yet."

"I am! I am ready."

"Nope," he said. "You know how I can tell? Because you can still form coherent sentences. We have to fix that."

He began unbuttoning his shirt. She watched, fascinated, as the sides of his shirt fell back, revealing toned pecs and rippled abs that narrowed to a vee before diving under that damn belt. It was by far the best-looking display she'd ever witnessed in person. She didn't try to touch, though. Not yet. She didn't want him to stop taking his clothes off.

And he didn't. He unfastened the belt buckle, and she had to admit, it was sexy to watch him do it. He took his time, drawing back the end, pulling the length of leather slowly from the loops of his pants so it hissed across the fabric. Her gaze hopped from the tease of that display to the action under his fly. His pants weren't keeping his secrets.

He unbuttoned them, and slid the zipper down, dropping them to the floor.

Boxer briefs. With an impressive bulge in them. Her hand involuntarily flew out to grab, and this time, he didn't stop her. She wrapped her hand around him and squeezed, and he jumped under her touch, warm and so, so hard. And big. Damn. Step aside, Jondalar.

When she let go, he eased the waistband of his briefs over the slick, dark red head of his cock, and replaced her hand with his. One long, tight stroke, skin-to-skin, from base to tip, while she watched and her pussy pulsed in sympathy and need.

"Soon," he promised. "Almost."

He crossed the room—hey, now *that* was a nice view— and came back with a condom.

She held out a hand. "Let me. I haven't ever. So, it's part of the V-card *package* deal, don't you think?"

He laughed at her negotiation, but surprised her by turning the packet over to her. She tore the foil, set the disk against the drop of moisture that had formed on his taut head, held the tip, and rolled it down. "Like a pro," she teased, looking up at him through her lashes.

"Indeed," he said, his voice rough.

She leaned back on the bed, opened her knees and pulled them up. "I'm right here," she said.

The look in his eyes was so raw and hot that for a split second she thought the power balance had shifted. She thought she might actually see Griff Ambrose lose control. And it was about the sexiest thing she could imagine.

But then he crawled over her, took himself in hand, and began using the tip of his cock to tease her. First, he nudged it against her opening, which made her clench involuntarily and try to bear down on him. Then he stroked the swollen head up to her clit and drew ever-tightening circles until she was panting again like she had been a few minutes earlier. He stroked his length through her lips, gliding on her wetness, while he bent his head to suck her nipples, and her clit felt raw and huge.

The tension in her belly drew and coiled until it was almost painful.

"I'm going to fuck you now," he said conversationally. "I bet the guy in your book had a more romantic way of saying it, but I don't give a flying fuck because I'm the one between your legs, and that's what I'm going to do to you."

What he did, though, didn't feel like fucking. It felt like—

Oh, *God,* it felt so good.

Just the head. Which, even that, was such a powerful stretch. Her heart was pounding and she kept thinking, *This is it! I'm not a virgin anymore!*

Her body was tightening around him, which was sending more sensation toward her clit and her ass and her nipples. He eased in a little more, and a little bit more. She kept waiting for it to hurt, but it didn't. It just felt *good.*

He bent again and took a nipple in his mouth. Sucked, flicked, licked.

She groaned and pressed toward him, wanting more. Needing more.

It was a stretch now, a little bit of a burn, but not bad.

With a thrust, he was all the way in her. Okay, *ow*, that was a lot of burn, but as she adjusted to the feeling, it started to subside, and—wow. He was in her to the hilt, which meant his body met hers right at her pubic bone and when he edged forward to seat himself more fully, he rolled and stretched *right* across her clit, and she cried out.

"You okay?"

"Do. That. Again," she instructed.

"Greedy," he said, with great satisfaction. "I knew you'd be greedy. God, that's hot." And he did exactly what she'd asked, with the added benefit that he propped himself over her and worked her nipple again with his tongue.

She got lost in the sensations, the chain of electricity linking her nipple to her clit, the winding up, reeling in, tightening down—

"I'm going to—ohhhhhh."

She never finished the sentence because he'd pushed her over the edge, and she was coming, coming so hard her vision went white and pleasure knotted her tight and unwound her again, in alternating waves. Vaguely, dimly, she heard him cry out, sensed him rigid above her, felt him pulsing inside her, thrusting deep and holding there, but all she could do was wrap her arms and legs around him and hold on for all she was worth.

17

He hadn't meant to go over with her. He'd meant to give her two or three orgasms and come when he was good and ready.

But she was—

She was too much. Too hot, too tight, too eager, too grateful, too greedy. She was all around him and she'd gotten *in* him, too: under his skin, in his head, rattling around in his chest. It wasn't just the slick heat that had taken him over the edge, it was how damn much she was into it.

He separated himself from her, taking care with the condom. He went into the bathroom and came back out with a warm washcloth, because even though his strongest impulse was to get the hell out of dodge before shit got real, there was no way he was going to be that guy. Everyone deserved to be treated like a princess and given a good cuddle afterwards.

He caught her examining a spot of blood on the hotel bedsheets, looking chagrined.

"Ah, no biggie," he said. "It's just so we can prove to the village elders that you didn't cheat your First Rites."

She laughed and stretched under his caretaking, that beautiful curvy body arching back against the bed.

"Feels nice," she murmured.

He dealt with the washcloth, then came back to bed and wrapped his arms around her.

"Griff?"

"Mmm-hmm?"

"That was good."

He smiled into her hair. "Glad to hear it. It was good for me, too."

"You virgin fetishist, you."

Yeah, that part had been fun, for sure, though there was more to it. He almost told her that wasn't why it had been good, but then he thought about how he'd been the one who hadn't wanted things to be complicated, which was still true, so he just left it alone.

"Do you feel different?" he asked her.

"Well, I feel like I just came really hard."

He chuckled. "Aside from that."

"Nope. Well—" she hesitated. "I feel relieved. That there's nothing wrong with me."

Shocked, he pulled away and sat up. "*Wrong* with you? Are you *kidding*?"

She bit her lip. "When you're twenty-four and you haven't —I know it's not true, but it just starts to seem like—maybe— it's you? You know? Anyway, it's just good to be over that hump, literally. So, at least now I know that all those times I wasn't that into it, it was just because I wasn't with the right guys. Now I'll know to be pickier. And maybe a little more—I'll have higher standards."

"Good," he said, pondering that. Her going after the right guys, having higher standards. Getting what she wanted. Getting off with a long cry like she had a couple of minutes ago. With the right guys. Who weren't him. "That's what you deserve, Becca—for it to feel amazing. Every time."

She blushed deeper, but she looked incredibly pleased with herself, which was at least as much reward as the rest of it for Griff. "One of New Becca's resolutions is to stop dating assholes," she said. "I decided it would be easier to do that if I wasn't constantly dealing with the virginity thing."

"Glad to help," he said.

"If you don't mind my asking, how'd you lose your virginity?"

He grinned. "It's such a teenage guy story. Are you sure you want to hear? It doesn't necessarily paint me in the best light."

"Go for it."

"I was fifteen."

"Fifteen!"

"Yeah. That wasn't actually that young in the town where I grew up. It was just the way it was. We didn't have anything else to do. By the time I lost mine, I already felt like I was behind the curve."

She rolled her eyes at him.

"Well, I know different now," he said. "Anyway, I was at summer camp. And there was this girl there. She was my age, and pretty, with—" he paused, trying to be truthful but not crude. "—she was well-endowed. All the guys were interested."

"You guys," Becca said darkly. "All alike."

"At fifteen, hell yeah." He eyed her admiringly. "Not so different now, maybe, either. Just able to see a few more good traits without tunnel vision." He smoothed her hair back and kissed her nose.

"So this girl? The curvy one?"

"Everyone said that she'd come to camp with a box of condoms. Like, her parents had put it into her luggage, just in case. And that, as you might imagine, made her the object of a lot of curiosity. Mine included. I made friends with her, and then I kissed her one night next to the lake, and a few nights after that, we used up the condoms. In the woods, on her sleeping bag."

"Did you take *her* virginity, too?" Becca asked, big-eyed.

He kind of wanted to say yes, just for the first rites cred, but the truth was, he'd been third in line. He shook his head. "Nope. Just mine."

"Was it good?"

"Not the first time," he said. "I mean, it was fine for me, but it was just like you'd expect. Over in a blink of an eye. The second and third times, though, I managed to do a little better."

"Just the small pack, then?" she teased.

"Yeah, that was what I said, too," he said, grinning. He hesitated, wanting to ask a question that had been on his mind, but not sure how to word it. "Hey."

"Yeah?"

"How *does* someone as hot as you end up a virgin at twenty-four?"

She smiled, a cat-who-swallowed-the-canary smile. "I had a slow start. When I was seventeen, I started dating this guy,

Todd. He came from a conservative Christian family, and he wanted us to save ourselves for marriage. I would have been fine with—" She bit her lip. "But he was adamant. Nothing below the waist. So that's how it was, and—you'd be surprised how hot that could be."

Her cheeks pinked up.

"I wouldn't," he said, thinking about the way Becca kissed and how she'd responded to his mouth on her nipples. His dick stirred back to life.

"We were together three years. After high school, he went to community college and I was working, and we were seeing each other a few times a week. He'd hinted a proposal was on the horizon. I thought maybe he'd even bought a ring. But then he—"

She bit her lip again, and he realized he was braced, anger tightening up his chest. Someone had hurt Becca, and he so, so wasn't okay with that.

"He quit waiting. He'd been having sex with someone else for several months. While I kept holding out for him. The worst part was, when I found out—" Her voice broke, but she sailed on through it and steadied out. "He said he still wanted to marry me, and he thanked *me* for staying pure even though he hadn't been able to resist temptation."

"What the *fuck*? Like, what the *actual fuck*? That *bastard*!"

The guy, whoever he was, was lucky that Griff wasn't violent by nature, because otherwise his days would have been numbered. Griff would have hunted him down and strangled him with bare hands.

"Shit, Becca, that *sucks*." *I know what that's like,* he didn't say aloud. But he remembered, with a rush of pain. The sense of loss and betrayal. Someone you trusted—hell, loved—

making you feel like none of it had ever mattered. Like *you* hadn't mattered.

She waved a hand. "It was a long time ago."

He'd seen that hand wave before, though. He knew—she didn't like to admit to anyone how much something hurt her.

Took one to know one, on that front.

She rolled away from him, toward the edge of the bed. She grabbed her phone and tapped an app.

"What are you doing?" he asked.

She gave him a look. "Ordering myself a Lyft."

He winced. She must have seen, because she said, "What?"

"Do you think that's how I roll? A *Lyft*?"

"Um—no. Sorry. I just didn't want you to feel like you had to drive me home."

He glared at her.

"Sorry! OK."

"Pour yourself another glass of champagne," he said. "Have some chocolate covered strawberries. Celebrate. *Then* I'll take you home. Also—"

He got up, crossed to his bag, and pulled out the gift he'd brought her from the lingerie shop. "Thought you might want something clean to put on. Since your underwear's all wet."

"Your fault," she said, shooting him a look that made his dick wake up and show interest in more action.

He watched as she pulled his gift from the bag. "Wow," she said. "That's *really* pretty. And you *really* didn't have to do that."

He shrugged. "Kinda wanted to see you in it."

"Should I put it on?"

The best part was watching her wriggle the red teddy bodysuit up her body. She shimmied to accomplish it and her tits were like something he would have dreamt up when he was a teenager.

Goddammit, he was going to fuck her again.

She reached for her dress, but he put an arm out to stop her. "Not yet," he said.

Her eyes got big at that.

18

The second time was even better than the first. He took a long time getting her ready, kneeling at her feet, her ass cupped in his big hands, his face buried against the lace of the bodysuit. She was pretty sure, from how seriously he took his job, that he'd planned this from the moment he'd first seen the scrap of red lingerie in the store.

He peeled her out of the bodysuit and laid her back on the bed and then he stroked into her until her world narrowed to the sharp sparkle of sensation where his body met hers. In, out, heat and light and that crazy spiraling tension that wound all the way to climax and took him with her. This time, she stayed aware enough to watch him, the way all his muscles went taut, the expression on his face one of pleasure bleeding right to the edge of pain.

Afterwards, he asked her if she wanted a shower.

"We could shower together. You know, save time," she suggested.

He grinned. "We'd be here all night if I got in there with you."

All night wouldn't be so bad, she thought, and then was annoyed with herself. What had he said to her? His threshold for complicated was so low that he didn't even stick around for donuts and coffee. She wasn't going to get sappy and want more. She wasn't going to be that dumb stereotype.

She got in the shower and washed herself clean, marveling at how wet he'd made her, and how swollen. How sensitive and greedy her body still felt.

Then she sat on the bed and toyed with her phone while he showered, and she tried not to break down the door to the bathroom and demand more.

It was just horniness, though. He'd gotten her going, and apparently now that she knew what she'd been missing, that particular genie wasn't going back in its bottle. It was up to her and her alone to rub that magic lamp.

The bathroom door opened, and he came out on a cloud of spicy wood-and-wilderness *Griff*. He smiled at her, but the expression on his face was different now. More remote.

Ah, so this was how he did one-and-done.

That was fine; she could do that, too. "Ready to head out?" she asked.

"Yup."

He must have blown the candles out when she was in the shower, and now he gathered his things and restored them to the duffle. It was strange watching it all go back into the bag, all of what they'd done undone—except for the act itself, which had permanently changed her.

He held the door for her on the way out, hit the elevator button and pressed door-open so she wouldn't be rushed—

but he didn't kiss her. He didn't even look at her, fiddling with his phone as they descended to the main floor. They crossed the lobby in silence, stopped briefly at the desk where he checked them out, and stepped out together into the night.

Traffic on Alaskan Way was surprisingly busy for after midnight, cars rushing by on the multi-lane street. He took her hand and stepped off the curb.

A car peeled out from nowhere with a screech, startling her. It must have been idling along the curb somewhere, and they hadn't seen it. Its headlights swept across their faces, and Griff jumped back, yanking Becca's arm so hard it hurt.

She was startled. The lights. The sharp pain in her shoulder. The harshness of a man who'd been so gentle with her body less than an hour earlier. It took her a moment to let go of her surprise and tune in to Griff.

He'd dropped into a crouch on the curb, and terror overwrote his features. His eyes were a million miles away.

She knew it immediately—she'd spent enough time around Nate and Alia, listening to them talk about Nate's struggles and the men Alia treated. This was some kind of flashback.

She knew not to startle him out of it. She knew he wasn't here with her and that he could be violent without realizing it, a reaction to whatever was in his half-conscious mind. She crouched beside him and murmured his name. Quietly. Over and over again. He was frozen in place, his gaze on a distant point, his breathing fast but quiet—as if he were hiding in the dark, waiting for his chance to—to what, she wondered? Attack? Defend? A strange tenderness caught at her, the two of them there, him suffering something she couldn't see— that no one could see. How awful to have been hurt in a way that could overpower his consciousness, so that the sweep of headlights could scare him into an animal retreat.

"Griff." Not trying to call him out of it, just trying to reassure him. She must have said it twenty times.

Finally something shifted in his gaze. A tiny flicker of awareness. His pupils shrank, and he was looking at her. The tenderness she'd been feeling for him was reflected right back at her. Something swelled in her chest, and she reached out a hand to touch his face.

He caught her hand and clasped it to his cheek.

"Marina," he said, his voice thick with affection and longing. "Thank God you're okay. I couldn't find you."

Becca jerked her hand back like his stubble was a cactus's quills.

"It's Becca," she said.

Her voice sounded cold and harsh, loud.

Then he was *really* back. His eyes focused, hard and tight, on her face, and she saw it: recognition followed quickly by disappointment and regret.

Well, of course. He'd loved his wife.

What had Nate said the morning after she and Griff had watched *The Princess Bride*?

You and he want different things.

And what does *Griff want?*

To bang enough women that he forgets his ex-wife. Which, I might add, is a lost cause. He's totally not over her. I think he'd take her back in a heartbeat if she asked.

She thought: *You hit the nail on the head, Nate.*

"Sorry—Jesus. Sorry."

Griff got to his feet, a little shaky.

"I have these flashbacks."

He was obviously sheepish, and at once, her compassion returned.

"PTSD," she said.

"That's—yeah." He shook his head. "That was probably really scary for you. I'm so sorry."

It had been, a little. Her hands were shaking now. But the last thing he needed was to worry about her. "I've heard about it, so I figured that's what you were going through. And you weren't—you didn't do anything. You just crouched down. Does it happen a lot?"

"It's happened before. When something startles me, usually. Loud noises, bright lights, things flashing. Look, um —if you could maybe just not mention this to Nate and Alia? Or Jake?"

"They don't know?" she asked, surprised.

He shook his head. "It just not something I talk about."

That struck her as odd—and not quite right—but she left it alone for the time being. He could do without the third degree in the state he was in.

He took a deep breath and sighed. "Thanks for not freaking out. For just bearing with me."

"Of course," she said. "Seems like the least I could do in exchange for a big favor."

That made him laugh, shakily. "Just so you know," he said, "that favor one hundred percent paid for itself. Seriously. You don't owe me anything, and you never will. Besides," he said. "Friends look out for each other."

It was her turn to laugh. "I guess that makes us pretty good friends then, huh?"

"Yeah." He took her hand firmly in his, looked both ways, and guided her across the street. "Yeah, I'd say it does."

His voice was warm, and it warmed her.

Friendship was good.

It was perfect, in fact. Safe. Simple.

Because Griff was obviously, patently, completely still in love with his ex-wife.

19

On Monday afternoon, Griff plopped himself down at R&R's peer support group.

He tried to make it to the groups as often as he could, even though he rarely, if ever, talked about himself. He figured someone had to do the listening. And that wasn't going to change today, even as his conversation with Becca from the other night echoed in his thoughts.

They don't know?

It just not something I talk about.

Most of the chairs in the circle were full, and Jake was already seated across the circle, making the folding chair under him look like a kid's potty. He was the perfect stereotype, physically, of an Army Ranger—over six feet tall and big, muscled, tough as nails. Except that if you looked closely —and *only* if you looked closely—you'd see that one of his legs was prosthetic from mid-thigh down. And Jake wasn't the only one; a bunch of the guys in group had prosthetics.

Griff had been coming to group for longer than anyone

besides Jake. Sometimes Griff half expected Jake to kick him out, or at least chastise him for still taking up space, two years on. But no, Jake greeted Griff with the same welcoming grin every time, the same one he was shooting him right now.

The door opened and CJ sauntered in. Griff raised his eyebrows in Jake's direction, and Jake nodded, a half-smile creasing his face. This was CJ's first time. It was a good sign when a guy showed up. It meant he was starting to open up, let the toxic stuff drain away, at least as much as any of them could.

CJ settled into a seat near Jake, then looked up, saw Griff, and gave him a friendly nod.

Jake called the room to order. "Most of you know how this works, but there are a couple of new guys here today—"

It was when Jake led groups that Griff admired him most. Anyone could run a hotel for wounded vets, but only someone with guts could tell and re-tell the story of how his own life had been shattered in order to help other people heal. Not to mention listening, without flinching, to all the other stories of pain, neglect, guilt, and betrayal.

Griff could do the listening part, but the rest he would leave to Jake.

"The only thing you have to tell us is your first name. If you want to tell us anything else—age, rank, life story—it's up to you. I'll start. My name is Jake. I'm an Army Ranger . . ."

He always said it in the present tense, and yet Griff knew Jake had no plans of returning to active duty. He'd loved fighting, but he didn't miss the army. He was serving now in the best way he knew how.

Griff had missed the army so bad in the beginning—the

sense of purpose, the ease of always knowing exactly what he needed to do next, the brotherhood. It felt like he'd lost part of himself when he left. But gradually, that feeling had dulled. R&R had its own routines. Its own ever-changing brotherhood.

Griff couldn't claim that doing odd jobs for Jake was his life's mission, though it was reassuring for him to know where he was going and what was expected of him each morning when he got up. He just didn't feel like he'd chosen his path. Becca had nailed it—he didn't know what he was going to do when he grew up.

Becca.

He'd been trying to put Saturday night out of his head. It wouldn't do him any good to dwell on it—not how good the sex had been and not how the evening had ended. Remembering how he'd cowered on the curb drenched him with shame, even though Becca had been unbelievably kind about it.

Becca had been fucking amazing on Saturday night. Bits and pieces of it kept coming back to him, vivid flashes of how hot she'd been, how eager. The noises she'd made, how the red lace had hugged her curves. He'd been wearing out his right hand in bed these last few nights, reliving it.

He was pretty pleased with himself. He knew he'd given her a first time to remember.

The only problem was, it had been equally memorable for him. Hence his wrist fatigue.

"—next thing I knew I woke up and they were telling me they'd had to take the limb."

Jake was telling the story of what he'd lost to that IED

that day—his buddy, his leg. He'd told the story tens of times, but everyone listened like it was new. Maybe because of the way Jake told it, like he was still looking for meaning in it himself.

They went around the circle. Everyone talked, at least a little. When it was CJ's turn, he haltingly told a story Griff could tell he hadn't revealed to many people. He'd been trapped three hours in a wrecked armored carrier. The two other men with him had been killed. He'd been badly injured, hallucinating that the dead men were trying to kill him.

CJ closed his mouth then, and then his eyes, tight.

No wonder the kid was a little jumpy.

"You did good," Griff said, without thinking. "You did good, telling us."

That was Jake's job, usually, but Griff jumped in from time to time. He knew Jake's lines as well as Jake did, and Jake was glad to share the mentorship role with anyone who felt compelled to step up to the plate. It was a brotherhood, after all.

Now Griff looked across the circle to Jake, who nodded. *Go for it.* Griff nodded back. "You have nightmares?" he asked CJ.

CJ's eyes found Griff's. "Yeah."

Griff nodded. "Anyone else here have nightmares?"

Hands shot up around the circle.

They talked about how it felt to wake gasping for air, your lungs flattened by an explosion that was years or decades old. How it felt to realize you'd struck at or throttled the person in the bed next to you, or even just flailed badly enough to hurt them. How dark it was in the middle of the night, and how long the hours were between one a.m. and sunrise, even on the shortest nights of the year.

Well, the others talked. Griff just listened.

Griff had each of them say one thing that helped him get through the dark hours. Deep breathing. Meditation. Food. Texting a friend. Counting down from a thousand. Jerking off.

"Whiskey," someone said, and Griff let it go, because, truth.

"Nothing," a guy named Reggie said, and they all laughed and then sighed.

If anyone noticed that Griff asked the questions but didn't give answers, no one said anything.

As the other guys were filing out, CJ stopped. "Thanks," he said to Griff.

"You're welcome, dude."

"No, I mean it. Thanks."

He took a step toward the door, then turned back. "And, um, I thought you might want to know. That girl, Becca—"

"Woman," Griff said reflexively.

"She said she wasn't interested in going out with me. But I appreciate the help."

Griff knew he should feel bad, but he didn't. Not at all. In fact, he mainly was thinking about the way Becca had raked her hands through his hair as he'd licked her clit, and feeling pure male triumph.

"You win some, you lose some," he told CJ. "Back in the saddle, right?"

"A bunch of us are going out tonight, if you want to come along. Play wingman. Or get some pus—action yourself."

Yeah, CJ wouldn't waste any time, and Griff wouldn't

waste any guilt. "Thanks. Not tonight—but I appreciate the invitation. You going to drive the Shelby there?"

As soon as the words were out of his mouth, he knew. Like his brain had been slowly cobbling the pieces together, and it had just needed one more push to click this last one into place.

"You don't drive," Griff said. It wasn't a question.

CJ's face had gone pale.

"You haven't driven since—"

"Look, man, I gotta run," CJ said, and he did. Like, literally.

Griff watched him go, musing.

Jake came over. "Hey. That was great."

"Thanks."

"You're good with them."

Griff shrugged. Too much praise made him squirmy, and he knew he didn't deserve any in this case. He'd just put his foot in it with CJ, in a big way. And how could he take credit for helping anyone else when he wasn't brave enough to admit to his own bullshit? Those men who wore it on their sleeve; they were the real heroes.

"How'd you like to lead the group, from time to time?"

Griff shook his head. "Nah. No thanks."

"Why not? You listen. You know what to say. It's because of you that CJ even showed up today. They trust you, Griff."

Griff shrugged. "I'm just imitating stuff I've heard you say. I'm the last one who should be giving anyone advice." *Not to mention, I'm the world's biggest hypocrite when it comes to this support group. Trying to get everyone else to spill their guts while I stay clammed up.* "I'm just here because I couldn't hack it in the real world." He said it lightly.

"That's not the whole story, and you know it. You lost buddies. You lost your *wife*."

"I didn't lose her." He'd always hated that fucking phrase. "She left."

"There are lots of ways to get the shit kicked out of you, Griff." Jake's eyes were knowing.

For a moment he let himself drift back there. To what it had felt like, flying in and looking around for Marina at the airfield. Scanning faces for the dark curtain of her hair, waiting for the flash of recognition and affection to light up a face turned toward him. All the other guys had people there, with signs and flowers and flags and gifts. Kids running up and throwing their arms around their waists or their legs. Women kissing them like they were starved for it.

He'd told himself something had delayed Marina. Traffic. He texted her but didn't get an answer. In the end, he hitched a ride home with a guy, his wife, and their kids, and the whole way, it was one big huge love fest with Griff on the outside, feeling more and more awkward.

And then they'd dropped him in front of his big house— new construction, like Marina'd wanted—and he could feel it. The deadness, the emptiness, of the house. Even before he opened the door.

Inside it was just *hollow*. His stuff was still there, but nothing of hers. And no *her*.

Just the note.

"Griff."

He shook his head. "I'm nobody's role model. I've been here two years and I still don't know what the fuck I'm supposed to be doing with my life."

Jake raised his eyebrows. "It takes time. You know that."

"Yeah, well. I don't feel like I'm making much progress."

"If you're beating yourself up about the job at Harbor Grill, you can quit that crap. You left because they treated you like dirt. That's not washing out."

Jake was referring to one of the two times Griff had tried to leave R&R and find a civilian job. But Griff hadn't been thinking about Harbor Grill. He'd been thinking about the *other* job that hadn't worked out, at the new hotel. The one he'd gotten fired from. He hadn't told anyone how that gig had ended. Not even Jake, who he'd trust with his life.

"I can't keep depending on you to create work for me forever."

Jake shrugged. "There's always work here for a good man."

Griff's impulse was to push the compliment away, but he just said, "Thanks."

"Speaking of work," Jake said. "We're going to need to hire again soon. I can't keep making Sibby do double duty on the reception desk and event planning. She did the Memorial Day picnic planning, and now she's jumping into the Fourth of July picnic and Fun Run. I either need to hire someone who can do event planning, or I need to just let Sibby run wild with the events and put someone else on the desk."

"I can help with whatever you need," Griff said.

"Thanks," Jake said. "Might take you up on that, until I can find a permanent solution. I know you don't love the desk stuff, though."

"I'll do whatever you need."

Jake gave him a look. "I need you to think about what I said earlier. About leading the group sometimes. Just sleep on it, okay, man?"

Griff nodded, but he was full of shit. He had no intention of sleeping on it. That would presume he was capable of sleeping at all, but between war nightmares and memories of a certain hot blonde moaning his name, he'd given up on the notion completely.

20

Becca strolled into Julia's Day Spa and Salon with her big handbag slung over her shoulder and her lunch in hand, set both down on the floor behind the front desk, and sat down to listen to the voicemails that had come in since the previous afternoon.

Hi there? This is Mary Rombard? I'm going to need to cancel my appointment today because my personal trainer can only meet with me between nine and ten and as much as I love my massages, I have to put my exercise first. . . .

She copied down the number and the message, verbatim, because she knew Julia would get a kick out of it. *As much as I love my massages, I have to put my exercise first.*

Julia's favorite of all time was when someone had canceled to take her dog to acupuncture. That had made Julia howl.

It was unfortunate that Becca had to find a new job in the next few weeks. She could probably land another salon gig, but the chances that her boss would be as sane and personable as Julia were slim. Plus, like she'd told Griff, the money and hours were about as good as things got in this industry.

Griff.

Since Saturday night when he'd driven her home, she hadn't been able to stop thinking about him. What he'd done to her, yes, but also what had happened afterward. She couldn't quite figure out how to make sense of both things. For that brief time in the hotel room, with his attention fully on her, she'd felt like the center of the universe, but—well, she wasn't. Marina was the center of Griff's universe. And she hated to admit how much of a slap in the face that had been.

It wasn't that she'd thought there was anything special between her and Griff—

It just stung that it was so *un*special.

It was frustrating, in light of those mixed-up feelings, to *still* not be able to stop thinking about the sex. She'd be minding her own business, and then, *whoosh,* memories would wash through her mind and heat would flood her body. Depending on what she was doing and where she was, she'd either have to take a break and catch her breath, or . . .

Yeah, she could admit it. She'd retreated to her room *twice* on Sunday to rub one out. The second time she'd—

She blushed, thinking about it.

She'd put on the bodysuit. Remembered him down on his knees in front of her with his face against her pussy, licking her through the flimsy red lace.

Recalling it, she'd come so hard she'd bitten her tongue.

For a moment, she thought about texting him. Telling him. *I'm at work and all I can think about is you on your knees with your face—*

But that would obviously be the worst idea in the world, given the Marina thing.

Damn, she'd completely missed that last message. She hit 4 to repeat it.

A shadow fell across the desk. It was Julia. She was a remarkably well-preserved fifty-something blond whose hair and skin shone with the light of a thousand suns and several hundred beauty products.

"Hey, lady," Julia said.

"Hey back atcha." She passed her boss the sheet of notes, and watched, with amusement, as Julia's face cracked into a broad smile. "Like that one, do you?"

"That's a good one."

"How's the Bainbridge plan going?"

Bainbridge Island was a short ferry ride from downtown Seattle. For several years, Julia had been living there with her husband and kids and commuting back and forth, and she'd been in the process of opening a branch of the salon there when she got the news about losing the Seattle space. So, she'd decided to throw everything behind the Bainbridge location. Becca might have considered following her, but she couldn't afford to wait for Julia's multi-month grand opening timeline to play out.

"Well, as much as this wasn't how I'd planned for things to go, it'll sure as heck make the commute easier. And maybe if that opening goes well, I'll do one in Poulsbo, too."

Julia was putting a good face on the situation—it was her way, after all—but Becca knew it wasn't that easy. Julia had been at the Seattle location for years. She'd expanded the spa from a single storefront into two, and bumped out the back of the building to make more space for a relaxation room.

Starting over again in another town—no matter how much she'd benefit from an easier commute—would be exhausting, risky, and difficult.

"Becca," Julia said quietly. "Let's talk about you."

"What about me?"

"You need to figure out what you're doing next."

"I'm fine," Becca insisted.

Julia shook her head. "I'm going to pay you for the next two weeks, but my daughter will cover the desk during that time so you can concentrate on finding something new. It's the least I can do. You've taken almost no time off, and I don't pay vacation, so this my way of making it up to you."

Julia's generosity made her stomach hurt. "You don't have to—I can—"

But the truth was, she'd be crazy to turn down the offer. Two weeks of freedom, paid. She could get a jump on her job search. And—she got excited thinking of it—she could be with Nate, Alia, and Robbie. Alia was always trying to get her to spend more time with Robbie while he was little—*they change so fast at this age, something new every week*. And she knew Nate and Alia could use the help. They'd been so grateful for everything she'd done to pitch in last weekend.

It would be fun to get more time with her family. *And Griff*, a little voice said.

Not Griff, her practical self shot back. *Two and through*. No need to set yourself up for another slap in the face—or worse.

"Thank you," Becca said. She squeezed Julia's hand.

"You're welcome. And kiddo, it's been great. You've been great. If you ever want a job on Bainbridge, it's yours. Although I hope you'll have found something amazing with someone else who appreciates you by then."

"Thank you," Becca said, knowing there was no way she could afford to be out of work for that long, especially if she hoped to get a place of her own someday.

No, she'd start the job search as soon as she walked out the door today.

From her temporary home base in Tierney Bay.

Where she would do her very best to stay out of the way of one Griff Ambrose.

And if their paths crossed, she would make very sure their compatible body parts stayed well separated.

She *would*.

21

Griff was helping JoJo Evans with her math homework in the big tutoring room at KidsUp. JoJo was a seventh grader with an absentee father, an alcoholic mother, and a shitload of unrealized promise. She was brilliant at math, but the instant anything got hard for her, she bailed. Griff's toughest job was getting her to stay seated at the table long enough to finish a whole problem set.

A couple of other kids were working quietly in adjacent booths. Griff was the only tutor today—Fridays were usually slow because only the most determined kids started their homework before the weekend.

Which didn't explain why Jed was here, slouched in a corner, earbuds in, swiping madly at some video game on his phone. But Jed was often here for no reason Griff could figure out. He never asked for help, and when it was offered, he flatly refused it. Griff figured things sucked at home and a quiet booth where no one gave him shit about screen time was probably bliss.

JoJo was on problem twenty out of thirty when a tall,

beautiful blond woman pushed Robbie's stroller through the door.

Griff's dick figured it out first. It grew heavy before his brain made sense of what he was seeing. Or tried to, anyway.

It was Becca.

What the hell was she doing here?

"Excuse me a sec," he told JoJo, easing himself up from his seat.

He and Nate stepped into the lobby at the same moment.

"Bex!" Nate said jovially. He'd obviously known she was here, but he hadn't mentioned anything to Griff. And that was actually *good* news, because it signaled that Nate hadn't suspected Griff would want to know, which meant he didn't know anything about their shenanigans. Which in turn meant that Griff would live another day.

Although Nate was looking at him a little funny right now. Right. Because he was standing in the lobby instead of sitting in the conference room with his student.

"Hi," Griff said, belatedly, to Becca. "Did you come down for Friday Night Dinner?"

She hadn't mentioned to him that she was coming into town, and she usually put several weeks between visits.

Becca looked from one of them to the other, and blushed. "I didn't think you'd be here," she said to Griff. "I mean, at KidsUp."

"I'm here most Friday afternoons. But that doesn't explain why *you're* here. Pushing Robbie."

He stepped around the other side of the stroller, crouched, and greeted the baby, who stuck his tongue out and kicked his feet.

"You know how I told you the salon's closing? My boss

decided to give me my last two weeks as paid leave, which is super nice, right? So . . . I figured I'd come do some babysitting for Nate and Alia . . ."

She bit her lip, and he realized she was worried that he'd be pissed that she'd shown up. Because of their *agreement*. And he probably *should* be pissed, but the truth was . . . well, his dick had said it first. He was glad to see her. Very glad.

Griff watched appreciatively as Becca leaned down and dug under the stroller for something. "Here's the folder."

"Thanks," Nate said. "I really appreciate it. Left the fundraising notes I needed at home," he explained to Griff.

"And Alia needed me to get out of the house with Robbie, so it made sense for me to walk him down here," Becca said.

Griff nodded. "I should, um, get back to JoJo," he said apologetically to Becca. "You want to come see how it works in there?"

"In—"

"In the tutoring room."

"Um, Robbie and I should probably—"

"C'mon. Check it out."

He could tell she was unconvinced, but she followed him to the big room, pushing Robbie ahead of her.

All the kids looked up when she came in, even Jed, who took his earbuds out. At first, Griff was sure it was Becca's smoking body that had gotten Jed's attention, but then he saw that the kid's eyes were actually on Robbie.

"You want to say hi to Robbie?" he asked.

Jed hesitated, then made his way over. The hard expression on the boy's face gave way to something much softer as he greeted the baby, who treated him to a smile.

"JoJo, Jed, this is my friend Becca."

JoJo's eyes got big. "Is she your girlfriend? Is this your baby?"

"No," Griff and Becca said at the same time, then looked at each other and laughed. At least it wasn't going to be awkward between them, which was pretty damn cool.

"What are you working on?" Becca asked JoJo.

"Math. I hate it."

Becca smiled at her. "Yeah? I liked math okay. I was better at it than some other stuff. Writing gave me the worst time."

Jed's head came up.

"I suck at writing."

Griff froze. Jed barely ever spoke. And when he did, it was barbed. *Stupid fucking teachers, stupid fucking homework, stupid fucking school.* His comment *I suck at writing* wasn't exactly drenched in positivity, sure, but—

It was an opening, that's what it was. *Take it, take it, take it*, he willed Becca.

"Yeah?" Becca said. "You probably don't suck as much as you think."

"Yeah, that's what teachers always say."

"I'm not a teacher," Becca said. "I could never be a teacher. School was too hard for me." She bit her lip, shot an apologetic look at Griff, then turned her attention back to Jed. "I know what you're going through is all I meant. Maybe you just need to focus on something you care about?"

He shrugged, and for a moment she thought he wasn't going to answer. Then he said, "I never know what to say. And if I have an idea, I don't know how to say it."

"Do you bring your assignments here?"

He shook his head.

"You should. I bet if you brought a writing assignment to Griff, he could help you."

"Or Becca could," Griff said. The words just popped out of his mouth. It was something about the way she'd described herself. *Could never. Too hard.*

She gave him a *what-the-fuck* look. "I'm not a tutor."

"Yeah," said JoJo to Griff. "If she did bad in high school, she's not going to be tutoring people to do better in high school."

"Right," said Becca firmly. "Okay. You guys need to get back to work, and I need to get Robbie home. You coming to Friday Night Dinner?" she asked Griff.

You'll be there? I'll be there.

But all he said was, "Yeah." Just like every week. Only, having seen her again, he was suddenly craving something he was sure wasn't on the menu.

22

G riff pulled up in front of Nate and Alia's house behind Becca's seafoam blue Toyota Prius, and just that was enough to make him half-hard.

For a moment, Griff let himself imagine that Becca's reason for choosing to spend her two weeks down here instead of in Seattle was because she wanted a second—make that third—helping of him. And wasn't *that* a nice thought?

Maybe her right hand was worn out, too.

Oh, *wow*, that was an appealing visual: Becca in bed, fingers working between her thighs, recalling Operation V-Card and—Griff allowed himself to believe—his cock.

And now she was *here*, which meant that their plan to leave Operation V-Card behind them was going to be harder to accomplish.

He wasn't nearly as upset about that as he should be.

The truth was, he wanted more. He wanted more of what they'd done the other night in the hotel. Lots more.

He banged his head on the steering wheel a few times in

case that would help, and when it didn't, he made his way inside.

Jake had beaten him there and was in the kitchen with Nate, Alia, and Becca.

"No Mira?" Griff asked.

"She's got some crazy revision deadline on her book she's trying to meet. We both decided it would be a good idea for me to get out of the house."

Nate drained the pasta, steam rising in the sink.

"Help me set the table?" Becca asked Griff.

"Of course."

She pulled out placemats and napkins and handed them to him, then grabbed a stack of plates and silverware. They converged at the dining room table and started laying items out. Every time her hand brushed his as she set something on the table, or they skirted each other close, shoulders or arms or hips a hair's width apart, blood surged in his veins.

He wondered—if he leaned in and breathed an invitation in her ear, would she pull away, or turn toward him, eyes bright?

His skin felt stretched too tight all over.

Once the table was set, Alia put Robbie in his bouncy chair, and they sat down to dinner.

Griff took a bite of spaghetti. It was phenomenal, the sauce rich and meaty. He was about to praise the chef when Becca moaned. "God, Alia, you're a genius."

Griff's dick chubbed up and his taste buds shut down. And he deeply regretted the one-and-done promise. He really needed to admit to himself that he was going to break the ground rules they'd set and go for round three. Three and free? Four and no more? He was hopeless.

"Thanks, sis," Alia said.

"Yeah," Griff said. "Really good." Not that he could taste his food at the moment.

"You guys. Let's do roses and thorns," Becca said. "Alia and I used to do this at dinner every night. The best and worst thing that happened to you that day. Alia, you go first."

"My rose is that one of my patients told me he slept all the way through the night last night for the first time since he came home," Alia offered.

"Because of you," Nate said, smiling at her.

She shrugged. "I like to think I had something to do with it."

"You know you did." Nate's eyes were warm.

"And my thorn is that Robbie is teething again, and he bit me on the boob," Alia said.

They all winced.

Nate twirled spaghetti. "My thorn is that I have a lot of business and finance stuff to figure out tonight. But it's all worth it because I have a kid who just got accepted at North Coast University with a full scholarship. He dropped out his sophomore year of high school, but we got him into running —cross country and track—and he ended up lettering in both *and* pulling off a B average."

"That's terrific, Nate!" Alia said, and they all murmured echoed support.

"Bex?"

"My rose is you guys," Becca said, beaming.

God, that smile. It was hard-wired—yep, exactly—to his dick.

"And my thorn is having to find a new job."

"You have to find a new job?" Jake asked.

"Yeah, sadly." She explained about the salon losing its building and the fallout.

"You looking for something in Seattle?" Jake asked. "Because I could seriously use someone on the PT office reception desk. Sibby's basically doing two jobs right now."

"Yeah, Seattle," Becca said. "But if you want some help in the meantime? I could totally do that."

"You're around for two weeks?"

"Yup."

"Yeah, I mean, if you could come in for the next two weeks and do, I don't know, four hours a day? That would be huge. It'll take a day or so for Sibby to get you up to speed, but then you could spot her at the desk and she could catch up on events stuff."

"If you're doing that, how are you going to have time to look for a job?" Alia asked. She sounded like, well, a mom—and Griff watched Becca's jaw tighten. He wanted to kick Alia under the table.

"Just half days," Jake said quickly.

"Becca, you need to make sure you're focused on looking for something permanent, not messing around with something temporary," Alia said.

"I can manage both," Becca said tightly.

"I can always have Sibby fill in for you if you need a day in Seattle for interviews. And there are long gaps at the desk when it's quiet. You can work on job stuff then."

Jake looked toward Alia for confirmation, which made Griff want to howl, *It's not her decision!*

Alia opened her mouth to respond to Jake, but Becca's voice cut across her sister's. "Perfect," she said.

Alia opened her mouth, then shut it.

"Thanks, Jake," Becca said. "That'll help the wallet."

"No, thank *you*. That's going to be a lifesaver."

They smiled at each other.

"You still need to do your rose and thorn," Becca told Jake. "And so does Griff."

"I guess my thorn is that I'm short-staffed, and my rose is that Becca is coming to my rescue."

"Griff?" Alia asked.

He sighed. He'd been hoping they'd get distracted before this came around to him. He'd never been a fan of these kinds of traditions, like going around the Thanksgiving table and saying what you were grateful for. "Well," he said. "I didn't erase the debt of any developing nations or stop nuclear war, but I will say that Jake and I did a *kickass* job at rearranging the dining room to make it cozier. But I think my rose is actually this dinner."

"Aw, go on," Alia said, flapping her hand dismissively.

Although he'd meant not just the food but the company. And especially—he admitted to himself—the pleasure of having Becca back in town. He let himself peek. At the long fall of her gorgeous hair, her straight nose with its slight upturn at the tip, and those goddamn red lips which—

He was *so* going in again.

"And my thorn is—I'm all out of dental floss." It was the first thing that popped into his head.

Becca raised an eyebrow, and he shrugged. "It was a good day."

My rose, Griff thought, as she smiled at him, *is that I am going to have my hands all over Becca as soon as humanly possible. And my thorn is that "as soon as humanly possible" isn't right this second.*

23

After dinner, Jake headed home and the rest of them watched the Mariners game.

Ever since Griff had stepped into the kitchen, her sister's house had felt *way* too small. At dinner, Becca's right knee had almost touched his. Never in her life had she been that conscious of someone else's *knee*. It was like now that her body knew what Griff's could do, it couldn't leave the idea alone.

And he kept finding new and more creative ways to unsettle her. Right now he had Robbie in his arms, and was swinging him up and rubbing the crown of his own head across Robbie's tubby belly, making the baby chortle. He did it again, and then again, and Becca's resolve began to crumble, in direct proportion to the fireworks going on in her ovaries. God, the two of them were so dang cute, the giggling, drooling baby and the big, tough soldier with the look of soft devotion on his face.

Robbie squirmed impatiently in Griff's arms, reaching out for Becca. "You want the baby for a sec?"

She took him, sniffing suspiciously. "Did you just give me a baby that needs changing? Because if so, you're a bigger asshole than I thought."

"Does he need a change?" Griff asked innocently.

Okay, so maybe he wasn't Future Dad of the Year quite yet. She gave him the finger with her spare hand. He grinned at her. The grin didn't help with her resolve, either.

"Give him to me," Alia said with a sigh. She collected him. "I'm headed to bed, anyway, and he probably needs to be, too."

A few minutes later, Nate yawned, stretched, and looked at Becca. "You guys mind if I head upstairs? I was up three times last night and I'm falling asleep. Griff, you can stick around and watch the end of the game, I'm not kicking you out. Becca, lock up behind him?"

"Yeah, no worries," they said at the same time.

Becca didn't dare look at Griff.

"Parents," Griff said scornfully, when Nate had gone. "No staying power. It's not even time for the seventh inning stretch. I remember a time when Nate wouldn't miss the end of a baseball game for sex."

Becca eyed him. He was on one end of the couch, legs spread, arms crossed, all alpha male occupying an absurd amount of upholstery and looking disturbingly hot doing it. A tingle of want flared between her legs and sent warmth into her belly.

Shut up, she told her body. *We're not doing that.*

He leaned toward her, narrowing his eyes. "Are we *really* going to pretend that what happened last weekend didn't happen?"

She'd been determined to do so, actually, for her own self-preservation. But the look in his eyes right now was downright predatory, and—well, her best intentions were in the process of paving the path to her pussy.

That was bad.

"'First rule of Operation V-Card is, there is no Operation V-Card,'" she reminded him.

"Right," Griff said. Wrinkles appeared between his eyebrows.

"One and done," she added.

"Right," he said again, but he was frowning now.

"Besides. There's even more reason now to stick to those ground rules. I'm going to be around a lot the next two weeks, at least as long as I'm working for Jake. Plus watching Robbie, hanging out at Friday Night Dinners. No way for us to avoid each other."

"Right."

"And I'm staying here, under Nate and Alia's watchful eyes."

"Right."

For a second, she thought the conversation was over, and she felt a wave of relief—followed immediately by an equal and opposite wave of disappointment.

"Becca," Griff said.

"Yes?"

"Come here."

"No," she said.

It was *definitely* the wrong answer, because Griff's eyes gleamed with mischief and his mouth quirked at one corner. Her nipples tightened.

"No, huh?" he asked. "Is that, like, *no means no*? Or is that more like—?"

"We said one and done," she said, but even she could hear the desperation in her voice as the last of her resolve vaporized.

He moved down the couch in a flash until she could feel the warmth of his body and smell the spicy goodness of whatever the fuck made him good enough to eat. "Take it back," he commanded.

"Take what back?"

"The *no*."

She closed her eyes. She had never felt anything like this. She had always sort of wondered what all the fuss was. And now she knew. She didn't *really* have to give it up yet, did she?

"I take it back," she whispered.

"Say it. Say yes."

"Yes," she said.

It was such a small word but it had so much power. Everything went into slow motion, so the time it took for him to move was long enough for her mouth to go dry and her body to open and melt. Then he grabbed her and pulled her leg over his so that she was straddling him. The breath whooshed out of her, which made him smile for real. He took her face in both his big hands and kissed her. The feel of his mouth—hot, knowing, and familiar—pulled a whimper out of her, and he groaned his response.

She pulled back.

"Do we need to make new ground rules?" she asked innocently.

He cupped the back of her head and drew her back into a

kiss, inviting her to open and teasing her with his talented tongue until she discovered she was gripping his arms and rocking against the erection that was fully in evidence under his jeans. If he wasn't going to make rules, she wasn't going to either. Not with that cock between her legs. She wedged herself closer so she could rub the seam of her jeans against the bulge in his. He cupped a hand around her breast and found her nipple through her t-shirt. The combination of the denim-on-denim friction between her legs and the spark he had set off through her center—piled on top of all the fantasizing she'd done about him since Saturday night—was potent. She was going to come just like this, rubbing off on him, in ten more seconds. And she couldn't make herself stop.

"Don't stop," he said, like he could read her thoughts, and that just made it worse, the perfect friction, the building heat, the gathering tension, and she tipped right over, biting the crap out of his shoulder and pounding one fist against the couch.

"Jesus," he said.

"There's nothing wrong with me," she said when she could talk.

"Nothing," he agreed.

"I just was never with anyone who actually turned me on before."

The orgasm had loosened her lips—what she'd said was one notch more serious than she'd meant it to be—but it was also *true,* and he didn't seem to mind. He was cupping her face and exploring its terrain with his calloused fingers, and holy *crap* that light touch felt good. Her body was already tuned in and ready to respond to him again.

"So you're not still hot for the prehistoric guy?" he demanded.

"Jondalar who?"

And she wasn't kidding. If the King of First Rites himself walked through the front door right now? She'd tell him she was busy.

She eased off Griff a little, just enough that she could outline the big, hot shape of him under his jeans. He made a rough sound that reminded her that he was still waiting for his turn.

"I missed out on the whole high school hand-jobs-in-backs-of-cars thing," she said. "Do you mind if I catch up?"

He groaned. "Are you *kidding* me?"

"You *are* a full-service operation."

"End to end," he quipped, as she went after the button and zipper of his jeans and freed him so he sprang up in her hand. She'd held several penises but his was definitely the winner. It was the longest and thickest she'd seen, the cut head a deep red, the slit wet with precum, and the whole thing as soft as velvet to the touch and as hard as steel underneath.

She gave it a few experimental strokes. His head tipped back and his eyes fell closed. Two more and his mouth opened in a silent groan and his hand found hers so he could show her how tight he wanted it—*tight*—and how fast—slower than she would have guessed.

She stroked him until he started thrusting into her hand and she was no longer in control of the speed and all she could was hold on. He throbbed and swelled in her palm and then came with a silent shout, his head thrown back, his body tense under hers, his hand reaching to cup himself and contain the mess.

At least that mess they could clean up. The mess that they were creating by prolonging Operation V-Card? Well, she wasn't so sure about that one.

She was, however, sure of one thing: She wasn't going to give up the way Griff could make her feel until she had to.

24

He was wrecked enough that his brain was wiped blank. It had been a long time since he'd come that hard with only a hand on him. He got up and went to the bathroom, mostly to clean up but also because it bought him a little time to think. He sorted himself out, zipped up, washed and dried his hands, then stood staring in the mirror. His pupils were still huge, his eyes glazed, his cheeks ruddy. And the thing was, he wanted to fuck her. He'd just come and he wanted to fuck her *as soon as possible*.

That wasn't going to happen in Alia and Nate's house, but it was pretty clear to him that it was going to happen. Again. And maybe again and again.

The jazzed-up feeling in his chest was split between *Bring it* and *What the fuck am I doing*?

He went back into the living room and sat in the armchair, just to give them enough distance to have an actual conversation.

She rubbed her fingertips over her cheekbones. "Maybe

I'm out of line in saying this but it seems like we're not actually *done*."

She was glazed and pink, too, and it looked a hell of a lot
better on her. Her mouth was tipped up at both corners, like
she was trying really hard not to smile. And he wanted to
lunge out of his chair and kiss that smile right off her face.

But she had a damn good point, and they needed to talk.

"You're not out of line."

She nodded, just one small, tight acknowledgment. "But
it doesn't have to be a big deal, either. I know you don't do
relationships, and that's fine. I'm here for two weeks and then
I'm going back to Seattle. So this is just temporary. Time-
limited. Right?"

Two weeks. Time-limited. Perfect. Right?

Why was he having so much trouble answering a simple
question? She'd obviously killed thousands of brain cells
with that hand job. "Right."

"What if we just say we're going to—whatever this is, fool
around, fuck—"

The sound of that word on her lips made his cock jump.

"—until I have to go back to Seattle, and then we'll call it.
And we can stick with the original rule that *there is no Opera-
tion V-Card*—I think the last thing either of us wants is for
Nate or Alia to catch wind of this."

That was true. So why did the secrecy thing suddenly feel
a little uncomfortable?

Probably because if Alia knew what he and Becca had
just done on the couch, she'd make him pay the upholstery
cleaning bill.

He pointed a finger at her. "And it's exclusive. For the next
two weeks."

Where the fuck had that come from? Maybe from the same primitive part of him that had wanted to kill CJ for making a pass at her.

She raised an eyebrow. "Okay. I think that rule mostly pertains to you. Hard to imagine, but there aren't thousands of suitors currently beating down my door for a chance at me. Unless you count CJ."

"You underestimate yourself," he said irritably. "You can do way better than CJ. And on another topic, you could totally help Jed. Stop selling yourself short."

Her mouth fell open.

He wanted to reel the words back in. They hadn't come out at all the way he'd heard them in his head. "I'm sorry. That came out harsher than I meant it to."

She closed her mouth and wrapped her arms around herself. For a moment, he thought he'd really made her mad. Then she said, "You're not wrong. About the selling myself short thing. I told you I'm turning over a new leaf, right? I'm trying not to do that anymore, but old habits die hard." She gave herself a hug. The smile was gone and the wrinkle between her brows had reappeared. "That said, I have to disagree with you on the Jed thing. I barely graduated high school. I don't have any experience with kids aside from Robbie, and the damage I do to him is the usual aunt stuff like embarrassing him in front of future girlfriends."

She got a faraway look on her face.

"Alia was an honors student. In, like, everything. I, on the other hand, had learning disabilities that took a long time for anyone to catch and diagnose. One teacher asked me straight out, in all seriousness, if Alia and I were actually related because—and I quote—'your sister has such a brilliant mind.'"

Griff winced.

"Right? And I think that woman is still teaching at our old high school." She frowned. "After the school figured out what was going on with me, they made accommodations, but I didn't suddenly thrive. I stayed in the lowest track, with kids whose desire to learn had been shit-kicked out of them at some point. A few of them were working hard, like me, but most of them had just given up. Those classes—they were where learning went to die. And I just felt like, I was killing myself—going to tutors, trying my hardest—and I *still* couldn't keep up with my peers. I still couldn't get Bs, or even Cs most of the time. I figured I must be really—"

She didn't say it, but she didn't have to for him to hear the word in the room.

Stupid.

"You're *not* stupid," he said. "You're smart, and funny—like how good you were at Taboo. That's intuition, and being able to read and interact with people. The stuff that will actually help you in the world."

She winced, which wasn't the effect he'd been trying for, not at all.

"Honestly? I hate that, the 'you're not stupid' thing. Alia always did that. She said I was street smart, and smart in all the ways that mattered—EQ, whatever—but you know, after a while, you don't believe it any more. You think people are just trying to make you feel better."

So basically, nothing he could say would make her change her mind about what she believed about herself.

This was why she was working a job that was "fine"

instead of one she loved. Because deep down, in the snakiest part of her snake brain, she didn't think she was smart enough for anything else. She thought she had to settle.

Well, that was bullshit, and he was going to do his best to make sure she saw it and believed it.

"All that, Becca, makes you the perfect person to get through to someone like Jed. You *were* getting through to him. He was listening to you, which he doesn't do to any other adults as far as I can tell."

"Even you?" she asked. He could hear the eager hope in her voice, even if she tried to sound nonchalant about it.

"Even me," Griff said, completely truthfully.

He thought about Jake, trying to talk him into leading the support group. Maybe Jake felt the same way, trying to convince Griff that he had what it took, as Griff felt now, trying to convince Becca.

"Jake wants me to lead the peer support group sometimes."

"Oh. Wow. You'd be great at that."

"I don't know. I'm the last person who should be giving anyone advice."

"Why's that?"

"You saw me the other night."

"The flashback?" she asked.

He nodded.

"Yeah, but that's the whole point, isn't it? You're supposed to be their *peer* and walk together through the darkness. They don't expect you to be perfect."

"I'm far from that," he said with a snort. He gave into an impulse that had been building for the last couple of minutes and said, "Can I tell you something?"

"Yeah," she said. She pushed her hair back, behind both ears.

Was he really going to do this? He literally hadn't told *anyone*.

But it couldn't have been easy for her to tell him she thought she was stupid. And she was waiting, hands folded, eyes as calm and unjudgmental and blue as the cloudless sky, and damn it, he *wanted* to tell her. So he opened his mouth and gave it a shot.

"I've tried to leave R&R a couple of times to figure out what I want to be when I grow up. Just like you. I had a good job at one point, but I lost it."

"Because of the PTSD?"

She said it so neutrally. The same exact way she would have said "flu" or "diabetes," which made it possible for him to nod.

"I froze up."

"Just, out of the blue?"

His hands were fisted, he discovered, and he tried to unwind his fingers. "I was working at a hotel, doing odd jobs and landscaping. There was a metal door out back, and the pneumatic hinge was broken, so when people weren't careful, it would slam."

"Like a gunshot," she said.

"Yeah." It hadn't sounded anything like any of the weapons he'd ever fired or heard fired, but that hadn't mattered to the part of his brain responsible for fight-or-flight.

"Did you ask them if you could fix it?"

"Several times."

"But—?"

"The part was expensive and that door was only for service people."

Lines appeared in her forehead. "Then they're just assholes."

It would have been so much easier for him to believe that, but he knew it wasn't true. He hadn't given them a chance to do the right thing. "I didn't tell them why it was a problem. They didn't even know I'd served."

She took that in quietly.

"I was going to fix it out of my own paycheck, when I had some spare time, but then one day the door slammed, and the next thing I knew I was standing in the middle of the lobby yelling something—I don't even know what—and I'd scared the hotel guests half to death. And it wasn't the first time something like that had happened, so they fired me."

"I know you said Jake and Nate don't know. Have you ever talked about it with anyone?"

He shook his head.

Her eyes moved over his face, assessing but not judging.

"What happens? When you have an episode?"

"I go back to—"

His throat was tight, and he wasn't sure he could get the words out, but her expression was so—calm.

"This one night. There was a surprise attack."

It was always that fucking night he went back to.

"Six guys died. I was the platoon sergeant, so the men were my responsibility."

He didn't—he *couldn't*—say the rest. That he'd had a chance, maybe a slim chance, but a *chance* to change the outcome, and he hadn't taken it.

She reached out her hand and he grabbed it, not caring that he was probably hurting her.

"We went to bed and everything was okay. And we woke up in the middle of a battle. That's what happens in the flashback. I'm in one place and then I'm in the middle of a firefight." He didn't explain the other part. How the flashbacks, like dreams, sometimes incorporated people who hadn't been there in real life. Marina, usually, but other people too, from time to time. Family, friends.

Becca squeezed his hand, which made him realize he'd been crushing her in his grip. He eased off.

"That sucks." Her voice was steady, level. Kind, but not pitying.

"Yeah," he said, smiling at the understatement.

"In the flashback—"

But whatever she'd been about to say, she shut her mouth abruptly, and when she opened it, she asked, "Do you think it would help to tell Jake?"

"Probably?"

She smiled at that.

On a whim, he pulled her hand to his mouth and kissed it. He barely touched her skin, but the now familiar spark leapt between them, setting his skin alight. He grunted, and her smile ticked up a couple of levels of intensity.

"So, um, thinking about the continued sexual education of Becca Drake," she said, a tease in her eyes. "I'm still a beginner. If you're really a *full-service operation*, I'd think you'd need to provide an overview of all the positions—"

Heat flushed him and swelled his cock as he did a quick mental review of what they'd left out. "Well, that's true. We only covered missionary."

"—and it's not really a complete *package* without blow job training—"

"Je*sus*, Becca."

"You don't want to send me out in the world less than fully prepared to give really, really good head, do you?"

His cock surged against the zipper of his jeans. He dropped a hand to the denim-clad bulge and gave it a quick rub. Just to ease the throb brought on by the thought of being in her mouth.

It didn't help.

Her eyes followed his hand, avid.

"I can help you out with that," she said.

25

Talk about blowing. The look on Griff's face was blowing her mind. He must have had a zillion other women go down on him, but as she climbed off the couch and settled herself on her knees between his, he was watching her with the ultimate *What did I do to deserve this?* expression. Gratitude was so fucking hot.

She was looking forward to this. She trusted him not to do anything freaky without warning her, like yank her hair or push hard into her throat. And she had a thing for his cock. She loved the feel of it, the satiny texture over the swollen head and velvet just below, and the whole thing so unbelievably rigid under all that soft texture. The thick veins and the way the skin shifted a little under her hand . . .

She was getting wet, thinking about it. Since when could she fantasize her way to ready?

Since Griff.

She unbuttoned his jeans and unzipped them, for the second time that night. He reached in and freed himself, and his cock jumped up at her like a jack-in-the-box. "Well, hello," she said, and wrapped a hand around him. "You want to grab the arrow low on the shaft," she said.

He bellowed a laugh. "I was wondering if you'd caught that."

"You weren't subtle."

"I never realized how suggestive archery was until that lesson," he said. "Or maybe it was just having the right student."

She ducked her head and licked the smooth cap. There was a drop of pre-cum gathering at the slit, and she cleaned that up. Then she thoroughly licked him, all over the head, where the head dipped toward the shaft, down the length of his shaft. She made her tongue flat and strong and braced him with a hand behind so she could use a little more force without hurting him. He bucked his hips up from the couch appreciatively.

She wanted to see if she was doing okay, so she looked up at him, only to find him looking back down at her with so much heat and, yes, gratitude, that she felt a surge of her own wetness. "Griffin Ambrose, Ruiner of Panties," she said.

He laughed, but it was kind of a dark half-laugh, half-groan. "Yeah? You're wet because you're going down on me?"

"Yeah."

She was wet from before, anyway, but now she was considerably wetter, and yeah, she was surprised to discover it, but it *was* because of this. It was turning her on to turn him on, and the better she was getting to know his cock, the more she appreciated it. The way it pulsed under her tongue and against her lips. How hot it was. The softness of his sac when she cupped it—

That pulled another groan out of Griff, so she played a

little, fingers and tongue, and then she went back to licking the head, and then, because she was tired of waiting and she *wanted* it, she sucked him into her mouth.

His hips bucked again, and his abs went rigid. She peeked, and his eyes were closed, his head thrown back. Okay, then. She knelt up and took him deeper. A breath hissed out of him. Deeper, then. And why not, *deeper*. She felt him against the back of her throat, and she swallowed, letting her muscles caress him.

"Holy shit, Becca," he growled.

She did it again. She moved up and down on him, still gripping him tight at the base, spiraling her tongue around his shaft, and, when she rose up on him, giving him extra attention all over the head. At the end of every stroke, she opened her lips wide around him so they nearly met her hand and let him push against the back of her throat. Not only did she not hate it, the sound he made every time, like air was being forced out of him, was *killing* her. The next few times, she heard her own whimper, chasing his grunt.

He touched her hair. Tentatively. He was asking for permission, and she knew—she *knew*—that he'd respect her wishes if she said no. Which made it so damn easy for her to say yes. She nodded, her mouth still full of him. He wrapped his fingers into the thickness of her hair, but he didn't pull on her head. He just cupped his hand there and moved with her. His cock had grown even bigger in her mouth, which she wouldn't have guessed was possible.

He was holding back, though. She could feel it, in the tension in his thighs and abs. What would it be like if he *didn't* hold back? She slid a hand under his ass and tugged him up to her, and she got her answer, because he sort of lost it, then, in the best possible way. His hips jabbed toward her, his cock surging into her, and she discovered she could use her tongue and her throat muscles and her hands on his hips to control his speed and let him thrust into her mouth, and oh my *God* that was hot, her pussy was all liquid, her panties drenched, and she really needed another hand so she could rub down there and ease the clamor.

He knew, though. He reached down and cupped her through her jeans, and she rocked against his hand. Yes, that, and she squeezed, too, to try to get more friction and more pressure, and he made a broken noise. "Becca, I'm going to—"

He tried to draw back, but she held his hips and wouldn't let him, and his cock jumped against her palate and he was coming, surges and spasms and the hot bitter taste of him in her throat. She was coming, too, whimpering against the fullness in her mouth, bearing down on his hand.

She let him slip from her mouth and rested her head on his thigh. His fingers moved gently through her hair.

She was still catching her breath when she heard the squeaky board at the bottom of the stairs creak.

"Did you hear that?" she whispered.

"What?"

She ran to the stairs and found Alia retreating up them, trying to be silent. Her sister's pained expression told Becca everything she needed to know.

"I'm sorry," Becca whispered.

She wasn't even sure what she was apologizing for. Misusing her sister's couch? Not telling her sister what was going on? Screwing around with a guy that Nate and Alia had warned her about?

"We'll talk in the morning," Alia said grimly, and she turned away, climbed the rest of the stairs, and disappeared.

Becca turned and slowly made her way back to the couch. Griff had zipped and was leaning back nonchalantly, doing his best to look innocent, but she could still see the deep flush in his cheeks, and he didn't seem able to hold back his blissed-out grin.

"I think the cat's out of the bag," she told him.

Griff's grin got even bigger. "Oh, baby. That pussy hasn't even *begun* to free itself yet."

26

Becca wrapped her hands around a cup of coffee while Alia spooned breakfast into the baby. Robbie had just started rice cereal, and it was not a clean process. More rice cereal was coating Robbie's chin than was going down his throat.

"I'm not mad," Alia said. "You don't need my permission. I'm just worried about you."

"That's why I didn't tell you. Because I knew you'd be worried about me. And you don't need to be. I'm a big girl."

Alia scraped rice cereal off Robbie's chin and recycled it into his little rosebud mouth. "Are you sure about that?"

"That I'm a big girl?" Becca said, trying to lighten the mood.

"That I don't need to be worried?"

"Positive."

"I don't want him taking advantage of you."

"He's—" For a second, she couldn't even finish the sentence because what Griff was doing with her was so far from taking advantage that there just weren't words. Not to mention that the whole thing had been her idea. "—not," she managed.

Alia looked unconvinced. "I don't want you to get hurt."

"I know what I'm doing. It's just a casual thing."

Alia's eyebrows scrunched together in the middle.

"I swear, Alia. We're just both, um, blowing off steam."

"Someone's blowing off something," Alia muttered.

Becca rolled her eyes. "Seriously?"

"Cut me some slack. I can never unsee what I saw. And I didn't even see that much. Just the gist. But ack." Alia's face twisted. "Just tell me he reciprocates and it's not always you down on your knees."

"God, Alia!" Becca's face flamed. "Don't do the mom routine on me right now. He reciprocates, okay?" She took a deep breath. "I'm getting mine." And wasn't *that* an understatement. She shivered, thinking of how easily she'd gotten off last night, straddling him like a horny teenager. Or rather, like the horny teenager she would have been if Stupid Todd hadn't asked her to wait for a promise that had never materialized. She was making up for lost time and the experiences she'd been robbed of. "Jondalar's got nothing on Griff," she told Alia.

Alia's eyes got wide. "Are you *having sex with him*?"

"I had sex with him, yeah."

It was impossible to keep the smile off her face. The best she could do was try not to betray her giddiness.

"I can't believe you didn't tell me you lost your virginity!"

"I didn't tell you because—"

Alia bit her lip. "I know, I know. Because you were afraid that I'd freak out, just like I *am* freaking out. I'm sorry. I'm just so used to—"

They both knew how that sentence ended. *I'm just so used to taking care of you. Being your mom.*

Not for the first time, Becca thought about the toll that being a surrogate mom had taken on Alia. All that lost childhood, all those missed opportunities to cut loose and have fun. Always having to be the responsible one. And Becca hadn't been an easy child with all her—challenges. She knew it had been hard for Alia, later, to let down her guard with Nate, to quit being the one doing the caretaking and let him in to take care of her.

"How did this all come about?" Worry lines still etched Alia's forehead.

Becca gave her sister the bare minimum details to fill her in—how she'd asked Griff for the V-card favor, how he'd refused, how he'd changed his mind.

For some reason, she didn't tell Alia that CJ's interest had provoked Griff's about-face. She left out dirty archery, the Met steak dinner, the beautiful hotel room, the flashback, last night's soul-baring conversation. Those details didn't feel relevant. They felt like they belonged to her and Griff alone.

"And it was—good?"

Becca settled once again on, "Yup."

"Look at you! You're blushing!" Alia narrowed her eyes. "But you're sure you're not going to fall for him." Her tone was fussy with anxiety.

"I'm *not* going to fall for him. Stop looking at me like that! It's the twenty-first century. Tinder. Swipe freakin' right. Women do this kind of thing all the time. And Griff was totally up-front with me. He doesn't do serious, he doesn't do relationships."

The last thing Becca wanted was for Alia to rip Griff a

new one the next time she saw him. It was going to be awkward enough for the two of them. Nothing like a friendship where you've seen the other person's O-face.

"Yeah," Alia said thoughtfully. "His ex-wife pretty much destroyed him. You know the story, right?"

"Sort of? Only what you and Nate have told me. He came home from Afghanistan and she was gone." She wasn't sure she wanted to know more. She'd *almost* asked him last night, *In the flashbacks, do you see your ex-wife?* But she hadn't wanted to pry. She'd been grateful for what he'd told her already—and afraid to find out just how much he still cared for Marina.

"That's the gist. They were high school sweethearts. Marina didn't want him to enlist and she hated that he was gone so much. It was during that period of long deployments —like eighteen months long, and then back out again almost as soon as he'd been home. She couldn't get used to being an army wife. She wasn't good at playing nice with the other army wives and she was lonely. They fought about it for years, and finally she gave him an ultimatum. Her, or the army, but he couldn't have both. He told her he cared more about her and that he'd get out."

For some reason, that detail made Becca's stomach hurt. Not that she needed more evidence than she'd seen on Saturday night that Griff had loved—*did* love—Marina with his whole being. But she didn't love hearing it said aloud.

"He'd finished his active obligation, so he made a clean break. Flew home all ready to make a life with her, have kids, really settle down. He walked into the house and—" Alia threw her arms open. "It was empty. Marina was gone, her stuff was gone. There was a note."

"What did the note say?"

She was torturing herself, she knew. She wasn't going to hear anything that would change the narrative. Whatever had gone through Marina's head, Griff had been heartbroken by her leaving.

Alia sighed. "That she'd met someone else. That she'd been too young when they'd gotten married and she hadn't known yet what she really wanted and needed. And now she did."

Jesus, she didn't even want to picture it. Griff walking into an empty house, finding only a note. The way she imagined it, it was night. And cold. She could see him, standing in the middle of the room, a slip of paper clutched in his hand, trying to make sense out of betrayal.

Who had that woman been, the one who'd made Griff want to settle down, who'd made him willing to quit the army? Who he sought with his eyes and his heart when he was most terrified?

Becca wanted to hate Marina for hurting Griff. He tried to come off as tough, and maybe most of the time he succeeded, but Becca had seen his tender side. He was the kind of guy who'd take a girl out for dinner before he took her virginity, who would buy her pretty lingerie so that she'd have something clean and dry to put on afterward. He was the kind of guy who would hold himself responsible for wartime deaths on his watch. The kind of guy who didn't want Becca to sell herself short.

That kind of guy was sensitive enough to get his heart torn apart and still pine for the woman who'd done it.

But there had to be another side to the story—Marina's side—and Becca thought she might be able to see it. It must have been hard to love a man like Griff and have him be gone for months, if not years, at a time. To have him choose that *goneness* over and over, when she was begging him to stay.

It hurt to think about.

Becca looked up to find Alia watching her. "He's a good guy," Alia said. "It's just, I know from Nate that he keeps himself—um—pretty *busy*, and in the time that I've known him, I've never seen him get emotionally invested in anyone."

Becca knew all that, but hearing Alia say it aloud made her feel sick.

He's totally not over her. He'd take her back in a heartbeat if she asked.

She knew Griff wasn't over his ex-wife. But what about the second part? She wanted to ask Alia if she thought it was true. Would Griff take Marina back in a heartbeat?

But she knew that if she asked that question, Alia would jump all over her for not being as casual as she claimed. And then she'd tell Becca in a thousand different ways to be careful, to protect herself, to make sure she didn't get hurt.

Worse still—

Becca was beginning to realize that this time, Alia's warnings would be justified.

"Seriously, Alia, don't worry about it. It's nothing. It's over."

If that wasn't precisely true, it would be soon. That much was obvious.

27

"Seriously, asshat?" Nate's voice rang out from the doorway.

Griff was perched on the highest legit step of the ladder, screwing an LED lightbulb into the overhead socket. Jake had asked him to go around and change over as many of the old-style lightbulbs to LED as he could to try to save the resort some money on electricity. It wasn't fun work, but it was satisfying, and the best thing about working at R&R was that no matter how menial the task was, it was always in the service of a greater good.

Unfortunately, CJ was also up on a ladder, on the other side of the room. Griff had been going out of his way to give the kid odd jobs, both because he knew how much it had helped him early on to feel part of R&R in that way, and because he figured an opportunity might come up to dig a little deeper into the driving thing. But—yeah, not the best timing, because at the sound of Nate's voice, CJ had turned his head and was watching them both intently. Since Griff was pretty sure he knew what Nate was about to tear into him about, he didn't exactly need an audience, and especially not CJ.

Nate leaned against the doorframe, his body language casual, but Griff could see the tension in the lines of his face. "Dude, seriously? On my living room couch? With *Becca*?"

"Becca?" CJ said, in the tone of someone who'd just been shot from behind by a teammate.

Griff gave him an apologetic glance. Well, mostly apologetic. He wasn't going to apologize for winning fair and square, or for doing his level best to make Becca's first time one to remember.

"Can you give us a minute?" Nate asked CJ, and to his credit, CJ did—although he aimed one more wounded glance over his shoulder at Griff.

Griff climbed down the ladder. He wasn't going to do this from ten feet over Nate's head. He'd face the music like a man.

"What the hell do you think you're doing?" Nate demanded, once Griff was standing on the floor in front of him. "Because if you hurt her, I will remove your insides with a teaspoon."

"What *is* it with you guys and Becca?" Griff shot back. "She doesn't need you to fight her battles. She knows what she wants. She's tougher than you think she is. And before you get all up in my business, who says I started this?"

"I don't give a shit who started it. You were the one with your bare ass on my couch."

"My ass was never in contact with your couch," Griff said, because he couldn't quite figure out what he *did* want to say, and that seemed like a point that needed to be made clear.

"Good, because then I'd really have to disembowel you,"

Nate said, reasonably. "And I know you weren't the one who started it. Alia told me that Becca asked you to help her out with her *little problem* and you jumped like a dog for a cookie."

It wasn't a problem, Griff almost spat back, but he stopped himself just in time. They weren't fighting over whether Becca's virginity was something to be mocked or worshipped or respected or ignored. They were fighting because Nate and Alia were worried for their girl. And even if he thought they needed to let her be her own woman, he *got* it. She inspired fierce feelings of protectiveness—it was just that he knew enough to back the hell off, and Nate and Alia didn't. As evidenced by the fact that there were still words coming out of Nate's mouth.

"I just can't believe you said *yes*. I mean, seriously, man, what were you *thinking*?"

"I was thinking she asked me for a favor and I was in a position to grant it."

It was the truth, but facing down his furious friend, Griff had to admit that it was a pretty weak argument. The truth was, he'd wanted her from the moment dirty Taboo had hit the table—and probably even before that. From the very beginning, Operation V-Card had been the perfect excuse to do what he wanted to do anyway.

The perfect, well-bounded, no-strings-attached excuse to get into his best friend's little sister's pants.

Yeah. Brilliant work, Griff.

"I have to go with *aaaanh*." Nate formed an X with his hands and made a buzzer noise like an old-style game show. "Becca's—look, I don't know how much you know about how Becca and Alia grew up."

"I know their dad died and their mom had issues with depression."

"*Had issues with depression* is putting it mildly," Nate said. "She was there in body, but sometimes she didn't get out of bed for a week. Or she got up for a couple hours, but by the time they got off the bus, she was back under the covers. They were basically on their own as teenagers. Other than the fact that she signed permission slips."

Becca's words came back to him. *When a lot of kids still believed in Santa Claus, Li was buying her own Christmas presents.* Yeah. His stomach hurt hearing it, and he wasn't even Alia's *person.*

Nate jabbed a finger in Griff's direction. "You know what Becca learned from her childhood? That she wasn't worth getting out of bed for."

"Whoa. If Becca's mom had depression, it wasn't like she *chose* not to get out of bed for Becca—"

Nate's expression softened. "Of course not. But from Becca's perspective as a kid? How it must have *felt*?"

"She had Alia, though—"

Nate nodded at that, but then his eyes grew dark again. "You know about Becca's high school boyfriend? The one who she waited for for three years and then he—" His face twisted.

"Yeah. I know that story."

Nate's expression said that if Griff wanted someone to help him rend that guy limb from limb, Nate would be ready, willing, and able.

"That guy taught Becca was that she wasn't worth waiting for."

Hearing Nate put it in such bald terms made the ache in

Griff's stomach spread up into his chest. He was no stranger to that experience. "And when you dumped her, you taught her that her sister was worth more than she was?"

To Griff's surprise, Nate didn't snap right back at him. He took a deep breath. And then he said, "I may feel some sense of responsibility for her shitty self-esteem, *yes*."

They blinked at each other for a moment. Then Griff nodded. "Okay," he said.

Nate rubbed a hand over his chest, sighed. "But seriously, tell me it's not true? That she sees herself through that lens, of never being worth the effort?"

"She knows that's not true—"

Nate waved it off. "She may know intellectually, but trust me, she doesn't pit-of-her-gut know."

Griff's insides twisted tighter with the knowledge that Nate was probably right. Like Becca's belief that she was stupid, this one could easily be buried where it was hardest to dig out.

Nate sighed. "Look. I need you to understand why Alia and I sharpen our knives when someone messes with Becca. The last, very last, thing either of us wants is for someone else to teach Becca a lesson about what she's *not* worth. And you're in the perfect position to do exactly that."

Jesus, was that true?

"You know she wants it all, right? White wedding, two-point-five-kids or however many it is these days. She was ready to sign on at seventeen with that high school asshole of hers. And you? You live in what's basically a dorm room and your shit is still in Marina's basement because in your heart of hearts, you're still hoping she's going to get sick of her new boyfriend and come back to you."

Griff opened his mouth to deny it, but when it came down to it, maybe Nate was right. Maybe he had left his stuff there in part to stake that slim, pathetic claim on Marina's territory. Maybe he'd deleted that email a couple of weeks back because he hadn't been ready to give up, not completely. He'd still been hoping. For another chance. A chance to prove he *could* make Marina happy.

"Tell me it's not true, Griff. Tell me it's not true, that you could see yourself marrying Becca and living happily ever after, and I'll change my tune."

What Griff saw, though, when he closed his eyes, was not Becca in a white dress and the two of them skipping off through green fields, hand in hand. It was himself, standing in the living room of Marina's house holding the note she'd left on the coffee table.

He opened his eyes and found Nate watching him.

"Yeah," Nate said grimly. "That's what I thought."

28

"Hey."

Jenina stood in the doorway to Becca's bedroom in their Seattle apartment. It was early Tuesday afternoon, four days after Becca and Griff had been caught pants down—one of them anyway—but it seemed like years had passed.

"Hey." Becca looked up and smiled at her friend. "Missed you, hon."

"Missed you, too." Jenina threw her arms around Becca and the two women clung to each other. "I'm glad you had enough time to stop by after your interview. You packing more stuff?"

Becca had a suitcase open on her bed and was folding some extra t-shirts into it. "Yeah. I didn't bring enough business casual outfits to do the temp job."

"The interview this morning was for something full-time, right?"

"Yeah. At that salon in Wallingford. It seemed great."

Jenina perched on the corner of the bed. "Do you think they'll offer it to you?"

"I think I have a good shot. They liked that I'd worked at a similar place before, and I think I made a good impression. And I felt like I had good chemistry with the other women." Becca tucked a few bras into the suitcase, then reached for the pile of socks and undies she'd tossed onto the bed. "I just don't know—"

"What?"

"I think I might be having a midlife crisis."

Jenina hooted. "I think you're having a quarter-life crisis, at most."

"I guess—I had this conversation with Griff—"

"Did you have any *time* for conversation with Griff? Sounds like your mouths have been pretty busy with other things."

"God." She closed her eyes at the thought. She'd texted Jenina last Friday after Alia had walked in on her and Griff, to try to process everything she was feeling. That night, the giddiness of being wanted by Griff—the power and pleasure she'd felt with him on the couch—had still outweighed the shock of getting caught. He'd made her come twice and she hadn't taken off any clothes. She felt hot all over, thinking of it.

Jenina laughed. "That good?"

"Neen, you have *no* idea. *I* had no idea."

"But between your multiple orgasms, apparently there was some *talking*."

"He just made me think. That there might be something I'd want to do more than taking another salon job."

To her surprise, Jenina nodded. "I wondered. What about the R&R thing?"

"That's just temporary."

Sibby, Jake's long-time receptionist, had trained Becca on the reception desk yesterday. Sibby was a grandmotherly woman who was kind and patient but tolerated no bullshit from anyone who approached the desk. *You train them like dogs,* she told Becca. *Consistent boundaries. No wiggle. If you do that, they'll learn the rules and they won't expect you to make exceptions for them if they're late or want to reschedule.*

The clients themselves—all men—were also a plus, different across almost every dimension from the clientele she'd worked with at Julia's. They were often young and easy-on-the-eyes and, as Sibby had reported, well-trained to give her no trouble. Some were gruff and no-nonsense, others were outrageous flirts, but all were respectful to her, and many were outright grateful to be where they were—without a speck of entitlement.

"Does it have to be temporary?"

"Are you trying to get rid of me?" Becca demanded, laughing.

Jenina rolled her eyes. "Yes. I am trying to subtly kick you out so my super-hot boyfriend can move in and we can convert your bedroom to a nursery for the baby I'm expecting. No, I'm not trying to get rid of you, you idiot. I want you to stay! I would sell my soul for you to stay. But this is not about me. This is about you. And I get it. I never thought you were that crazy about the salon job. I mean, Julia was great, but—yeah, there are lots of jobs out there. Plus," Jenina said, waggling her eyebrows, "if you looked for a job down there, you could have more of those *deep conversations.*"

"I don't think that's going to happen." Becca shook her head. "Alia and I had a big talk on Saturday morning, and I'm guessing Nate must have lit into Griff, too, because I haven't heard from him since."

"But it's none of their business!"

"No, it's not," agreed Becca, "but—the stuff Alia said to me —she wasn't *wrong*." She gave Jenina a brief rundown of Griff's relationship past, then filled her in on how Griff had mistaken her for Marina during his flashback, and what Nate had said about Griff trying to bang Marina out of his head.

"Well, shit," Jenina said. "But did *Griff* tell you that? That he's not over her?"

"He didn't have to. You should have seen his face when he thought I was her, Neen. And when he realized I wasn't." She squeezed her eyes shut, but she couldn't quite get the image out of her head.

When she opened her eyes, Jenina was regarding her sympathetically.

"Yeah."

"But maybe you're . . . different."

Becca sighed. "Don't we all tell ourselves that? *He'll leave his wife, He's over his ex-wife, I'm different from all the other women he bangs and dumps?* But, no, I don't think so. And yes, he *did* say the thing about not wanting to be serious. To my face. He told me that he's so anti-commitment that he doesn't stick around for donuts and coffee. Can't make it any clearer than that, can you? Plus, where's he been all week? Not even a text? Pretty sure the same place I've been, which is having second thoughts about whether this is a good idea."

It was Jenina's turn to sigh. "Why are the hot ones always commitment-phobic?"

"Maybe because if you can have any woman you want any time, you don't need to pick one?" She bit her lip. "Anyway. It's just a fling. And that's all I *want* it to be. I belong in Seattle. And probably I should just take this salon job if I get it. I worked hard at a lot of shit salons to get myself that job at Julia's, and, like you said, I'm too young for a mid-life crisis. I finally have enough money to have my own space and not to depend on Alia for anything. If I stayed in Oregon, it would be that old routine of Alia feeling like she has to take care of me, which isn't good for me *or* her. I'm done with that."

"That's not true anymore, Becca. They love having you there. And you're watching Robbie—you're taking care of them now, not the other way 'round."

Becca rolled her eyes at that. "Mantra of couch-crashers everywhere: 'I'm doing them a favor.'" She tossed another dress into her suitcase and zipped it closed. "You have time for lunch?"

"Lunch with my best girl?" Jenina demanded. "That's a big fucking hell yes."

29

G riff approached the desk where Becca sat with Sibby, their silver and platinum heads inclined toward each other as Sibby showed Becca something on the computer.

It was Wednesday afternoon and the first time he'd seen her since Friday. He'd spent the last five days trying to make sure their paths didn't cross, telling himself he was going to leave her alone. Because Nate had asked him to, and Nate was his best friend. Because Nate was *right* that he didn't have anything to offer Becca. Because even though Nate underestimated Becca's strength, the last thing Griff wanted to do was pile more hurt on her.

But as soon as he saw her, her hair a glossy fall of blond, her lower lip caught in her teeth as she followed Sibby's instructions, he knew it was a lost cause.

He wanted her to look up and smile at him with that sunshine smile. He would do just about anything to make it happen.

Two weeks. They'd agreed, they'd set the ground rules.

There was still a week and a half left, and he wanted the time with her. Nate didn't know everything.

Sibby looked up and smiled at him. "Hello, Griffin. How are you feeling?"

She was probably the only person at R&R who insisted on calling him by his full name, because that was how all his appointment slots on the computer had read when he'd first come here. Also, she still always asked him how he was feeling, despite the fact that it had been a long time since he'd needed an appointment.

"Feeling great, Sibby, feeling great."

"Hi, Griff," Becca said, not quite meeting his eyes. So much for the sunshine smile. He'd have to earn it back. Alia had definitely gotten to her.

"Can I use the copier?" he asked Sibby. "I have to make a stack of fliers for the Fourth of July Fun Run." He flashed the poster he'd been working on.

"Absolutely," Sibby said. "Actually, Becca needs a copier tutorial and I haven't gotten to that yet. Can you give her one? I'm going to run downstairs and see if I can get some mac and chili."

"Oh, is it mac and chili for lunch today?" Griff asked. "Get me one too?"

"Of course," Sibby said, grinning at him. "Becca?"

"You want one," Griff supplied. And not just because it would give him great pleasure to watch her eat it. Because the mess hall's mac and chili was an epic experience.

Sibby pushed back from the desk, crossed behind Becca, and patted him on the arm on the way out.

Becca got to her feet more slowly, still not looking straight at him. Alia must have made him out to be a total man-whore.

The problem was, Becca's hesitancy didn't make him want to lay off. It made him want to use every tool in his arsenal to melt her resistance.

She came out from behind the desk and he caught his breath. She wore a royal purple dress that clung to her breasts, nipped in at the waist, and swung loosely around her hips, ending at mid-thigh. Her legs beneath the hem were long, tanned, and smooth, and the urge to reach out and swipe his palm over one was almost overwhelming.

She saw him looking and caught the plump red flesh of her lip between her teeth.

God give me strength.

She followed him into the closet where they kept the printers and copier. The scent of vanilla filled the small room and wrapped itself around him. He was not going to be a good person here; he already knew it. He could still feel her mouth on him, her hand wrapped tight.

"I'm sorry I disappeared for a few days there."

"It's okay," she said, with a shrug. "I figured you got the same speech from Nate that I got from Alia."

"I did," he said wryly. "He made some mighty good points."

"Yeah. Alia, too."

"I was pretty determined to behave myself after that," Griff said. "But—"

One corner of her mouth turned up. "But?"

"Then I saw you."

Her breath caught, her cheeks flushed, and heat slammed him.

"It made me think . . . Nate and Alia don't get to decide this for us," he said. "Unless . . . Unless that's what you want, too?"

She shook her head.

"I figure, I still have millennia of sexual experience to convey, and we only have a week and a half to do it in."

Her half-smile grew into one of those all-out sunshine smiles, and he resigned himself to going to hell. Happily.

He turned toward the big copier. "It's pretty basic," he said. "One copy, on the glass, hit this button. If it's not on, it takes a fucking age to warm up, but otherwise there's nothing to it. If you want to do a bunch, like a packet of papers, you can do the doc feeder, but that's easy, too—just put them here and push the button and it'll detect. If you run into trouble, text me and I'll come rescue you."

He laid his original on the glass. "Multiple copies you can type the number you want, like so—and then you just have to kill time while you wait for them to finish."

Not giving her time to think, he turned, backed her up against the wall, and kissed her, muffling whatever she'd been about to say.

She gave a little sigh and her body softened between his and the wall, yielding. Not so for his. He went from plotting his next move at half-mast to raging, and there wasn't enough space between their bodies for him to be coy about it.

There was no need, anyhow. She wriggled her hips—putting pressure on him right where it counted. As he kissed her, she parted her lips and let him sweep his tongue in so he could savor her.

He tore his mouth away and, with more difficulty, his

body from the warmth of hers, crossed the room in two strides, and closed and locked the door.

She made a sound, and he turned to see her leaning against the wall, looking like she was about to slide to the floor. He strode back and caught her in his arms.

"We're going to kill two birds with one stone," he said. "'Standing' and 'Quickie.' Unless you have an objection."

She moaned.

"I'll take that as 'no objection.'" He reached down and pushed up the hem of her dress, his hand finding the silky smoothness of her bare thigh. She whimpered. He slid his palm up further and his fingertips met lace, then damp fabric. "Ah, Becca, God—"

"Griff, hurry."

"The door's locked."

"Not that. Hurry because I need you now."

Damn. Damn. Damn. "Get these off."

She pushed her panties down—black cotton boy shorts edged with lace—and stepped out of them, while he wrestled the button and zipper of his jeans, then dug out the condom he kept tucked in his wallet and sheathed himself. With one hand he gripped his cock; with the other he found her curls, parted them, and breached her entrance with his fingers to make sure she was ready for him. She was, slick and enticing; he groaned at the feel and she made a matching sound and wriggled against his touch. He pressed a thumb to her clit, easing back and forth over the slippery nub.

"Come for me."

Obligingly, she did, huskily calling his name.

He picked her up and urged her to wrap her legs around his waist. She gathered up her dress with one hand and wiggled her ass, seeking him. He didn't need a written invitation. He slid into her like she'd been made for him—which to be honest, it felt like she had—and she settled down on him, taking him as deep as she could and moving her hips in time with the last pulses of her orgasm. That was all it took—that and one hard pistoning of his hips—and he was coming deep inside her.

They stayed like that for a long time. Long enough that he honestly wasn't sure what they'd done could qualify as a quickie anymore. He just didn't want to move. Not quite yet. He told himself it was post-sex hormones. If they were horizontal, he'd be asleep.

Whatever the damn reason, he kept his face against her hair, breathing in the vanilla scent of her, and his arms wrapped tight around her, keeping her close and safe.

After he'd set her down and they'd done everything they could to put themselves back together again, the condom crumpled in a sheet of copy paper, he said, "Anyway, that's how the copy machine works."

"Thanks for the lesson," she said wryly. "I'll let you know if I need future assistance. It's obviously a two-person job."

They both dissolved into helpless laughter.

30

W hat are you doing?

Griff's text sounded an awful lot like the prelude to a sexting session, and Becca's whole body flushed hot in anticipation. She was still wet and swollen from their lunchtime encounter.

I'm sitting at the reception desk trying not to fall asleep.

If she was right about Griff's intentions, his next question should be either *What are you wearing?* Or *Where are your hands?*

Would it be really, really wrong for her to drop one hand under the desk?

She decided the answer was *yes* and squeezed her thighs together instead.

Any chance you could get Sibby to spell you for a bit? Someone's asking for you.

Her brain did an abrupt, tire-screeching stop. Unless he'd started referring to his dick as an autonomous being—she had known guys who did, but Griff didn't seem the type—she'd been barking up the wrong tree.

What? What are you talking about?

Her phone rang.

"I'm at KidsUp," he said. "I'm putting Jed on the phone."

"Wait—"

She could hear the sounds of the phone being shuffled around, and then the slightly awkward breathing sounds of a teenage boy.

"Is this Ms. Drake?" A man's voice but with that just-into-puberty husk to it.

She almost didn't recognize her own name. No one ever called her anything but Becca or Bex. "Yes."

"I brought my English assignment in."

She squinted. What was this about? Griff trying to make her feel better about herself?

"Griff can help you with that." She squeezed her phone, too hard. It hurt her hand.

More breathing. "He said I could ask you to help me."

"I'm not a tutor," she said, but the protest sounded weaker than the last time she'd made it.

"You said writing was hard for you. I thought you might know how to get me through this."

Either Jed was a damn good actor, or his voice shook on that last sentence.

And why the fuck not, right? Why couldn't he mean what he was saying, what he was asking for? If Griff could be wrong about how good he'd be at leading that R&R support group, she could sure as shit be wrong about this.

But what if she couldn't do what Jed was asking her to do? What possible right did she have to think she could help someone learn to write a high school essay, when she'd sucked at it herself? Writing had stayed hard for her, and that was how she'd gotten herself and Alia into trouble with Nate. Alia had ghostwritten Becca's letters to him, and he had found out.

That was a whole other story, though.

The point was that she still didn't think of herself as a particularly competent writer. She got through by dictating pretty much everything longer than a text—emails, letters, Instagram posts. She let her natural voice flow rather than getting hung up on the process, but she wasn't exactly writing the next Great American Novel or anything.

Somehow, though, there was a kid on the other end of the phone who thought she might have some useful advice for him. And she couldn't quite bring herself to say no.

"Let me see if I can get someone to cover the desk for me," she told Jed.

He was silent on the other end of the phone. She imagined he'd nodded.

"I'll be over there in fifteen minutes if I can. I'll text Griff either way."

"'Kay," he said, and hung up.

She texted Sibby, who said she could easily make the phone calls she was making from the reception desk. Ten minutes later, Becca pulled up in front of the KidsUp office, and a minute after that she stood, heart pounding absurdly, in the big room that housed the study booths.

Griff looked up from where he was working with a thick-set, towheaded boy to smile at her. The smile did nothing to slow her heart rate down, but it did steady her a little.

She spotted Jed, unruly carrot hair and wall-to-wall freckles. Giving Griff a small wave, she slid into the booth across from her student and said, "All right. What's the assignment?"

Without looking at her, he muttered, "We have to write about something that scares us."

Typical high school composition idiocy. What high school student wanted to talk about what scared him? "What did you choose?"

"Nothing scares me." He shrugged.

"Yeah? Really? What about spiders? Snakes? Guns?"

He shook his head. "Nope."

"Girls?"

He smirked, and she could see a hint of the man he'd grow up to be. "Nope, nope, and nope."

"Come on, Jed, something's gotta freak you out. At least a little. How about stupid English assignments?"

Jed's eyes flicked up to Becca's face. "I'm not *scared* of them. I just think they're a waste of time."

She didn't try to argue with him. Maybe the pit-of-her-stomach dread she'd felt when she'd been faced with a high school composition assignment wasn't the same for him. But she doubted it, somehow.

Across the booth from her, he took a deep breath.

"I don't like being home by myself in the afternoons," he said.

It was just a sentence, but she felt such a rush of adrenaline that she got dizzy.

"Write that down."

"Write what down?"

"Write down what you just said. 'I don't like being home by myself in the afternoons.'"

"That's not how you write a paper. You write it fancier than that."

"No." She remembered thinking the same thing, especially when she'd sat down to write letters to Nate. "The words in your head are good. And they're way better than no words at all. If we put them down on the page, we can make them better, after. We can polish them. But if they stay in your head, you don't have anything."

She could see how hard he was thinking about that. The stillness in his face, the far-off look in his eyes.

She held her breath. She could feel it, the thread between them. She could see him thinking about it, a small wrinkle forming between his eyebrows. Her own heart felt like it was in her throat, she wanted this so bad.

"That's probably why you couldn't write worth shit in high school, either," he said darkly.

Then he rolled his eyes, pushed his chair back, rose to his feet, and grabbed for his backpack.

"Wait!" He *couldn't* leave.

He gave her a hard look. "You know what? You were right. You can't help me. Because no one is gonna be able to help me. This is fucking stupid. I'm outta here." He turned and fled.

"Don't go—"

She got up and hurried after him, out into the main lobby.

"Jed, wait—"

But he didn't. Instead, he slammed the door in her face.

31

When Jed ran out of the study area, Becca on his heels, Griff almost ran too.

He'd been watching her as she worked with Jed. She'd been smiling. Lit up. Full of energy, leaning across the table, talking with her hands. She loved it. Anyone could see.

So when Jed ran—

Yeah, Griff had wanted to chase that kid down, snatch him by the scruff of the neck, and shake him.

Instead, he made himself sit still and finish up the lesson with his student, Hal. He made himself put a big fat bow on Charlemagne's empire and send Hal away feeling like they'd made some progress.

Then he went out into the lobby and found her sitting in a chair in the waiting room, looking like—

Well, like her light had gone out. Like someone had doused her flame in cold water.

He was going to give Jed a piece of his mind the next time he saw him. About not appreciating what people were trying to do for him. About not appreciating a woman who really and truly had something to offer.

What he could do now, though, was try to help Becca see it differently. "Hey," he said. "Don't beat yourself up. Jed's tough."

"I thought I was getting through to him."

"Tell me what happened."

She told him. When she got to the part where Jed had told her, more or less, that she didn't know what she was talking about, she looked at him with big, sad blue eyes that said, *See? I'm stupid. Thanks for putting me in this position so that I could be humiliated, just like I said would happen.*

You're not *stupid*, he wanted to howl.

"He's just pissed. You know how teenagers are. They get angry at themselves and take it out on everyone else. He lashed out to bring you down to where he was. You can't let him get to you."

She bit her lip.

He couldn't help it, he reached out, touched her lip just below where the tooth dug in, and freed it. Rubbed his thumb back and forth. Leaned in, kissed her.

She accepted the kiss but didn't return it.

"Hey. Him running away doesn't mean you didn't do a good job. He hasn't even been willing to let anyone else help him yet, but he let you in. That's something."

"But now he'll never come back."

"Doubt that," Griff said. "He'll be back, because he's not an idiot. He knows you've got something good to say to him."

"But I *don't*," Becca said. "I don't know how to help him."

"You *were* helping him, just by listening to him and

sharing what you know about struggling. And he'll figure that out."

She rolled her eyes. "Bet he won't."

"You want to bet? Fifty bucks—no. The best head you've ever had says he'll be back, asking for you."

She rewarded him with a dark blush, which won an answering surge of blood to his dick.

"Hey. You want to get some dinner?"

"Like, just us?"

The shy way she asked that—given everything else that had happened between them—made him smile. "I was thinking we could invite Nate, Alia, Robbie, Jake, Mira, Sam —you want me to call Hunter and Trina, too? And their girls? CJ? Yes, just us. That okay with you?"

"Yeah," she said, lips tipping up.

He kissed her again and this time she kissed back. He had to call a hard stop on it several beats later before he ended up with both his hands up her shirt and the two of them panting audibly in the KidsUp lobby.

"I have to go back to the desk for," she consulted her watch, "an hour and a half. But you could pick me up after that?"

He grinned. "Deal."

HE MET her when her day ended and drove her to the Tierney Bay Diner.

"This place used to be a dive, and then my friends Lily and Kincaid bought it and fixed it up really nice."

She looked around at the decor, big and brightly lit with a

nautical theme, like someone's ritzy beach cottage. A sign said *Please Be Seated*, so they slid into an empty booth across from each other, and a red-headed waitress with freckles and a ponytail brought them menus.

Lily was cooking, but she came out anyway and greeted them, trailed by Kincaid. "Hey," she said.

"This is Becca," Griff said. "Becca, this is Lily. And Kincaid."

Becca shook their hands. "This place is beautiful."

Lily smiled back at her. The two were an incongruous pair—Kincaid an ex-con and lawyer, tattooed and as big as a linebacker; Lily, a chef by training, petite and pixie-faced. They were crazy about each other and their restaurant.

"Wait till you taste the food," Griff told Becca.

"Wish I could sit for a minute with you guys," Lily said, "but it's crazy back there."

"No worries," Griff said. "We'll come some time when it's quieter and eat pie and chat."

"I'd like that," Lily said. "We both would."

Kincaid—who hadn't said much—put his arm around her waist, tugged her close, and nodded.

A few minutes later, Lily brought them a couple of special burgers. "Just for you guys," she said, and winked at Becca.

"She's nice," Becca said, after Lily left them.

"You're nice," Griff said, and he meant it, in the best possible way. She was sweet and kind and good, and it made him feel so fucking great to spend time with her.

She beamed at him and he didn't know what to do with his hands or his feet or the surge of feeling in his chest.

Lily's burgers were like no others—thick, tender, and juicy, and these were loaded up with caramelized onions, bacon, blue cheese, and some special sauce that made Griff's mouth water obscenely.

"There's a job I think I have a really good chance at," Becca said, when she could talk between bites.

"Yeah?"

It made no sense to feel surprised and a little disappointed. He'd known she was looking for a job in Seattle, but he guessed he hadn't expected it to happen so fast.

"Nice salon not too far from where I live. I liked the people."

"Ah. That's great." Because he was happy for her. He *was*.

"I'm *not* selling myself short."

Shit, she'd mistaken his confused feelings about the fact that she was leaving for something else. "No, I know. I didn't—I know you're not."

"I'm not," she repeated.

"When I said that, it wasn't really what I meant," he said. "I just—"

He had to stop because the sentence that had been about to come out of his mouth felt too serious. But then he decided to say it anyway, because it was true:

"I just want you to do something that makes you happy."

Her face got pink. She gave him the sweetest smile. "Thank you," she said. "That's—That's really—"

They both stopped and just *looked* at each other for a long minute.

Griff thought maybe one of them was going to say something, but then neither of them did. When she broke the silence, she moved them back into safe territory. "This job'll make me happy."

"Then it's good. Then that's good."

She took a long drink of her chocolate shake, and he watched her mouth form a sweet little O around the straw. Hell yes. Only bigger and better.

"So when Nate gave you his big lecture, what did he say? About us, um, screwing around?" she asked.

He didn't like that phrase. Screwing around. Their fling might be casual and it might be temporary, but it didn't feel like *screwing around*.

"He didn't say anything I didn't already know. He told me about your mom, which you'd told me, but—I guess I didn't realize quite how bad her illness was. Was she always like that?"

Becca tilted her head. "Um—well, mostly. But I remember some times—when we were little and before my dad died— that were really great. All of us together as a family, sure, but also just my mom. She used to do a lot of craft projects with me, and she had the best stuff, the best ideas. Glitter and feathers and sequins and googly eyes and pom-poms in all different sizes, and she would get so, so excited . . ."

Her voice, which had brightened as she reminisced, trailed off, and she looked into the distance, chasing the memory.

She took a bite of her burger and he thought she was done, but then she set it down and began speaking again. "And sometimes she'd have good stretches. Like, the year I was twelve, she came out of her depression. Before that, she'd surfaced from time to time, enough to take on chores and driving and stuff, but this was a whole series of months that she really came back, like she'd just woken up from hibernation. She'd sit down with me after school—I was getting home an hour earlier than Alia then, because we were in different schools—and she'd make me cinnamon-sugar toast, and we'd talk. Really talk. I told her about my friends and guys I had crushes on and which classes I was having trouble with, and she listened and gave advice, and—I remember, I felt—"

She paused abruptly, and took a deep breath. "Like, *Is this is how other kids feel all the time?*"

Griff, who had grown up with a mom who did craft and cooking projects with him and his sister, a mom who had fed him a snack every day after school for thirteen years, could not find words.

"But it didn't last long," Becca said. "Just before Christmas that year, she got back in bed, and—" She sighed.

Griff reached out and covered her hand with his. It didn't feel like anywhere near enough, but he had to touch her. Offer twelve-year-old Becca some speck of comfort in a world where parents could die and be lost in their own suffering without warning.

Becca's gaze flashed to his, surprised, and gratitude warmed her eyes.

"Do you ever see her, now?"

"After I graduated from high school, I saw her at holidays, but I haven't seen her for a couple of years. Alia thinks I should visit. And maybe a year ago I would have caved, but I'm in a good place, and, I don't know, New Becca doesn't need that, you know?" She didn't wait for his confirmation, but picked up her burger again. "What else did Nate say? I'm sure you guys didn't talk about my mommy issues the whole time."

"He also brought up your ex. The one who made you save yourself for him and then—"

He could feel the expression on his face morph into murder, which made Becca smile. "Todd," she said. "Yeah. He probably said I was a hot mess after that, huh? I mean, not that he saw it for himself, but I know Alia's told him. Something like that really screws with how you think about promises, you know? We were both saving ourselves for the rest of our lives. And then—"

"I really want to hurt him," Griff said quietly.

"You wouldn't though, would you?" she asked uncertainly.

That made *him* smile. "Nah. Lately I've wanted to hurt a lot of people on your behalf. But I'm not really that guy. I mean, war, yeah, obviously, but I've never even punched someone as a civilian. Not even—"

He stopped.

"Alia told me about what happened with Marina."

That socked him in the middle of the chest. Maybe because she'd guessed it was Marina's boyfriend, Scott, who he'd fantasized about hitting. Or maybe it was hearing her say Marina's name. Like Marina was supposed to be completely separate from Becca. Or maybe it was the other way around.

"That must have been awful."

Her expression was soft. It made the ache in his chest worse.

"Pretty bad, yeah."

"You got blindsided."

Startled, his eyes met hers. And he didn't have any time to hide either the surprise or the truth, which was, *yes, that's it exactly. Blindsided.*

She saw him so clearly. It was fucking unnerving. "Yeah."

"You must hate surprises, now."

"Guess I do."

Her eyes searched his face. A little worried, if he had to guess, like maybe she shouldn't have gone down this path. But then her expression changed. She got a mischievous look on her face.

"So if I told you I wasn't wearing any panties . . ." she teased.

She barely had the sentence out, but he could already see, feel, and smell it: her bare ass against the fabric of her skirt, the silk of her pussy touched by the cool air between her thighs, spread just a little, her clit stiffening. He imagined he could catch the sea-salt scent of her from here.

All the blood in his entire body had detoured to his dick, leaving him light-headed. "Are you really not?" he demanded.

She laughed, cheeks pink, eyes bright. "No. I mean, I really *am* wearing panties. I was just testing how far your hatred of surprises goes." She smirked. "Although they have had kind of a . . . damp day, what with the copier room and all."

"Oh, Jesus, baby." He leaned back and gave her a lazy perusal. She folded her arms over her peaking nipples and then, with a deliberateness that made it even sexier, crossed her thighs. He leaned over the table. "What if I said you should go to the bathroom and take them off?"

"I'd do it," she murmured, leaning in. "Of course. In the interest of my sexual education."

He was having some trouble breathing, on account of how much of his body's resources had been diverted south.

"Go," Griff said, his voice barely more than a rasp.

And she went.

32

She was glad she'd worn a slip under her dress, because the way he looked at her through the rest of dinner, eyes burning, she would have had a wet spot when she stood up.

"Do you want dessert?" he asked her, when a waitress—not Lily—had taken their dinners away.

"Would it be painful if I said yes?" she asked.

He shook his head. "I'm enjoying the anticipation," he murmured. "I hope you are, too."

She was. The cool air between her legs and the silk of her slip against her bare skin.

She had Boston cream pie, licking the custard off the fork in a way she meant to turn him on. He never took his eyes off her, like *she* was his dessert, and her body was all confused between the taste and sensation on her tongue and how lit-up the rest of her felt, like sex and food couldn't figure out how to coexist in her brain.

Afterward they walked out to his truck. She snuck a look his way and saw that he was watching her.

"Ever had sex in a pickup truck flatbed, under a blanket, in a field, beneath the stars?"

She shook her head.

"Want to?"

She grinned at him and nodded.

On the drive out on Route 26, the anticipation was sweet, the two of them side by side in the dark cab, knowing what was going to happen.

"Are you thinking about it? What it's going to feel like?"

"Yeah."

"Tell me."

"I think about me being really wet and you being really big and how good it feels when you first come into me."

"I think about that, too."

"I think about when you're in all the way, like really all the way, so you're stretching where it feels best."

"God, Becca." His voice was rough.

"I think about you kissing me and fucking me at the same time. And being really wet both places."

"It's probably not safe for me to drive while you talk like that. Because there's no actual blood in my brain."

She laughed. She hadn't really talked like that to anyone before, and she liked it. A lot. She figured there wasn't anything she and Griff could do that she wouldn't like.

She laid off the dirty talk, then, knowing he was right about it not being safe, but she didn't stop thinking about what was coming.

He spread blankets for them in the back. He boosted her up onto the bed and came in after her. They lay down together face to face and he kissed her and kissed her, his mouth hot in the cool night air. There were stars overhead, a scattered mess of them across a black sky.

His fingers found her—her nipples, then her curls, her slit, her clit, her wet heat, bringing pleasure everywhere. He kept kissing her. She went to work on his jeans, button, zipper, working them down, freeing him so she could wrap a hand around his thickness and squeeze. "Yeah," she said. "Yeah, yeah, yeah. Love this."

She felt a little self-conscious about having said love, even if it was just about his penis, but she figured it was probably okay, because he kissed her again, even deeper, after.

He produced a condom from somewhere in the depths of the blankets and covered himself, then kissed her some more. His tongue teased and probed and promised. Then he was nudging her open with his hands and his cock, and she rolled onto her back to give him better access. She kicked his jeans down further, which made him laugh. Then he was inside her. His tongue tangled with hers and his cock was buried in her pussy and she groaned her satisfaction into his mouth. He growled back. Or really it was more of a grunt. His hands were much rougher on her nipples now, but she didn't mind. She liked it. He was kissing her gently. And he moved slowly in her, a sweet glide and retreat. Tension was gathering itself, not so much between her legs but in some complicated space in her belly that was taking feedback from everywhere else in her body. Her mouth was sending pleasure there, and her nipples. Her clit, and the walls of her pussy.

Everything was going to that one spot and coiling up and getting ready to unleash itself on her, and she felt, suddenly, a little afraid. She grabbed Griff's arms. Clutched him around the back. Like whatever was coming for her was bigger than she knew how to contain, and he was the thing that could keep her safe.

And that was just how it felt, when the orgasm broke over her, like surf breaking over her head. Like it was bigger than her, too big for her body to contain so it had to get outside of her and she couldn't stay serene in its turbulence. Like her hands in his hair and grabbing handfuls of his clothes and her voice calling his name were the only things holding her to the earth.

He was holding on, too, hurting her with the strength of his grip, and her name on his lips was a crooked, broken sound that unleashed itself into the dark night.

33

Griff knocked on CJ's door the next afternoon, and the kid opened it. "What do *you* want?"

"I'm sorry about the Becca thing." No point in beating around the bush.

"Some wingman," CJ said, giving Griff a hard look.

"I should have told you right off she wasn't available. That's where I screwed up."

CJ must have caught something in Griff's voice, some measure of *no bullshit*, because instead of snapping back, he nodded. "So it's like that."

Was it? He wasn't sure. Lately it felt like there was so much he didn't know, like he couldn't get his bearings. And last night hadn't helped. He'd come so hard that the stars had spun overhead, and afterwards, driving Becca home to her sister and Nate's house, he'd wanted something he didn't want to want.

More time.

He left it at that, though, and said, "I gotta go to Home

Depot. Thought you might want to come along. Kill a few hours, do a favor for Jake?"

CJ nodded.

Griff tipped his head and CJ grabbed his wallet, locked the door to his room, and followed Griff out of the building. When they got within spitting distance of Griff's truck, he pulled his keys out of his pocket and flipped them to CJ. The kid caught them—reflex kicking in—looked down and then at Griff, then tossed them back.

"Hey," Griff said. "Give it a try?"

CJ shook his head. "I've tried."

"But you're fine when you're a passenger."

"It's the being in control part that wrecks me," CJ said. "I freak out. Shake. Sweat."

"That doesn't sound so bad."

"Easy for you to say. You aren't the woman sitting in the passenger seat backing further and further into the corner, like, *get away from the psycho.*"

"Has that happened?"

"Not with anyone else in the car. But, yeah, I mean, I can't even drive two minutes to the grocery store without it happening."

"And if you do it more? Like, longer stretches, or more often, you know, get used to it?"

"Fuck that," CJ said. "You try driving drenched in sweat, shaking, and cryi—fuck that."

Griff didn't argue any further. He just climbed up on the driver's side, started the car, and drove them to Home Depot.

They stepped inside and were instantly hit with sensory overload. The visual clutter, the hollow, echoey sounds, and the smells—lumber, peat, chemicals, new carpet. Griff hesitated, trying to sort himself out, then grabbed one of the big orange plastic carts.

"You want to split the list?" CJ asked.

"Sure," Griff said. He did it literally, tearing the list into two pieces and giving half to CJ. "It'll go faster that way." Griff quickly scanned the items he was responsible for. "Hose nozzle?" he demanded. "Jake's just messing with me."

CJ snickered and sped off towards lumber.

Griff headed to gardening, took one look at the selection of hose nozzles, and pulled out his phone, snapping a photo and then dialing Jake.

"What kind of *hose nozzle*, your highness?"

"One of the fancy-ass ones with different settings for spray, mist, and *pound the shit out of some vegetation*."

Griff laughed. "Will do." He hung up. Huh. There was a voicemail from a call he hadn't caught earlier. He paused to listen.

His heart did a funny skip-beat thing as soon as he heard her voice.

Marina.

Hey, Griff. Long time no talk. Um, so, I know we talked about this a while back, but it's a little more urgent now. If you could get your stuff out of the basement, it would be super helpful. Maybe text me some times that would work for you?

He sighed and shook his head. He didn't even give a shit about that stuff anymore. He should call her back, probably, tell her to just throw it out or something.

Later. He'd do it later. He had other, more important shit to contend with right now, like hose nozzles.

Ugh, who was he kidding? He just hated the idea of having an actual conversation with Marina.

He put his phone away and found the "fancy-ass" equipment that Jake had spec'd. The thing looked like a deadly weapon, not a gardening tool.

And of course, the next thing on the list was on the other side of the store. Maybe he and CJ should have made some effort to split the list by location.

He took a step away from the nozzle display and the world shattered into sound.

He was on his feet before the last reverberations, before he knew his name, his chest heaving, his mouth dry, reaching for his SIG Sauer. He woke up fully then to the mud hole of a combat outpost where they'd been sleeping, to the swearing of the men around him, everyone grabbing for Kevlar and NVGs, for weapons, for positions, tripping and stumbling over gear and each other and shouting—Fuck, Wake, where are you? The fuck was that? Jesus, Teo, get the *fuck* down! Gregger, call that shit up, call it up, call it up! The fuck are you thinking?! *He could hear mortars, no incoming Hollywood whistle to warn them, no big budget explosion they could see by, just the boom*—Fucking fuckers! *someone shouted.* Where are they? *And* Over there, over there, no, behind that big ledge. North! The other fucking north! *And he kept thinking,* I knew, I fucking knew, I fucking *knew.*

"Whoa, you okay, man?"

Someone was shaking him gently. An older guy with an unkempt beard and an orange Home Depot apron pushing one of those store carts around.

"I dropped a load of PVC pipe," the guy said. "It hit the

ground with a clatter, and you swung around and aimed that thing at me. At first, I thought it was a gun. You scared the *shit* out of me. I almost called for security backup. We coulda both gotten shot."

The guy was breathing hard, Griff realized.

"And then you were just standing there. Staring."

Slowly, the world rearranged itself and began to make sense.

He'd been back there, the night of the surprise attack. Again.

"I'm—I'm okay," he said.

The Home Depot guy didn't look convinced. "Do you need me to call anyone?"

"No. I'm fine. It happens, sometimes."

The attendant was still staring at him with concern in his kind brown eyes.

"I'm okay," Griff said again. He took a breath. Tried it on for size. "I get these episodes. PTSD. Army."

The guy's eyes softened even more. "Yeah. My nephew has that. Marines."

The thing of it was, Griff had been trying for days to find the words to tell Jake about his episodes.

He'd thought of about ten different ways to start, but in the end, he hadn't been able to get the words out. *Any* words.

And then he'd gone and told a stranger.

That was ten kinds of fucked up and also made some weird-ass sense.

"Thanks for your service, man," the Home Depot guy said.

"Thanks for checking on me. I'll be fine now."

The guy nodded and went back to his own business.

"Hey."

Griff turned to find CJ standing behind him.

"You hear that?" Griff asked. He knew he was pale, his face damp with sweat; he tried his best to control the shaking that always followed an episode, but he could see from the way CJ's eyes carefully avoided his hands that he'd failed.

CJ nodded.

They stared at each other for a minute. Then CJ shrugged. "You said it. We all have our shit." He dumped a bunch of short two-by-fours in Griff's cart. "I should probably get my own cart, huh? Meet you up front in a few?"

Griff finished his shopping—still shaking, damn it—and met CJ at checkout. They paid, then loaded the contents of the cart into the back of the truck. Griff could feel CJ's eyes on him as he tried his best to steady himself. "You okay to drive?" CJ asked him.

Griff was a hair's breadth away from snapping back at him, *Of course I'm fucking okay to drive*, but stopped himself just as he was opening his mouth.

Huh.

He'd just had an idea.

"Not sure," he said, hamming it up a little. "Feeling pretty shaky. And, um, disoriented. A little—" What was that word Jake used a bunch in group? "Dissociated." It was when you lost touch with reality. Definitely not compatible with safe driving. Way worse than sweaty and shaking, or at least Griff hoped CJ would think so.

"We could hang out for a little, until you're better," CJ said. "Or call someone to come get us."

"No," Griff said. "I gotta get back ASAP. I've got tutoring in forty minutes. You'd better drive," he said, tossing the keys to CJ.

CJ's eyes were big as he caught them. "Uh, this is a really bad idea."

Griff looked away so CJ wouldn't see his expression. "I think it's our best bet."

Unwillingly, CJ hauled himself up into the driver's seat. Griff took shotgun. Now he just had to hope that he wasn't actually going to get them both killed.

CJ started the truck, backed out of the space, and started toward home. True to his word, he began to sweat and shake. His hands gripped the wheel so hard it must have hurt. Griff felt his own hands clenching into fists in sympathy. "You're doing good, man," he said quietly.

"This *sucks*," CJ said.

"Hang in. And thanks for saving my ass."

CJ sat up a little straighter at that. And he turned onto Highway 101 without any visible further freak-out.

At the first traffic light he shook his head ruefully and said, "Well, it's not pretty, but I'm doing it."

"Doesn't have to be pretty."

"Tell that to the woman riding shotgun."

"You ever thought about just owning it?" Holy *shit*, he was a hypocrite. He almost shut his hypocrite face before he could go any further, but then he thought about it for a minute. Maybe he wasn't as much of a hypocrite as he used to be. He'd told Becca, after all. And the guy in Home Depot. And CJ. So he went on, plowing through, because even if he *was* a hypocrite, he owed it to CJ to make sure the kid didn't make the same mistake he had, didn't spend years clammed up. "Just tell her. *I was in*

Afghanistan, this crazy thing happened, and driving makes me a little jittery."

CJ just grunted—but Griff knew he'd heard. And when they reached the light at Seaside, CJ said, "You were right, it gets a little easier. I guess I never tried more than a couple minutes. Never gave myself time to, you know, settle in."

Griff smiled, an invisible, internal smile.

By the time they pulled into R&R, the sweat had dried on CJ's face. He unlocked his hands from around the wheel. "They're going to be permanently in this position," he said, holding them up like claws for Griff to see. They were shaking, too—but only a little.

"But you did it."

"I did it."

Griff felt a surge of triumph. "And it *will* get easier."

"Yeah," CJ said. "Yeah."

"You could give me a ride in the Shelby soon, and start using that baby for the purpose for which God intended her. As lady bait."

That made CJ smile—not a full-on smile, but a hopeful one.

Griff suddenly realized he had completely stopped shaking. He looked down at his hands, and they were rock steady. Huh. Apparently, helping someone else was the best cure.

CJ looked at Griff's hands, too, and a funny expression crossed his face. Then he squinted up his eyes. "You're full of it, aren't you?"

"Who, me?"

"Dissociating? Dizzy?"

Griff gave CJ his best sheepish face.

CJ sighed. "You are an asshole, man, you know that?"

"Been told that," Griff said, grinning.

"Did you do all this because you wanted a ride in the Shelby?"

"Nah," Griff said, clapping CJ on the back. "Just being a good wingman."

34

*J*ed's here.

She stared at Griff's text for a long time before tapping back, *So?*

I thought you might want to come in and talk to him.

She thought she'd made herself clear the last time they'd talked—she'd given it a try, but now she was done. *Nope,* she texted back.

Her phone rang.

"Griff, don't," she said, before he could say anything else.

"You have unfinished business with him." He was whispering, so she knew he was in the big tutoring room and that Jed was in there, too.

"I really don't."

"C'mon, Becca, give it one more try."

She pushed a stack of insurance claims forward on the desk, then pulled them back toward her. "Did he ask for me?"

There was a long silence. That would be a *no*, then.

"Did he ask for help at all?"

"He—no." Griff's last word came out on an exhale, almost a sigh.

"He doesn't want my help. He made that abundantly clear. And one of the things I like about New Becca is that she knows who she is, and she's happy with that version of herself. She doesn't need to prove anything to anyone, especially if it means banging her head against a wall."

On the other end of the phone, Griff took a deep breath. "Hang on a sec." His voice moved further away. "JoJo, I'm going outside for a minute, can you handle that on your own?"

"Yeah. I got this." JoJo's voice drifted to Becca.

There was the sound of shuffling and then Griff's voice, closer to her ear than before. "You can do this Becca. Not to prove anything. Not because I say you should. But because Jed wants your help, and I know you know what it's like to be a kid who's finally fessed up that he's vulnerable."

She wrinkled her nose. "Griff. Are you trying to emotionally manipulate me into helping Jed?"

He blew out a short snort of a laugh. "Ha! No." There was a pause, and then he said, "Why, is it working?"

She laughed. "No. Nope. I cannot be emotionally manipulated. And you cannot use those Jedi mind tricks on me."

"Dang," he said. "Because if there's a way to get you naked on my bed using Jedi mind tricks—"

"Mmm," she said. "Suddenly I find myself drawn toward my car . . ."

"Keep going," he teased. "Turn the key in the ignition . . ."

"I think that's your job," she murmured.

He blew out another breath, one that was halfway to a groan. "I should probably get back upstairs."

I know you know what it's like to be a kid who's finally fessed up that he's vulnerable.

She loved that he knew her like that. She really did. Even if she didn't know what it meant that she loved it, or how this was all going to play out.

"Okay," she said, finally. "Okay. I'm coming over there. Don't tell Jed, though. Promise."

She thought he was going to crow a little over his victory —he was entitled—but he just said, "I promise."

She got Sibby to take over the desk and drove to KidsUp. When she came into the study room, Jed looked up and saw her. A look flashed across his face—it might have been the pinched fear of a trapped animal, she couldn't say for sure— but he didn't run away. He sat still, watching her warily, as she came and slid in across from him.

She motioned for him to take his earbuds out. She half thought he'd ignore her, but he didn't; he wrapped the earbud cords around his phone and set the whole thing aside. Then he surprised her by reaching into his ratty back-pack, pulling out a tattered sheet of paper, and dropping it on the table between them.

"I wrote it down, like you told me to. It sucks. A lot."

His eyes challenged her to argue.

She touched the piece of paper, her heart pounding. "That's okay," she said. "Let's look at it."

She read it, slowly working through his almost indecipherable handwriting.

I dont like being home by myself in the afternoons Everything is too loud, I can hear the refridgerator huming and the floors creking, sometimes I think I can here the fight my parents had last nite still echoing. The house feels like the shades are drawn even tho there not.

She caught her breath.

Across the table from her, he was waiting, watching her face, unable to make himself not care.

"Do you know why we write?" she asked him. "I mean, what the point is?"

He gave her a look that was one notch short of an eye roll, but she didn't give a shit. What she was about to tell him was something her tenth grade teacher had told her. At the time it hadn't made a lot of sense to her—but after she'd seen what Alia's letters had meant to Nate . . . Well, now she thought she understood. And she thought Jed might, too.

"We write because we're trying to reach into someone else's head and make them feel the same thing we feel."

Jed's eyes were on hers, a little less guarded than they'd been before. And she was pretty sure Griff was right. She *was* getting through to him, for whatever weird reason. Maybe because like recognized like.

She took a deep breath. "My house wasn't empty, like yours, when I came home from high school. My mom was home. But she was—she was, um, hurting too much to come downstairs. So it was just like you said. Just like that. It felt like the shades were drawn, even though they weren't." She closed her eyes, because she could still feel it—that sense, beyond sight or smell or hearing, of something *wrong*. "You nailed it."

His eyes widened. If she hadn't been watching so closely, she would have missed it.

"Would you let me help you with the capitalization and

punctuation and spelling? I'm not a super genius at it—" She paused for effect. "But I don't suck as bad as you do."

A small puff of breath escaped his mouth—the closest thing to a laugh she figured he had in him. Then he put his sullen teenager expression back on and shrugged.

"I'll take that as a yes," she said.

She tried not to, but she couldn't keep herself from looking over at Griff. Sure enough, he was looking back and the expression on his face really *was* going to kill her. She knew that expression, even though very few people had ever looked at her that way. Alia, sometimes. Her mother, on a really good day. A teacher here and there.

He was looking at her like he was *proud* of her. And it lit her up, partly because who didn't want someone looking at them like they'd done something good? Or important. Or smart. Or all of the above.

But right then, it wasn't that Griff thought she was good or important or smart that mattered most. Maybe she was, and maybe she wasn't. Maybe she'd helped Jed a ton or maybe he'd just been ready to figure it out for himself, and maybe she'd never know which. She was pleased she'd made a difference, one way or the other, but that wasn't why Griff's expression made her feel like fireworks were going off in her belly.

It was because when you were proud of someone, it had two parts. The part where you were all, like, *That person did a good job.*

And the part where you were like, *And that person?*
She's mine.

35

JoJo left first, followed by Jed, and then it was just the two of them in the study room. Becca got up from the booth where she'd been working with Jed and came to sit across from him.

"That . . . seemed like it went well," Griff said.

She had a bright glow to her that he knew was satisfaction at having cracked the code that was Jed. And it made her ten times as beautiful as she already was, which in turn made it hard to look at her.

"Thank you," she said, unexpectedly. "For—" She hesitated. "For texting me to say he was here. For having faith I could do it. For—being generally awesome in a way that made me want to be awesome too."

Oh, Jesus, she was—too damn much. He couldn't fit the way she made him feel under his skin anymore.

"I wish—" He stopped.

She put her hand on the table and he covered it with his. He wrapped hers up, small in his grip. "I wish you could stay longer. I know I'm a craptastic friend for not being a hundred percent gung-ho about the salon job—"

She shook her head. "No. I'm not a hundred percent gung-ho, either."

"You could stay here. Work for Jake. And Nate."

She smiled weakly. "One successful tutoring session doesn't suddenly make me qualified for this kind of thing."

"You loved it, though. Admit it."

She couldn't hold back her smile. "I loved it."

Watching her smile like that was battle victory and a military parade, a Memorial Day picnic, *The Princess Bride*, the best bitter hoppy beer, Robbie's unconditional affection.

This was how he wanted her to be all the time. He wanted her to have a life full of things she loved that much.

"God," he said, because it was actually painful to want that. To feel like this again. He was walking on a tightrope and he was going to fall, any minute. "God, Becca, that makes me really happy, you know?"

She reached out and rubbed a hand over his jaw where afternoon scruff was sprouting. Then put the same hand in his hair and gave it a little tug, so he was forced to lean across the table and meet her kiss. She bit his lip and he groaned.

She pulled back and gave him a look, the one he now recognized as loaded with his favorite kind of trouble. "We still haven't done it with me on top. Or you behind me."

All that was true, but it wasn't what he wanted. He wanted—

"What if I said—?"

She was very still across the table from him, picking up on how serious he was.

"What if I said I didn't want to do you any favors or work

on any projects or fulfill any kama sutra fantasies or one-up Jondalar the Wonder Schlong or play any more fucking games? What if I said I just wanted to take you back to my room and make love to you?"

"Oh," she said, softly.

"Would that totally freak you out?"

She shook her head. "No."

"Good," he said. He put his hand out, and she slipped her small, soft one into his again. He tugged her out from her side of the booth, close to his side.

"Griff," she whispered, coming into his arms.

He couldn't help himself—he kissed her. Her mouth was soft and hot and so, so hungry. As if up to this point, she'd been holding something back, and now she was giving everything to him. He wasn't sure he could take it. He was going to catch fire and burn up.

But he kissed her back anyway, because he couldn't *not* do it. Her tongue was eager and bossy. Her hands grabbed his clothes, his ass, his hair. She was whimpering and murmuring things he couldn't understand, and he was going to do something very, very bad if they didn't get out of here.

He put his hands on her shoulders, held her away from him. She didn't like it. She clutched at him, which almost made him give in.

"We have to stop, just for now," he said. "I don't like it either. I want to fuck you on that table right there. Right now. But I want to make love to you in my bed more than that, so that's where we're going." He paused. "But I need an hour, first. There's something I have to do."

She raised an eyebrow. "I have condoms."

He laughed. "Not that. I'll tell you afterwards, okay? Meet me at my room—" He looked at his watch, "at six fifteen."

He could tell she didn't understand, but that was okay. She would.

JAKE WAS JUST LEAVING his office—perfect timing.

"I need to talk to you," Griff said.

His boss raised an eyebrow.

"If you have a minute," Griff amended.

Jake turned back into the office and gestured for Griff to follow. They sat in the waiting room in comfy chairs, which were a little too deep for actual comfort, the arm rests a little too high. So Griff stood again, and paced.

Jake watched him, patient, curious. Big, badass Jake with his one "meat" leg—as he called it—and the other one, prosthetic from the thigh down. Jake, who—long before the incident that had taken his leg—had gotten a medal for dragging some guy to safety under a rain of PK fire.

No two ways about it, Jake was a hero. Bravest guy Griff knew.

But there were all different kinds of brave. Like CJ driving because he thought Griff needed him to.

And Becca showing up and powering through with Jed. Killing it, really, the way she'd killed everything she'd taken on since she'd decided to slough off Old Becca.

"You know why I lost that hotel job?"

Jake stood up, then, too, and leaned against the wall. Watching Griff, not saying anything, just waiting.

It was still, after all this time, tempting to back off. Until the words were out of his mouth, he didn't have to say them. But he wanted to say them. He wanted to be as brave as Becca deserved for him to be.

"I flashed back because a metal door slammed shut, and scared the shit out of a bunch of guests. I did it earlier today, too—minus the big audience—in Home Depot. Next thing I know a guy's shaking me and telling me I was threatening him with a fucking hose nozzle."

Jake just nodded. "Yeah. I thought it might be something like that."

Griff's mouth fell open. "You knew and you never asked me about it?"

"Figured you'd tell me when you were ready."

Griff closed his mouth and nodded. Then he opened it again and said, "Guess I am."

"Same flashback every time?"

Griff nodded. "Battle in the mountains where we got woken out of a dead sleep by a surprise attack that shouldn't have been a surprise. The kids were off. Quiet. Not out playing. You know?"

Jake closed his eyes. Griff had heard him tell that part of his story enough times to know how well and how personally he knew: The kids could tell you everything. Kids where they shouldn't be, no kids where they should be. "Something bad was coming. I told my platoon leader—" There was a tight band around Griff's chest. "He convinced me that we were all jumpy from nothing happening for so long, that I was looking for something that wasn't there. He dismissed it. And —I let him. I didn't—"

His voice cracked.

"I should have trusted my gut. I should have stood my

ground till the end of time, dug myself in so deep Knapp would have had to listen. Or gone over his head. Talked to someone who *would* hear me out."

"But you didn't."

"No, I didn't. I knew. I fucking knew, and I didn't stop it—"

This—this was what he'd been trying to avoid, being weak in front of Jake, in front of anyone, but all Jake said was, "I'm sorry, Griff." He didn't say anything else, just put his palm flat against the center of Griff's back while Griff hunched over and got the rest of his grief out, in shudders and sobs.

When Griff pulled it back together and swiped his sleeves across his face to mop up the worst of it, he felt purged, like he'd hurled up bad food instead of years of held—whatever. And Jake looked as unsurprised and unconcerned as ever.

So, thought Griff, *that* was what he'd been afraid of all this time. Opening his mouth and losing his shit, and—the world hadn't, in fact, ended.

He took a deep breath. "Six men."

Jake nodded. "I'm sorry, Griff."

They had kind of an impromptu moment of silence then, or something, Griff remembering: *Toff, Hanamalu, Mike, Jay, Regis, Teo.*

Maybe the first time he'd let himself tick them off, one by one, like that. Mourn them all.

Jake crossed his arms. "Can I say something?"

Griff nodded.

"Hindsight's a bitch. It always tells you that you should have known. And maybe so. But you knew what you knew, you did what you did. And here we fucking are. It's not pretty, but it's how we keep on going."

"You get paid to sell that shit?" Griff asked. A choked, tear-sodden laugh came out of him, unexpectedly.

Jake smiled, too. "Damn straight."

"Nice work, if you can get it."

"You can get it. You can lead the support group from time to time like I asked."

Griff took a deep breath. Nodded. "As long as you know I'm no expert. Just a guy with his own shit, ready, willing, and able to hear out other guys about their shit."

That made him think of CJ, and he smiled.

Jake's grin spread. "Glad to hear it. So what made you decide to tell me all this now?"

Griff hesitated. "Dunno. Maybe enough time just passed."

Jake raised an eyebrow. "Or maybe you have a new friend?"

Griff tried to give Jake a blank look in return, but Jake just shook his head and smirked. "Don't you know by now that I know everything that goes on at R&R? Besides, last Friday at dinner, the amount of energy you and Becca spent *not* looking at each other could have powered Portland for a year."

Griff could feel a rare deep blush coloring his face.

Which reminded him—

"I should get the hell outta here. I'm, uh, meeting someone."

Jake raised his eyebrows.

"Yeah, yeah, yeah. You know everything about everyone, Mr. R&R. I know."

"IT'S NOT MUCH," Griff said, as he opened the door to his R&R room. It had nice carpeting, had been recently painted, and was well-lit—but it was still a dorm room.

If Becca was disappointed—if she thought a guy his age should have more to his name, more to show for himself—she didn't say so. Instead, she gave him a little shove into the room and pushed the door closed behind them.

"We're alone, aren't we?" she asked.

He nodded.

"Then it's perfect."

All of a sudden, it really did feel that way. As if the only thing that mattered was the four walls around them and the way she was looking at him, like he was everything she could possibly ever want in the world. And right at the moment, he felt pretty damn good. As if maybe he was someone she could want like that.

She sure as hell was someone he wanted like that.

"So where'd you go just now? If it wasn't to get condoms?"

She looked a little worried, which made him want simultaneously to laugh and to wrap her up in his arms. And that captured in a nutshell his feelings for Becca.

"I was in Jake's office."

She tilted her head.

"I told him. About the episo—flashbacks."

Her eyes got big. "You—that's so great!"

He filled her in on the flashback in Home Depot, then about getting CJ to drive home.

Then he told her exactly what he'd told Jake. All of it.

The grief came back in the retelling. It choked him and filled his eyes, but he kept the words coming. And she listened quietly, the way she always did, absorbing it. She came and stood with him and rested her head against his chest like she was listening to his heartbeat, and that made it easier.

"He's right, you know," she murmured, against his shirt. "So easy to think you should have done it differently. And maybe you should have, but you can't know."

"I know."

"I mean, it might not change how bad it feels."

"It does and it doesn't."

"Was it hard, telling Jake?"

"It wasn't so hard, once the words started coming out. And—I also told him I'd lead the support group sometimes. If he wanted me to."

She stepped back and looked at him. "You—I'm so—" She inhaled deeply, her eyes bright. "Is it weird to say I'm so proud of you?"

His breath kept threatening to flit away from him, like some wild bird. "No. Not weird at all. I, um—I think I did it *to* make you proud of me."

In the silence that followed, *her* eyes filled with tears. "You're going to kill me, Griff Ambrose," she said.

His chest felt full of light. "You're going to kill me first, Becca Drake."

They were both quiet for a little bit. He wondered if her chest ached, too. If she was trying to think about what she wanted to say and how to say it, like he was. If there really was even anything to say. Maybe there was just this, the fact that they made each other feel good and made each other try harder to *be* good and would always be able to look back and be grateful for that.

He took a step toward her, which backed her up against

the door. He put one hand on each side of her head. Her eyes got big and her lower lip softened, and a little breath slipped out of her. He bent his head to kiss her. Just their lips touched, soft and sweet, but she whimpered. He took a step in and pressed her against the wall, bending his knees and lining the bulge in his jeans up with the seam of her leggings so he could stroke her with the friction he'd learned she liked.

"I'm going to make you come once like this," he said contemplatively. "And then once more on the bed with my fingers and my tongue. And *then* I'm going to make love to you."

Her eyes were huge.

He cupped her cheek, feeling so much tenderness for her, for every part of her, that it *hurt*. Like your toes getting feeling back after being frozen, but he was pretty sure in this case that the thing that had been frozen was his heart. He touched one part of her after another—her hair, her lips, her ear, her throat, and each place he touched her, she made a different sound, like he was playing her. It was the sexiest, most beautiful thing he'd ever heard.

He stroked her nipple, settled his mouth on hers again, and began very gently rubbing himself against the heat between her legs. One slow, sure tilt of his hips, clench of his ass, after another, while he alternated between kissing her and watching her. On a kiss, she bit his lip, gave a sharp cry, and came. He pulled back and cupped her tight in the palm of his hand so he could feel the flutters, like a trapped bird, and she breathed and sobbed into his ear.

His cock surged and for a second, he thought he was going to lose it, too. Like a high school kid. Like a virgin.

What have you done to me, Becca?

He scooped her up, carried her to the bed, laid her down, and stripped her leggings off. She was wearing a barely-there thong—really just strings—and he moved it to the side so he could see her. She was beautiful, every shade of pink God had ever invented, and slick with desire. And when he bent to lick her—she tasted so good. Clean and briny. He took his time, sliding first one finger into her slickness, then another, crooking them to find the spot that made her arch and cry out.

"Come again for me, baby," he urged.

He looked up to find that she'd propped herself up on pillows and was watching him. She'd pushed her sweater up and her bra down and she was playing with her nipples, toying, pinching, twisting, almost absently, like she couldn't help herself. Holy *fuck*.

"Keep doing that," he said roughly. He hadn't meant to speed up what his fingers were doing, but he was fucking her now, and she didn't seem to mind. Quite the opposite. She was fucking back against his hand.

"Feels better when you do it." Her voice was a low murmur.

Who was he to resist a request like that? His left hand was free, and he let it play over her nipples, which she'd teased to beads. Jesus. He pinched one nipple. She moaned, and reflexively, he grabbed her hand and flattened it over the bulge of his cock in his jeans. She squeezed him. "Griff. Please."

"I'm supposed to make you come one more time, first."

"What if I said I really just want you inside me? What if I said I—"

Her voice tightened and choked off the words.

"I feel so much right now, Griff. I just *need* you. I need you to be inside me so I can *show* you."

He knew what she meant because he felt it too, at the painful thawed achy middle of his whole fucking self. It wasn't the kind of thing you could say. You had to *do*.

He pulled away from her, unbuttoned and unzipped his pants, dropping them, kicking them away. He tugged the nightstand drawer open, pulled out a condom and rolled it on. Now that he had abandoned his plan, he was in a hurry—he needed her like he'd never needed anything, like now that the deep freeze was gone, all the held-back life in him had to pour itself into her.

But he wouldn't rush it.

He crawled over her, bracing himself, and kissed her. Her mouth was open, helpless, out of rhythm. Wet and hungry. He was the same way. She spread her thighs and opened to him, so his painfully hard cock slicked through her folds, long, slow, blissful strokes. If he didn't stop, he'd come all over her belly, and he wanted to give her what she was asking for too much to do that. He wanted to be inside her, like she'd asked him. He wanted her to show him how she felt, and he wanted to show her.

"Griff, *please*."

He lined himself up, grabbed the base of his shaft to hang onto his fleeing self-control, and eased in, just enough to feel her soft, slick flesh part and give way.

She made a sound so needy and primal that he almost came right then. She wrapped her arms around him and held him close, her cheek pressed against his, her breath in his ear. She raised her hips and he eased deep inside her.

"Like that, Griff, feel it?" she murmured, her arms tightening. "But even more. Give me more." And she slid her cheek along his until their mouths caught, hot and wet. Her tongue found his and stroked, so he was in her and she was in him.

It was so good, the heat, the sweet fucking slippery *glide* of her, but mostly how tight she was around him, all of her, holding him, *showing* him. "God," he said. "God, Becca—"

"I know. I know."

She held on and held on, and he thrust, hard, and then again, giving up completely on trying to be gentle or thoughtful or any of that.

And she thrust back just as hard, lifting her hips, jamming herself against him, rubbing herself when he was in her to the hilt, tightening down on him. She was coming, he realized, suddenly, shaking in his arms, pulsing around him, whimpering, until the whimpers turned to words and the words were, "Like that, Griff, like that, like *that*."

The long pulses of her orgasm pulled his out of him, and he was coming, too, and he knew *exactly* what she meant, even if he couldn't say it, not yet: *This is what I wanted to show you, how much I like you, how goddamn much I like you—*

This, baby, this is how much I love you.

36

"Hey, sleepyhead."

Becca rose through layers of tufty cotton dream sleep to find Griff sitting on the edge of the bed with two to-go coffee cups and a bag that she prayed contained something that tasted as good as it smelled—of fried dough and sugary frosting.

He was wearing a dark green t-shirt and jeans. His hair was rumpled, as if he hadn't bothered to comb it when he'd gotten out of bed. They'd spent the night spooned with her back to his front. Not that she'd slept a whole ton, because they'd gone three rounds and eaten a ridiculous amount of Thai food before falling asleep probably only about four hours ago. She was going to have to do a walk of shame to work today, and the thing was? She didn't give a crap.

"Hey, beautiful," he said.

"Hey, yourself."

They smiled at each other. Becca felt even happier, which seemed almost impossible, because she thought she'd maxed out last night. Not that she hadn't freaked out a little bit, after that first time. She'd come down from the crazy heights he'd taken her to, feeling a bit like some kind of wind-up toy that had been disassembled so its gears and cranks were strewn on the floor. She was pretty sure she couldn't be put back together, not the way she'd been before.

At that moment, she'd wished for a do-over. Just so she could hold a little, tiny part of herself back. Just . . . to be careful.

Sex with him in the Edgewater Hotel room had been amazing, but she had definitely kept herself at a distance. She'd known where she was and where he was and how wide the space between them was, the whole time. Even so, when he'd said Marina's name in the street outside afterwards, she'd wanted to throw up. She could admit that to herself now.

And if that's how vulnerable she'd felt *before*, he could *destroy* her now. He could make what Todd had done to her look like a bee sting in comparison.

What she'd also realized last night, though, was that it hardly mattered anymore, because she couldn't stop. She couldn't stop wanting him, and she wasn't going to stop being with him until he wanted to stop being with her. Worst—or best—of all, she couldn't stop loving him, which, she was pretty sure, was the feeling that had broken her apart when he'd made love to her, and the thing that made it feel like her heart was trying to beat its way out of her chest.

He *had* to be feeling it, too. The way he'd looked at her across the table in the study booth, what he'd said about not wanting her to go. Telling her he wanted to *make love* to her.

The way he was looking at her now, like she was the best

thing ever, as opposed to ratty-haired and raccoon-eyed from not taking off her makeup.

So that was what she was going to hold on to, for now. If she gave this thing between them some space—and the rest of the time they had left together—everything would work itself out. Somehow.

Meanwhile, she was going to enjoy every last solitary minute she had with him.

She accepted a cup of coffee, took a slug, and then kissed him good morning. A long, hot kiss that almost made her forget everything else—but not quite.

"Need my donut," she said.

"What flavor do you want?" He held up the bag.

She licked her lips. "What are my choices?"

"Ah. We have the official pink Dundee donut, maple bars, chocolate bars, bismarks, and glazed cinnamon twists."

"Can I have one of each?"

"You can have two of each if you want. Especially if I get to watch you eat them. Damn," he said. "If I'd thought of it, I would have gotten you something with cream inside so I could watch you lick it out."

"You are a dirty, dirty man."

"And you know you love it."

He slid onto the bed beside her.

"Are we going to eat them in bed?" she asked, startled.

"Were you never allowed to eat in bed?"

"Alia was a surprisingly strict parent," she admitted. "But one time, when my mom was in a good period—I think I was about nine—we ate takeout in her bed. She called it a picnic, and she let us have Oreos, and she—" She bit her lip, remembering the delight of that evening. "She laughed. She didn't laugh very often, but she laughed that night."

He squeezed her hand.

"Alia is never going to let Robbie do anything like that. I'm going to have to be one of those aunties who sneaks him candy and stuff."

"I'm in, too," he said. "You and me. Between the two of us, we'll make sure the kid grows up right."

He tilted his head after saying that, probably realizing how it sounded. "More immediately, though, have you decided which donut you are going to defile the bed with?"

She giggled. "Glazed cinnamon twist."

He handed it to her and she took a bite.

"Oh. Oh, God. God, that's good."

"Becca," he said suddenly.

She thought he was going to make a crack about the donut, which was rather phallic in shape, or her outburst, which had definitely sounded orgasmic, but he said, "What did you tell Nate and Alia? About why you didn't come home last night."

She squinted at him. "Just not to wait up for me."

"Did you say you were with me?"

"They don't know we're still—" She gestured at the bed around them.

"You going to tell them?"

"Depends, I guess."

"On?"

"On what it is we're doing," she admitted. "I mean, if this is going to end in a week, then no. Because they'll just make a fuss about it, and it's just not worth it. But if—"

She stopped. Once she said it aloud, it would be impossible to take back. And the ball would be in his court, and she would know.

"Becca," he said.

"Uh-huh?"

"Do you know what we're doing? I mean, literally, right this second, in this bed."

"Eating donuts and—"

Suddenly she got it.

"Eating donuts and drinking coffee." Her voice cracked.

He nodded and reached for her hand. Squeezed it. "You killed my fear of complications. Killed it dead. I *want* complications with you."

Her heart was pounding. Hard.

"Would you think about—? I know this is a big ask, but would you at least think about sticking around here a while? Maybe seeing if Jake could give you the receptionist job long term? Doing a little more work for Nate? I know," he said, "one successful tutoring session and all that, but—"

The way he was looking at her, almost pleading, it was hard to breathe around the lump in her throat.

"Yes. I will think about it," she said.

He looked startled. Like he hadn't actually expected her to say yes, let alone so quickly. And then he broke out in a grin so big it made her smile, too, and the two of them just did that, beamed stupidly at each other until he took her donut and her coffee cup out of her hand and set them on the night stand.

Becca was very late to work, which she supposed didn't make the best impression under the circumstances, but it had been the best morning she could remember. And she didn't want to waste a crumb of it.

37

"Hi, Becca," Jake called, rushing past her into his office. "Overslept!"

He'd come in even later than she had, but unlike her, he was *not* wearing the same clothes he'd worn yesterday. He was, however, looking every bit as flustered. Becca got the distinct feeling that whatever went on in Jake and Mira's house, it was off the charts. She didn't like to think about the details, but it did make her smile, seeing this big, tough, in-charge man still acting like a teenager in love a decade into his relationship. It made her feel hopeful about romance.

Or maybe she was just so happy herself that other people's happiness felt like icing on the Dundee pink donut.

His first patient was waiting for him, so she knew she wasn't going to get a chance to ask Jake now about a permanent job, but maybe she could snag some time with him later. She got up from her desk and peeked her head into his office.

"Hey, Jake?"

"Yeah?"

"Can I grab fifteen minutes with you later today?"

"It's going to be a crazy one, Becca," he said. "Tell you what. Is it something we can talk about tonight? At Friday Night Dinner?"

She shrugged. "Sure." He'd made his last job offer to her at the dinner table in front of her family members, so she didn't see why not.

"Okay. Remind me."

BECCA'S PROJECT that day was to clean out the desk, the perfect thing to do on only four hours of sleep.

Sibby might have been a stern taskmaster, but she wasn't a neat freak. Becca tossed out, among other things, a half-eaten candy bar and a *People* magazine from five years ago. She found twenty black pens that still worked, threw away nine that didn't, then turned up a brand-new unopened box of pens. *Note to self, no office supply orders until you do an inventory.*

She chatted with several repeat patients—she was getting to know them now: Garcia and his knee, Jaquizz and the neck pain that made him hold his head brittlely at an angle, McElroy who wouldn't talk at all or even make eye contact—and met three new ones. She let Yuri Osterich see Jake even though he'd arrived ten minutes late. Sibby might have the ovaries to send away a guy who was clutching his hand and walking with a limp, but Becca was, for better or for worse, a softie.

She went to lunch, spotted Alia, and set her tray down.

Her sister looked up, raised both eyebrows and said, "Yesterday's clothes."

"Don't be judge-y."

"When were you going to tell me that you were still sleeping with him?"

Becca sighed. "I wasn't in a hurry to tell you, because I knew you wouldn't approve."

Alia closed her eyes. "I just—"

"I know. You just don't want me to get hurt. Well, I'm not going to get hurt. It's not like that. He asked me if I'd think about staying here."

Alia's face went blank, and Becca's stomach clenched. She pushed the tray, with her spaghetti-and-meatball lunch, away.

"Things are really good with him, Alia. You need to be happy for me."

"I *am* happy for you," Alia said. She did a creditable job of sounding and looking like she meant it. If the words—and the accompanying body language—had come from anyone Becca knew even slightly less well, she might have bought it, but she wasn't convinced.

But there wasn't much she could do about it, was there? Aside from hope that Alia was wrong to be wary.

"So are you going to stay?" Alia demanded. Now she was smiling for real. "Because you know that would make me really, really happy." Then her look sharpened. "What are you planning to do for work?"

"I'm hoping Jake can find me something permanent."

"Something with growth potential?"

"I didn't ask him that," Becca admitted. "But I will, *Mom*."

"I just want what's best for you."

Becca gripped her sister's hand, but she heard the warning behind the warmth in Alia's words, too. And while part of her wanted to brush it off, another part of her curled in on itself, as if her sister's wariness were catching.

THE AFTERNOON WAS PEACEFUL, with the retreat winding down towards the weekend. Just before five, Becca's brain ran out of steam for organizing the office space, and she began scrolling through the retreat's Facebook page and making notes on how Jake could improve it. That's what she was doing when the knock came at the door.

It was a woman, which was unusual. Almost everyone who walked through that door was a man and would be until the retreat opened its doors to female veterans, which was slated to happen next spring.

The woman was young—not much older than Becca— and strikingly pretty. She had long straight glossy black hair, dark wide-set eyes, and a rosebud mouth. She was like a Disney princess come to life. Her eyeliner winged at the corners and her lips were painted bright red. She wore skinny jeans and a metallic silver button-down shirt. Her body was lean but curvy. Becca couldn't say why, but she knew this woman meant trouble for her.

"Hi," she said.

"Hi," Becca returned.

"I'm looking for Griff. Griff Ambrose."

Something clicked, gears slowly grinding into action, and Becca's stomach tumbled. "I—he's—I'm not sure where he is right now."

"Is there any way to get in touch with him? Let him know I'm here?"

"Is he expecting you?"

And who are you? Are you who I think you are?

But she didn't ask, partly because she wasn't sure she was ready to hear the answer.

"No, but I'm—I'm an old friend. Marina Potter."

The ground Becca had been standing on shifted. Lurched.

"I could try to reach him," Becca said. What she really wanted to do was demand, *How can you just show up here, after what you did to him?*

She was unexpectedly furious, but there was nothing she could do that wouldn't make the situation worse, so she picked up her phone. Griff was so rarely at his desk—he didn't even really *have* a desk—but she tried anyway to call the extension where he occasionally sat. As she'd expected, it rang through to voicemail. She didn't leave a message.

When she hung up the phone, the other woman's face fell. Which made Becca's stomach feel even heavier. Knotted around itself.

"I thought about calling ahead," the woman said, as if to herself. "But I knew if I gave him a heads up, he'd figure out a way to avoid me—"

Becca was aware of being on a precipice—she could withhold the fact that *she* knew Griff's cell number, and there was a fighting chance Marina would leave without ever speaking with him. She certainly didn't look like a woman who was determined to stick to her guns. She wore a wavering expression that Becca—at least Old Becca—knew well.

But if Becca did keep Griff in the dark, she would always wonder. If she had stood between Griff and what he really wanted. She would always hear Nate's voice in her head, stating in no uncertain terms that Griff still sought reconciliation. Wouldn't it be better to know the truth, now?

"I'll text him," she said.

Marina's eyes got big. "Would you? Thank you so much."

Even once Becca had said it aloud, committed herself to it, her body didn't want to execute the moves necessary. Her arm didn't want to reach for her cell phone. Her fingers didn't want to swipe the phone open, tap the message app, find Griff's texts. The last text was him telling her he'd gone to get donuts and coffee. She stared at it for a minute, remembering. The thrill of waking up in Griff's bed, the sheets scented not just with him but with them. The sheer, pure joy of the hot coffee, the funny mix of donuts, and his affection.

She couldn't give it up.

Shh, New Becca told Old Becca. *You're getting way ahead of yourself. You were the one in his bed last night. You were the one he gave three orgasms to. And coffee and donuts. Chill the eff out.*

But Marina was the one he married, Old Becca countered.

She was also the one who broke his heart.

C'mon, kiddo. You got this, New Becca said. *He cares about you.*

She made herself type the text. *Marina Potter is here to see you. In the PT office.*

The reply came back instantly. *I'll be right there.*

Couldn't he have taken a few minutes to think about it?

Or better yet, asked her to tell Marina he wasn't available? To send her away?

The disappointment she was feeling—the *fear*—made it hard for her to repeat Griff's message aloud to Marina, but she did it. "He's on his way."

"Thank you," Marina said. "Thank you so much."

It would have been so much easier if Marina had been unforgivably rude to her. If she'd marched in here, demanded to speak with Griff, betrayed no insecurity. But she seemed so *human*. Except for the enormous and unforgettable fact that she had broken Griff, Becca actually *liked* her.

The door of the office swung open and Griff stepped in. Becca's eyes went straight to his face. She couldn't look anywhere else.

"Hey," Marina said.

Becca had seen him look like this once before, on a dark street in the middle of the night outside the Edgewater Hotel. She'd seen the same potent mix of recognition, regret, hope, and longing.

She gripped the edge of the desk so hard her knuckles cracked.

"Hey," Griff returned.

Becca wanted him to say something else. Anything else. She wanted him to move, to speak, to get that look off his face.

"Can we—can we talk?" Marina asked.

Please, please, please say no. Say you're busy, you're in the middle of a project, you have to go to Friday Night Dinner. Say she had her chance to do the right thing, you don't need her, you don't want her, you're done.

Griff opened his mouth, and Becca let herself hope for one long, freighted moment.

"Sure," he said, and the hope curled away like water spiraling down a drain.

38

Even though he'd had plenty of warning, his first sight of Marina still caught him off guard.

She looked the same as always—still tall, slim, curvy, and beautiful—but when she turned to greet him, her face was different. She was wearing makeup, and it made her look—older. More sophisticated. She was all grown up, but even beyond that, there was a quiet under her skin, a peace, that he'd never seen.

He knew it for what it was: happiness.

She was happy now, and it made him realize, with a sharp twist of regret and remorse, that she hadn't ever been when they were together.

"Where do you want to go? Bob's Tavern, maybe?" Marina asked. "That's a good place to talk."

"Sure," Griff said again. It seemed to be the only word he could manage.

Something, a slight sound maybe, drew his attention toward the reception desk, but Becca wasn't looking at him, and her expression was cool and unruffled. He took a step towards the desk, thinking he'd give her a quick explanation and some reassurance. He'd tell her he'd see her later at Friday Night Dinner.

Before he could speak, the desk phone jangled. She gave him an apologetic look, picked up the phone and put her headset on, pressed a button. "R&R physical therapy offices, can I help you?"

He'd text her as soon as he had a chance, explain what he could, promise to explain the rest later, once he knew more about why Marina was here.

"Lead on," he said to Marina.

He followed her down to the parking lot to where her car was parked, the same zippy little Mazda she'd driven back when they were together.

"Meet you there?" she said.

"Sure." He rolled his eyes internally at himself.

Driving down 101, he tried to gather himself, but he felt like a leaky scarecrow, bits and pieces of his straw brains poking out everywhere. What the hell was she doing here? What did she want? What was there to talk about?

For so long, he'd been hoping—not even admitting to himself how hard—for her to realize she'd made a mistake.

Was that what was happening?

If so, she—and the universe—had the world's most fucking awful timing. Because things with Becca were—

They were going somewhere, somewhere good. Somewhere right. What he'd let himself think and feel last night, that had to mean something.

That's what you thought once, a long time ago, about Marina, a cruel, tight part of himself chided.

The parking in town was bad—it was Friday and midafternoon, and thus peak by beach town standards—but not nightmarish. He found a space on one of Tierney Bay's little cross streets down by the water and walked back to Bob's. Marina wasn't there yet, so he pulled out his phone.

Sorry, that was probably really weird for you. I don't know why she's here, but I figured I'd better hear her out. See you at FND?

Becca sent back a thumbs-up.

He wanted to say something more, something reassuring, something like *Don't worry, this is no big deal, I'm totally over her—*

But wouldn't that be kind of opening a can of worms? Or, like, protesting too much? He and Becca hadn't talked much about Marina, but it felt like trying to reassure her that Marina wasn't important to him might make Becca more worried than she would otherwise be.

So he just left it at that.

Marina was watching him, waiting for him to finish, when he looked up. They headed inside and slid into an empty booth along the fireplace side.

"Sorry to just show up like this, but I kind of figured you were never going to respond to my emails and messages," Marina said, right away.

It appeared they weren't going to make small talk or anything.

"Probably not," he admitted.

The waitress set waters down in front of them. "Can I get you some drinks?"

"A Hoptastic," Griff said.

"Root beer."

"You guys want food, too? Or just the drinks?"

"Um, I'm all set," Marina said.

"Me too," Griff said.

The waitress smiled at them and headed back toward the kitchen.

"Look. I should probably have said more in my messages, but I was hoping to at least get you on the phone so I could explain. Scott and I—we're getting married."

So much for the notion that she'd come here to ask for a reconciliation. He couldn't quite make sense of the tangle of emotions in his chest. Old hurt, but also, maybe, relief? Because wouldn't that have been the craziest thing, if she wanted him back, now, just when he was falling for Becca.

"Griff?"

"Congratulations," he said. And he even managed to sound like he sort of meant it. "That's—that's really great, Marina."

She didn't even try to hide her relief. She just let it break out all over her face, and in the big breath she let out.

"Did you think I was going to throw a temper tantrum?"

"I didn't know, Griff. I honestly didn't know."

"I'm not. I'm—I'm okay, Marina. I'm actually—I'm seeing someone."

Although "seeing someone" seemed as feeble as "screwing around" had when Becca had said it yesterday.

"Oh, Griff, I'm glad! I'm really glad. Is it serious?"

"Yeah," he said, thinking of the donuts and coffee and how late he'd made Becca to work this morning, and suddenly he discovered he was smiling. Beaming, actually. Robbie would have been proud.

Right then, sitting across from the woman who'd once brought him to his knees, thinking of the woman who made him want to get down on his knees, he realized just how much he needed Becca to stay.

She couldn't leave. That was all there was to it. He wanted her to have coffee and donuts with him every morning.

Somehow, despite his best intentions, despite the lesson he'd learned from Marina, he'd gone and done it again.

He'd fallen in love. He'd put himself at another woman's mercy.

The waitress came back and set down their drinks. He took a long slug of his beer, bitter and cold. Marina sipped her root beer through the straw, daintily. He'd once thought that was super cute. Becca's appetites had recalibrated him.

He smiled.

"Griff," Marina said. "I really am happy for you. And—oh, God, I'm—I'm sorry. Sorry, not for what I did, but for how I went about it."

"It was pretty shitty," he said, without rancor. "I came home and you were just *gone*."

"I know. I know. I'm so sorry. If I'd been brave enough to do it any other way, I would have. But I was a coward."

Tears filled her eyes.

"If it makes it any better, and I know it doesn't, really, but I tried every way I knew to warn you," she said. "I tried and tried to tell you. And I still don't know if I wasn't saying it out loud like I thought, or you just weren't hearing it. I felt like I was telling you, but—"

He could see her, suddenly, in his mind's eye. Crying. There were words coming out of her mouth, but he couldn't hear the words. He could just see the pain. So many times when he'd been home on leave, it had been like that—her pleading and crying, the two of them yelling and fighting. But had he ever *really* listened?

He shook his head. "I didn't do a good job of hearing you. You *did* say how bad it was and I just didn't want to believe it. I let you down."

And he saw, with a needle of pain to his chest, that he'd known that all along. That was what Marina had been doing in his flashbacks—trying to tell him how much he blamed himself for letting her down. For not hearing, for not seeing, for not trying harder to save what was between them.

Her eyes held gratitude. And he wondered: If he'd been able to say that when she'd first left, would things have turned out differently? Would she have walked away from Scott, back to him?

As if he'd spoken the question out loud, she spoke, seeming to answer. "I'm not sure it could have gone any differently," she said. "I was so young." Her voice was wistful. "You were my first and I thought all that great sex had to mean something. But maybe it didn't? Maybe it was just great sex and we should have been smart enough to walk away from it when our lives were so obviously going in different directions."

He wanted her to stop. Not because it wasn't true. It *was* true. But great sex made him think of Becca, and Becca was young. He hadn't thought that about her recently, but he'd definitely thought it that first night, that Friday Night Dinner when they'd played dirty Taboo. He'd told himself that she was too young and innocent for him and that he wouldn't make the mistake he'd made with Marina again.

Becca *wasn't* Marina. She wasn't.

Marina was watching him carefully, searching his face for

something—he didn't know what, but it made him uncomfortable and he picked up his beer.

"Griff. There's more. Scott and I are moving to the East Coast. Connecticut. We're selling the house. The open house is Thursday. That's why I had to come by. Aside from the fact that I didn't want to leave without saying some kind of goodbye, I need you to get that stuff out of the basement."

He winced. "I'm sorry I left it there so long."

"It's okay," she said. "I get it. I really do. But we need to be able to put stuff down there to stage the rest of the house, so —I don't mind if you want me just to have someone come haul it away, I just didn't want to do that without letting you know."

He shook his head. "No. I don't want you to have to hassle with that or spend money to do it. I'll come get it. Look—" He drained the rest of his beer. "Can we just get it over with now? I don't have anything super important to do the rest of the afternoon. My boss'll understand. And then I'll be out of your hair, and—"

And it would be a fresh start for him. For him and Becca.

She nodded. "Works for me. It might take a couple of trips?"

"Okay. Let's get started."

39

B ecca's cell phone vibrated on the desk where she'd set it, indicating a phone call. She glanced down, and her heart skipped a beat. It was the salon where she'd interviewed on Wednesday.

"Becca speaking."

"Hi, Becca. It's Wendy, at Wallingford Wellness Salon and Day Spa."

"Hi, Wendy! Good to hear from you."

"Everyone here really loved meeting you. We think you're great, and we want to offer you the receptionist position."

"Oh, wow," Becca said. "Thank you! That's great! Wow, that's great news."

The enthusiasm was reflexive. It just poured out, because she'd been trained to be polite and she was a natural people pleaser.

Not because she'd been feeling painfully uneasy since Marina and Griff had left.

She hadn't heard anything from Griff since that first text message, which was—three hours ago, now? The day was almost over. Not that he usually checked in with her a ton during the work day, but she would have expected some-thing. *Looking forward to FND!* maybe, or *Hey, sexy, can't wait to see you!* or *Don't freak out, even though I just walked out of work to go have a "talk" with my ex-wife and never came back, there's nothing to worry about.*

There's nothing to worry about, New Becca said, but her voice had been getting fainter all afternoon.

"So, can I take that as a yes? We'd love to have you!"

She should say no. *No, I'm sorry, I've decided to stay where I am, on the Oregon coast; I won't be coming back to Seattle after all. There's a guy—*

Why wasn't she just saying no?

There's nothing to worry about, New Becca insisted, now barely more than a whisper.

What if he's changed his mind? What if she *changed his mind? What if she wants him back?*

He'd take her back in a heartbeat, Nate's voice said.

He wouldn't, New Becca said. *He wants you to stay. He cares about you.*

Did he say that? Old Becca asked. *Or does he just want more sex?*

Becca took a deep breath. "Can I—can I take until tomorrow morning to think about it?"

There was a small but fraught silence on the other end of the line before Wendy said, "Of course. If you need to."

"You're in on Saturdays, right?"

"Yes. I'll be in tomorrow morning from ten till noon." Her buoyantly friendly voice had tightened down, and Becca regretted the loss of the warmth, even though—

Even though she didn't want the salon job. She wanted to

stay here and be a real auntie to Robbie and all of Nate and Alia's kids who came after him. She wanted to work for Jake, helping the veterans restart their old lives or jump-start their new lives. She wanted to volunteer with Nate—maybe even take a part-time job with him—tutoring kids like Jed. Kids like *her*.

And she wanted, oh *God*, she wanted, to give this thing with Griff a chance . . .

She heard herself explaining to Jenina why there was no "thing" with Griff. Why there was nothing to give a chance *to*.

But things had changed since then, hadn't they? Last night, she'd felt it: Everything had changed.

"I'll call before noon. I promise," she told Wendy.

"Okay. I'll look forward to hearing from you."

They exchanged friendly goodbyes, and she hung up the phone.

Jake poked his head out of his office. "I have a few more things to finish up," he said. "And then I'm going to head over to Friday Night Dinner. But you should go. There aren't any more appointments and it's five-oh-five on a Friday and—" He grinned. "Get the hell out of here."

"Thanks," she said.

She shut down her computer and cleaned up her desk, surveyed the waiting room to make sure it would be ready for Monday morning's appointments, and headed downstairs. She was hurrying across the parking lot toward her car when a flash of silver caught her attention in the direction of the veterans' lodgings. She turned her head to look.

It took a minute to make sense of what she was seeing—a man and a woman coming down the stairs from the rooms, which by itself was unusual because so many of the men who came here were single and there were so few women around. Maybe it was the unusualness of the sight that held Becca's attention, or maybe some part of her brain that recognized, even from a distance, the rumpled hair, the black T-shirt, the well-worn jeans, the build that had become so familiar to her that she could pick him out of a lineup with her eyes closed.

It was Griff, with Marina by his side, the two of them caught up in an obviously intense conversation. Coming back *from his room*. Three hours after they'd left together "to talk." And there was intimacy in every line of their bodies, the two of them leaning toward each other, eyes locked on each other's faces.

She was going to throw up. Or pass out. Or just stand here staring at them until they caught her, and that would be awful.

As she watched, they reached the bottom of the stairs, and Griff opened his arms and pulled Marina in.

Move! New Becca bellowed. And Becca did, turning toward the car, clicking the door remote, sliding into the seat, pulling out of the parking space and out of the lot.

Did he see you?

She looked back in the mirror just before she lost sight of them, but Griff was too intent on the woman in his arms to notice anything else.

40

There was a knock on the door of his room.

"Come in," Griff said.

Jake appeared in the doorway and surveyed the room. It was crammed with Griff's stuff. All the empty space —and there had never been much—was occupied now, with Griff's clothes, books, CDs. His skis leaned against one wall, golf clubs against another. Griff himself was sitting in the recliner he'd loved and Marina had hated, which was covered with some slightly shaggy velvety blue material. Two bookcases flanked him, one on either side. They'd been the only furniture he'd owned before Marina.

He'd been sitting in the recliner for probably forty-five minutes, feeling too flattened to move.

"Having a yard sale?" Jake quipped. Then he must have gotten a better read on Griff's expression, because his smile slipped away. "Dude. What's going on here?"

Griff closed his eyes. "Marina is getting married."

"Oh, *shit*," Jake said.

"No. No, it's okay. I think."

"You don't look okay."

Griff didn't *feel* okay. He was exhausted from the emotional conversation with Marina, which had bled over into the drive to Astoria. Then he'd had to see the house—the living room where he'd stood, note in hand, the kitchen where he and Marina had eaten dinner on the floor their first night in the house. And yet, the house now was *not* that house, because it had been transformed into something completely different by Scott and Marina. They'd repainted, remodeled the kitchen—made it super homey and super personal, just like he might have done one day with Marina if—

If things had turned out differently.

Scott hadn't been around—he was still at work—so Marina had single-handedly helped Griff carry stuff up from the basement and load it into his truck and her car. With effort and both vehicles, they'd been able to get the whole thing done in one trip, but even so it was after five by the time they finished unloading everything into Griff's room.

And now it was all here, crowding him, making it hard to breathe.

"It started out so well," Griff said. "You know? I mean, we were crazy in love."

Jake nodded.

"But she's right. We were young. When we first met, I didn't even know I was going into the army, and she didn't know—I mean, how would she have—that she was going to want someone who could be around so much more than I could be."

"It happens," Jake said. "Mira and I didn't get it right the first time."

Griff closed his eyes. "Maybe that's part of it. That part of me thought I was going to get a second chance, but the truth is, you don't, always. I'm not going to. This is just *it*." He gestured to the roomful of stuff. "Me and all my shit in this— couldn't you have built these fucking rooms a little bit bigger?"

Jake laughed, and it eased something in Griff's chest. "And what if I—what if I don't get it right with Becca, either?"

"You will," Jake said. "You have to. I bet Mira you guys would make it work. I have both money and sexual favors riding on it."

Griff rolled his eyes. "TMI, man, TMI." He hesitated. "But seriously. I—I don't think I can do it again, you know? Survive it again."

To his chagrin, his voice broke. Apparently once you let it all hang out, it was out there for good.

"You could," Jake said simply. "You're a survivor."

"I know, but what if I don't want to be? What if I don't want to do that ever again? I asked her to think about staying and she, I don't know, she said she would, but I'm not sure she meant it."

Jake's eyes were sympathetic, which only made Griff feel worse.

"You've had a tough day, Griff. Let's go to Friday Night Dinner and get some amazing food and as soon as you see Becca, you'll know it's going to be all right."

Griff wished he had Jake's faith, the faith of a man who'd been happily married now for a long time, who'd won the woman he'd always wanted and who never doubted it. But right now, he just wanted to sit in this recliner by himself for the rest of his life.

Jake held out a hand. "C'mon, man. Let's go."

Griff grasped the hand and let himself be yanked unceremoniously upright.

"On your feet, soldier," Jake said, and despite himself, Griff smiled.

41

As soon as Becca stepped into her sister's kitchen, the tears she'd been holding back clogged up her throat and threatened to fall, and she knew she'd been dumb to think she'd be able to pretend nothing was wrong.

"What's wrong?" Alia asked.

"Nothing," Becca said.

"You're full of shit," Alia said, narrowing her eyes. "What's wrong?"

Becca shook her head. If she told the story—Marina showing up in the office, Griff and Marina going somewhere "to talk," seeing them, three hours later coming out of Griff's room together—Alia would look at her with a face full of pity and she would fall apart into a million tiny pieces. New Becca expressly forbade that.

"Does this have to do with Griff and Marina?" Nate asked quietly.

Alia's gaze flew to her husband's face.

"I saw them in the parking lot earlier this afternoon. Just talking," he clarified, because Becca's expression must have broadcast her horror. Nate's eyes scraped over her face, concerned, and Becca felt the last of her reserves crumble.

"They weren't just talking when I saw them." It hurt to say the words out loud, and the tears she'd been trying to hold back flowed and streamed down her face, soundless. "They were coming downstairs from his room."

Alia shot an alarmed look at Nate.

"Maybe it wasn't—" she began, but Nate's voice cut across hers.

"That *asshole*. I'm going to *kill* him."

"No," Becca said. "Don't do that. I was the one who didn't listen. You guys warned me."

Her tears slowed down, and she felt suddenly calmer. Almost numb, in fact.

Nate was right, she thought.

Alia was right.

They saw the writing on the wall.

And I was stupid.

But the good news was, she hadn't done anything permanent. She hadn't turned down the Seattle job or asked Jake for a job. She hadn't even told Griff she'd stay. She'd gotten lucky this time. She'd seen the truth before she gave herself over so far that there was no going back.

New Becca could still keep this from turning into a disaster.

The doorbell rang, and they all turned toward the front of the house.

A big, familiar voice rang out. "I'm here, people! The party can start!"

And Griff appeared in the doorway, a little dusty, a little scruffy, and so painfully beautiful that Becca's stupid, stupid heart crumbled into a pile of ash.

42

They fell silent when he stepped into the kitchen, Jake right behind him. In that way that people do when they've been talking about you and then you show up.

Becca's eyes met his. It struck him, seeing her, how very, very young she was. Young and vulnerable and confused. The opposite of Marina, with her makeup like war paint.

And that *definitely* wasn't happiness shining from under Becca's skin.

He couldn't keep from shooting Jake a look, like, *What, dude? You promised me it would be okay when I saw her.* And it didn't help that the look Jake returned was one of alarm.

Alia turned away from him and began stirring something on the stove. Whatever it was, it smelled amazing. Moroccan, maybe—cinnamon and nutmeg and a bunch of darker spices. And he thought that was rice steaming in the cooker on the counter.

"Do you need me to make the salad?" Nate asked Alia, pointedly not looking at Griff.

"Salad fixings in the fridge," Alia said, and Nate flung open the door and buried himself in the salad drawer.

Without asking, Jake grabbed the placemats and began setting the table.

Griff took a step toward Becca, wanting to—he didn't know. Do *something*. Touch her, kiss her, ask her a question, *answer* the question on her uncertain face.

"Why don't you two take a walk before dinner?" Alia said, suddenly.

A cold fear gripped Griff in the pit of his stomach. He looked at Becca, but she didn't look back at him.

"Becca?" he asked.

"She's right. Let's take a walk."

He followed her out into the street, and the cold fear accompanied him. He tried to put an arm around her, but she pulled away, just far enough that she was out of his reach.

"Are you mad?"

She shook her head.

"Talk to me, Becca. Tell me what's in your head. I need to know what's in your head."

He stopped, made her stop with a hand on her arm. Turned her so she was facing him, forced her to look at him.

She opened her mouth. He had a million ideas about what might come out, but what she actually said still managed to surprise him.

"I got the job."

"The job—?"

The fatigue he'd felt, the weight that had threatened to pin him to the recliner earlier, suddenly descended over him like a heavy cape. His body and brain felt like they were moving at the speed of molasses.

"The salon receptionist job in Seattle," she said wearily. She sounded disappointed, but not surprised, that she'd had to explain that to him.

"Oh." His stomach clenched. "Congratulations, that's— what are you going to do?"

She was walking faster; he had to speed up to stay by her side.

"I think I should take it," she said. She was talking fast, too, like she could slide that sentence by him without him noticing what she'd said.

But there was no chance of that. The cold knot in his stomach doubled and redoubled.

"What's this about, baby?"

The endearment made her flinch, which hurt somewhere in the pit of his gut.

"I just—I just think you were right from the beginning when you said that this would get more complicated than we wanted it to."

It was his turn to flinch, hearing his words flung back at him.

"You're my first, and I'm barely twenty-four, and, I don't know, it feels stupid to turn down a job that's perfect for me in a city where I already have a great apartment and a fabulous roommate, on the strength of a few weeks of—whatever this is. It's been good, Griff. *So* good. But I've let myself think it's more than it is, and I don't think I should give up what's right for me."

"No."

The word came out before he could stop it.

"You don't get to do that. It's not 'whatever this is.' It's more than that and you know it."

He was going to tell her what it was. Dirty Taboo and filthy archery. The best sex he'd ever had. Conversations that helped him make sense of what he wanted and who he was.

The first time in two years that he had let himself *feel*.

Like an idiot, the mean tight voice in his head said.

"What's this really about, Becca?"

"I saw you. And Marina. Coming out of your room. I saw you, holding her."

"Holding—?" Then he figured it out. She'd seen them coming downstairs after the last trip to unload furniture, when he'd hugged Marina goodbye. It had been a long, warm hug, because—well, because they'd cleared the air between them and it felt like they could be friends now. And honestly? Because he'd probably never see her again.

Becca's lower lip trembled, and he saw that he'd hurt her. Badly. Damn, he'd been stupid and insensitive, but he was going to make it up to her now. For the first time, the knot in his stomach loosened, because he was going to explain and apologize and fix this.

"I'm sorry I didn't stop to explain who she was or try to tell you why she was there—everything happened fast, and I just wanted to get it over with. I'm sorry. That was dumb. But please—I don't know what you're thinking, but whatever it is, that's not how it went down. She just showed up. And she wanted me to get my stuff out of her basement—"

He was doing this wrong, he realized suddenly. He wasn't saying the important stuff. He was just babbling.

"Your stuff." She took a breath. "In her basement? What, is that a metaphor?"

"No, for real, my actual stuff. I—I never got it out."

"You never got your stuff out. Of her house."

Her voice was flat, and he could see how ridiculous it sounded now. And how damning.

"You left your stuff at her house for *two years*. Clearly, you *wanted* to get back together otherwise you would have gathered up your stuff and moved on. Nate said—"

"What? What did Nate say?" He was cold again.

"That you were trying to bang enough women to forget her, but that you'd take her back in a minute if she'd have you."

She looked like she was one sentence away from bursting into tears, and he reached out and tried to tug her into his arms, to comfort her with his body and warmth, but she wouldn't come.

That was when he really started to get scared.

"Becca. Listen. There was a time when what Nate said was true. There was a time when my stuff was at Marina's house because I thought maybe, one day, that would be our house again. And I would have done just about anything to make that happen. But that was a long time ago. She's marrying Scott now. And moving to the East Coast. We *can't* ever get back together."

"And I'm supposed to feel like that makes it okay. You wanted to get back together with her until you couldn't, and now that you can't? I'm the next best thing?" She was shaking her head.

"That was *before*. I haven't felt that way since I met you."

"I can't, Griff. I just—I promised myself. I promised New Becca I'd never do that again. Put my life on hold for someone. Wait and wait for someone who couldn't deliver. And, Griff, I saw your face today. When you came in and she was there. I've seen you look like that before, so don't try to tell me—"

"What do you mean, you've seen me look like that before?" His heart was pounding so hard it was difficult to think straight.

"That night in Seattle, after the Edgewater—"

"What are you talking about?" He willed himself to breathe, willed his pulse to slow down, as he once had during battle. *Breathe.*

"When you had the flashback. You said her name."

"What?" A feeling was barreling down on him. A familiar and terrible feeling. Something coming he could prevent, if only he could say the right words.

"When you were coming out of the fog, you thought I was her and you looked at me—at her—like she was all you needed in the world to be happy."

"Wait—I what? Why didn't you tell me that?"

Panic had risen up, and it was making him slower and dumber.

"You mean, tell you that I think you're still in love with your ex-wife on the night that you took my virginity? I'm sorry, but I couldn't quite find a way to work that into the conversation."

It wasn't her words that made the panic rise and twist, like a vine around his throat. It was her tone of despair.

"And that's what you thought you saw on my face today, when I saw her in the office."

She was nodding.

"You're wrong, Becca. It was just shock, and the weirdness of seeing her again after so long. That's all it was."

But she was shaking her head, and his chest tightened. It

was like he'd stepped into the middle of a situation he'd
already lost control of. It was beyond his reach, the moment
to salvage it already missed, receding into the past. His mind
calling out, *too late, too late, too late, I knew, I knew, I* knew.

"Jesus, Becca, be *reasonable*." He heard the edge in his
voice and tried again to bring himself down, but the anger
was rising with the suffocating fear, the two emotions twined
around each other like bittersweet around the branches of a
tree.

"I am being reasonable, Griff. I know what I saw."

"You—God, Becca! You know what you saw? You saw
what you wanted to see. You never feel like you deserve to be
happy. You never feel like you're good enough. You never feel
like you deserve anyone to love you, so you take one look at
the situation and you see what you need to see so you can run
far and fast in the other direction. Damn it!" The words
spilled out in a hot, angry slew, before he could stop them. He
was so hurt and so mad and so frustrated, and he could see it
all—the note in his hand and the empty living room, and his
dorm room full of his useless shit, and how good it had once
been and how bad it had felt tonight when torpor had pinned
him to that ugly chair. "I can't do this again! I can't be with
someone who isn't enough of an adult to know what she
wants."

He'd stunned her, he could see. And hurt her. He wanted
to take the words back as soon as they'd left his mouth—

But he couldn't. And he wouldn't, because they were true.

He knew he'd lost her even before she started shaking her
head.

He stood there, panting, and she stood there, looking
back at him, her eyes full of hurt and her teeth worrying that

sweet, plump lower lip, and she didn't have to tell him that it was over.

But she did, anyway.

"No," she said. "No. You're wrong about me, Griff. For the first time, I know I'm good enough, and I'm going to treat myself like I deserve the best. And in this case?"

Her hair shone in the moonlight, and her eyes were blazing, and she was possibly the most beautiful thing he'd ever seen.

"It means I won't set myself up for failure."

And she turned and ran back to the house.

43

They were all in the kitchen when she came back, starting to dish the dinner into bowls and pull out serving spoons and carry things to the table. They looked up from what they were doing, took her in, and did their best to look away. All except for Alia, who came towards her.

The soft look on Alia's face was the last straw for Becca.

"No," she said. "Don't look at me like that. I'm not twelve, and I'm *not* breakable. You may have been right about Griff, but you were wrong about me. You were wrong that I don't know how to take care of myself. You were wrong about my ability to make good decisions. And you were wrong to make me feel like a twelve-year-old. You and Nate both. This was not your business. It wasn't ever any of your business."

Their friends, even Nate, had melted away during her speech, leaving the sisters alone in the kitchen. There were tears in Alia's eyes. "Bex—I—"

"I know you need to do this. Take care of me. Believe me, I

understand. But I need you to *not* right now. So, we're going to have to find some middle ground."

Tears streamed down Alia's face, and part of Becca wanted to let her sister off the hook, but she knew that it was now or never. She would never know, so deeply in her heart, that it was time for her to do exactly what Griff had said she hadn't: grow up.

"I love you. You know I love you. But no more. I'm a full-fledged woman and have been for some time. You can be my friend. You will *always* be my sister. But you. Are. Not. My. Mother."

"I'll try," Alia whispered. "It's hard."

Becca touched her sister's arm tenderly. "I know. I'm not angry. I just—this is me. This is my life." She took a deep breath. "I'm going to go back to Seattle."

Alia's mouth opened, then closed, like the last turning of gears in a windup toy running down. She stayed silent.

Becca smiled and touched her sister's hand. "Thank you."

"What are the rules, exactly?" Alia asked.

"The rules?"

"Of being your sister and friend but not your mother? Can I comfort you?"

"Of course."

Alia opened her arms and wrapped her sister up. "Then this is me, being your sister."

Becca began to cry.

"Can I tell you it's going to be okay?"

"You can tell me," Becca said, between sobs. She buried her face against her sister's shoulder. "But I might not believe it for a long time."

Alia squeezed her tighter and Becca cried until she ran out of tears.

HER FRIENDS WERE boisterous at dinner, cracking jokes, giving each other a hard time. Becca thought it was mainly to cheer her up, but it didn't work. No matter how much noise they made, no matter how many jokes they told, there was a big empty space at the table where Griff was not. It hurt her, that empty chair.

She wasn't sure she ever wanted to be at Friday Night Dinner again. Not without Griff.

Even Alia and Nate's amazing Middle Eastern feast tasted as bland as sawdust.

Midway through dinner, Robbie got fussy.

"He doesn't need to eat any time soon, does he?" Becca asked.

"No," Alia said. "I was hoping he was going to fall asleep and sleep through dinner, but he's overstimulated and over-tired now and I think I'm out of luck."

"I'll take him for a walk."

Nate slowly unwrapped the kicking, drooling baby and handed him over. Becca wrapped him to her chest, facing in, and he protested at the loss of his view, fussing and trying to free his bound limbs.

"Shh," she told him. "You and me, dude, we're going to take a nice, long walk."

She left her friends behind, and stepped out into the night. Robbie was still fussing, his unhappy sounds starting to escalate.

"Shh," she said. "Shh, shh, hey, baby, shh," she said, and started to cry again.

Robbie caught the thread of her misery and wailed. She added a bounce to her step, hopelessly out of sync with how she felt, which was like lead. After another block, the motion started to get to him and his sobs subsided to hiccups and then to loud breaths which lengthened as he relaxed against her, warm and pliable.

She walked for a long time, until she was sure they'd be done eating back at the house, done with their roses and thorns and teasing and affection.

The whole time, her tears fell, occasionally landing on Robbie's sleeping head, leaving long wet tracks in the pale fluff of his baby hair.

44

It was not a good day for Griff to be in charge of the mental health of ten other men. He'd gotten very, very drunk the night before with liquor snuck into his room, the first time he could remember drinking alone since those lost days right after Marina had left. Now he was hungover and sluggish and unhappy. Everything filled him with regret—the sight of his belongings crowding his small room, the fact that he was pretty sure he could still catch a whiff of Becca's scent on his sheets, even the view of the lake with mist rising off it, because it reminded him of the simple delight of flirting outrageously with her.

But he'd come this far, and he'd come this far because of her, and he wasn't going to crawl back into a hole.

"Hey," he told the circle. "Most of you know how this works, but there are a couple of new guys here today . . ."

He gave the rest of Jake's intro spiel, then said, "I'll start. I'm Griff. . . ."

It didn't take him as long as he'd thought to tell his story, even though he started at the beginning, at the moment when he'd first noted the absence of the children, and even though he told it all the way through to the end, when morning came and they assessed their losses.

"I felt like, God gave me this huge responsibility. And I blew it. I fucking blew it, and six men died. And then I came home and my wife was gone and there was just a note, and I felt like—"

Oh, *shit*. He was going to break down. At his very first support group, he was supposed to be in charge, and he was going to cry.

He looked up and from across the circle he saw CJ watching him and nodding. And Griff thought, *Fuck it. In for a penny, in for a pound.*

"I felt like it was what I deserved," he said, and his voice broke, and the wall in his chest broke, and everything fucking broke, and he was, in fact, crying.

He didn't sob or anything. He pulled it back together and looked around the circle, his gaze challenging them to give him shit about it, but they were all pretty much just nodding and meeting his eyes, theirs full of sympathy and understanding.

"So," he said. "I am just going to try to work on feeling like I didn't deserve to be punished and like I deserve to be happy. And if anyone wants to work on that with me, we can set some goals around that together."

There was a moment of surprised silence—Jake had never really said anything much like that—but then the men started shifting in their seats and raising their hands and calling out. Just two or three, but it was enough, and they said they'd come back next week having tried to notice all the times in a week they told themselves they deserved to feel like shit.

Afterward, as the men were filing out, Jake came in.

"Hey," he said. "How'd it go?"

"I feel like—" Griff looked to the ceiling. "I feel like I've been wrung out and run over."

"It gets easier."

"Does it? Doesn't feel like it'll ever get easier."

"The more times you tell the story, the less power it has over you."

Through his exhaustion, he could feel the truth of that. He'd relayed the events to Becca, the stranger in Home Depot and CJ, Jake, and now the men of the support group, and each time, he'd felt a tiny bit of grace trickle into the dark space of his guilt and remorse. He could imagine that someday, there would be enough light for him to see clearly. Someday, he wouldn't hate himself when he thought of that night.

Someday.

Jake eyed him sympathetically. "Hey, man. I've been meaning to say. I'm sorry about Becca."

The sound of her name made his heart feel twice as heavy in his chest. He shook his head. "Not half as sorry as I am."

"Have you tried talking to her?"

"There's nothing to talk about."

"You sure about that?"

"Pretty sure we both said everything there was to say."

It was Jake's turn to shake his head. "You know you're making me lose to Mira for the third time, right? Can't you take pity on me?"

"If I could fix this, I would. I tried."

Jake tilted his head. "I was listening just now when you were leading the group, you know. You did good. And that's how it was for me, too. Feeling like I never deserved to be happy, after what I'd let happen. It's a dangerous feeling. It can keep taking and taking from you, if you let it. Don't let it."

Griff just stared at him. He knew Jake meant well, but he couldn't absorb any more right now. His whole body felt bruised. His soul, too, if he believed there was such a thing. Whatever part of him Jake's words had just poked at, anyway.

"Enough touchy-feely shit for one day, huh?" Jake laughed. "I get it. Well, let me know if I can help. Not because I'm your friend or anything. Just because I want to win a fucking bet with Mira someday."

"Thanks. I think."

Jake put his fist out for a bump, and Griff left feeling just as hungover and miserable as when he'd come in.

He went out to the archery range and shot until his arm muscles trembled and his fingers felt raw where the strings dug in.

He'd come to the range to distract himself, but it wasn't working. He kept thinking of the day of the picnic. The feel of Becca in his arms, the tease of their words, the promise that had simmered in the air.

Usually, archery made him feel better. It was something he could control. It was simple, forceful, and precise.

But today, it just made him remember how off the mark he was, and what he'd lost.

45

She sat behind the reception desk at Wallingford Wellness and chatted amiably with a parade of beautiful women who had come into the spa to get more beautiful. To become their best selves, which, to them, was something they could buy. She envied them their conviction that it was possible.

And she didn't begrudge them their happiness, not at all. She didn't resent how blissed-out and relaxed all the spa's patrons looked as they ambled out the door, having put aside their to-dos for an afternoon. She just didn't feel very much of anything else, either.

She kept hoping against hope that some shaggy vet would walk through the door, seeking the massage that would give him the first relief from pain he'd had in days or weeks or years.

"I think we should give a veteran discount," she told Wendy one day, a week into the job.

"A *veteran* discount?"

"Or free massages to veterans, maybe. We could even do a

special clinic for them. Maybe have all the massage therapists come in Thursday afternoon and evening when we're open late, and they could volunteer, like, half their fee, and the spa could donate the other half to veterans' services."

"I'll think about that," Wendy said, in the tone of someone who had no intention of wasting a quarter of a brain cell on the topic.

When Becca wasn't working, she mostly hung out with Jenina, who had been doing everything in her power to snap Becca out of her down mood. But Becca wasn't interested in Jenina's cure of choice, swiping right.

"I thought the whole point of sleeping with Griff was that now your sex life would be a hundred percent less complicated. And what point is there to that if you don't take advantage of all the no-strings sex the world has to offer?"

Becca shrugged. They were sitting cross-legged on her bed, their phones tossed in the space between them. Becca had just swiped left until she had tendinitis.

"Can I ask you a question, Bex?" Jenina said.

"Sure."

"Are you sure this is what you want?" Jenina gestured around her at the apartment, and then a broader sweep that seemed to encompass the whole city of Seattle. "You haven't seemed happy since you've gotten back here."

"I'm fine," Becca said.

"Do you think it's possible you had more feelings for Mr. Pop My Cherry than you've told your good friend Jenina?" She gave Becca an innocent open-eyed look.

Becca heaved a big sigh, closed her eyes, and leaned back on her pillows.

"Yeah, that's what I thought. What actually happened

down there?" Jenina always talked about the Oregon coast as if it were on the other side of the world, as opposed to just a four-and-a-half-hour drive. And the truth was, it felt that way to Becca, too. She missed her sister and Nate and Robbie, Jake and Mira, and Sibby, as much as she had ever missed people in her life. She kept having dreams where she was playing with Robbie, and he was giving her his single-toothed, drooly grin.

And then there was Griff. Who she didn't allow herself to think about much, except that he had a way of creeping back in whenever she let her guard down. Like late at night, when she would remember the way he touched her. Kissed her. Teased her. Filled her. Or worse—when she would remember the simple pleasures of being with him, watching *The Princess Bride* or the Mariners game, playing dirty Taboo and learning naughty archery, eating donuts and drinking coffee.

Confessing, confiding, soothing. Poking and prodding each other to take one more step, to try one more thing, to wake up the next day better and stronger.

Damn it, her eyes were filling up with tears, and Jenina, who didn't miss a thing, was watching, her face bright with sympathy.

"I don't *want* to miss him," Becca wailed.

"Of course you don't."

She told Jenina about the last conversation she'd had with Griff in the street outside her sister's house.

When Becca was done, Jenina made a humming sound.

"Can you believe he said that?"

Jenina tilted her head to one side and gave Becca a long, hard look.

"Shut *up*," Becca said.

"I said nothing," Jenina said. But she was smirking.

"I don't do that. I don't do that *anymore*," Becca amended.

"So you're sure that the look on Griff's face that day was because he is still in love with his ex-wife?"

"I—"

But Jenina, relentless as ever, plowed on. "Do you think it's remotely possible that he was just really, really surprised to see her? And maybe trying to wrestle with coming face-to-face with a ghost from his past? And that maybe the hug was just a goodbye hug?"

Becca opened her mouth, closed it, opened it again. Saw, in her mind's eye, the two of them coming down the stairs.

She tried it on for size: They'd been moving Griff's stuff, and then they'd come down the stairs, and he'd given her a hug goodbye.

She took a deep breath and looked at her friend. "Why do you refuse to ever, ever let me get away with my shit?"

"Because I love you madly," Jenina said, blowing her a kiss. "And one more question, while we're at it. Has it occurred to you, my friend, that maybe the problem isn't that you're too weak, but that you're too strong?"

"Me? No way," Becca said. "I mean, you remember me before New Becca. I had the shittiest self-esteem. I let people walk all over me."

"So you *say*," Jenina said carefully, "but I never really thought you were weak. And New Becca, she's great, but do you think maybe sometimes she is a little bit of an ice princess?"

"I don't know what you're talking about."

"Like, 'I'm not going to let anyone in, and that way, I can't get hurt?' Like, 'I'm not going to set myself up for failure' is really just another way of saying, 'I'm not going to risk getting hurt by you?'"

"That's *exactly* what I'm saying."

"But if you don't take the risk of getting hurt, you also can't set yourself up for success. It's like with the tutoring thing, right? If you never tried it, you'd never suck at it, but you'd also never discover you loved it. Same with Griff. If you push him away, you don't have to think about whether maybe, just maybe, you're actually *in love* with him—which is, admittedly, terrifying because heartbreak and disaster and ugly crying. But you'll also never get to find out if maybe? possibly? he's also in love with you?"

Becca's mouth opened, but no words came out.

"Just think about it, hon," Jenina said kindly. "Meanwhile, if you're just going to let the wide, beautiful world of Tinder go to fucking waste, let's at least watch a movie or something. Or," Jenina said, as Becca burst into tears, "we can do the ugly crying. I'll get the tissues."

46

"Just you and me, dude," Griff said to Robbie, who was sitting on his lap, facing him. It was Nate and Alia's first date night out in a while, and Griff had been pressed into service. He'd protested lamely when Alia had asked him—but he hadn't meant it. "What do you say?" he demanded of the baby. "Should we head out to the bar and pick up women? No? Play Trot Trot to London again? Okay, man, you got it. I wasn't in the mood for conquest anyway."

He bounced the baby on his knees, then tipped him backward off his lap, his hand behind Robbie's head, and Robbie's mouth fell open into the biggest baby belly laugh of all time. It even got Griff, despite his dark mood of late, to crack a smile.

It also made his craving for Becca about a thousand times worse. Because Becca would love Robbie's ridiculous belly laughs. And Robbie's all-in, no-holds-barred smile reminded Griff of Becca's sunshine grin.

He wondered how she'd been doing in Seattle the last

couple of weeks, whether the job was going well for her, whether she was happy. Jake still hadn't hired anyone to permanently fill the reception desk position. Griff had offered to take on more of the Fourth of July planning—the picnic was this weekend—so Sibby could be available on the desk. He tried not to question his own motives, whether there was a part of him that wanted to make it easier for Jake to delay hiring to fill that position. A part of him that still thought Becca might change her mind and ask for that job back.

And bloody hell, was he doing the same thing now that he'd done after Marina had left? Sitting around, *waiting* for something to miraculously change?

"Robbie, my man," Griff said to his drooling charge, "do not, I repeat, do *not* grow up to be as much of an idiot about women as I am. Actually, may I suggest the Catholic priesthood? Or, just go ahead and be a monk. I'd say you should be gay, but you'd probably still be an idiot about love, and I think you would miss breasts. Although I'm probably just projecting."

For sure, he missed a certain set of breasts, and the perky nipples that went with them, as well as the moans he could draw out of their owner. And everything fucking else, too—smile, blue eyes, long legs. But really most of all just *her*. Everything, and he meant *everything*, was more fun with her, from movies to watching baseball games, to eating Friday Night Dinner to putting an arrow in a target—*in both senses*, he thought wryly, and with a pang of sadness, because he could have made her laugh by saying it.

When he'd showed up tonight to babysit, Nate had opened the door, and for the first time since Becca had left, he didn't glare at Griff. Instead, he surveyed him, long and hard, and said only, "You look like shit, man. I don't know which one of you guys is the bigger idiot, you or Becca."

"Do you think I'm an idiot?" he asked the baby.

Robbie gave him a sly sideways smile, screwed up his face, turned red, and delivered payload.

"Seriously?" Griff asked him. He reached for the set of changing things that Alia and Nate kept under the side table. He had Robbie securely under one arm, the changing pad in one hand and a diaper in the other when sound crackled around them, sharp as thunder.

He jumped. Robbie burst into surprised sobs.

"My man," he told the baby. "You are *okay*. We are *okay*."

And that was when he realized that he was still in the living room. He hadn't traveled through time and space to the northernmost reaches of Afghanistan, but was actually in Nate and Alia's house, a baby under one arm and a bunch of changing paraphernalia in his hands.

Also, Robbie still stank.

Another crack came, and Griff flinched but stayed firmly planted in the present. Robbie gave another shriek and buried his face against Griff's chest.

"It's fireworks, bud," Griff said. His heart was slowing down. He took a deep breath and sighed it out, willing Robbie to respond to his calm. And the baby did seem to be settling down, his cries softer and spaced further apart. "Early Fourth of July fireworks," Griff told Robbie.

I gotta tell Becca, he thought. She was fucking right. All that talking about it—telling Jake, leading the last few Saturday groups and fessing up to the other men—it was *helping*. Maybe it wasn't a miracle cure, but look at him. He was in the living room, holding it together, wasn't he?

"I gotta tell Becca," he told Robbie.

It was probably just coincidence, but at that moment, Robbie stopped crying and smiled.

"Yeah? You think?" Griff asked the baby. "We had a pretty big fight the last time we talked. What was it about? I honestly can't tell you. I think it was about the fact that most of the people she's ever really cared about have let her down—"

He caught his breath with the sudden realization.

"I let her down," he told Robbie. "I mean, I didn't, but she thought I did, and she got scared. And then, instead of trying to make her feel better, I basically told her she was being stupid. Which is the thing she hates most in the whole world, except maybe for being told she's not stupid."

He set Robbie, now just hiccupping, down on the floor and began to change his stinky diaper.

"I love you a lot, man, you do know that, right? Because I would not do this for most people."

Robbie gave him another smile, and Griff closed his eyes against the overwhelming tightness in his chest.

"And you know why I told her she was being stupid? Because I was scared. Because she was breaking up with me and I just couldn't. I couldn't do it again, man. I couldn't lose—"

He was choking up, and there were tears in his eyes.

"Don't judge," he told the baby. "You cry more than I do."

He thought suddenly of what Jake had said, about how the feeling that you didn't deserve happiness would take and take from you as long as you let it. And he thought of telling Becca that she was pushing her own happiness away.

Griff looked down at Robbie, who was calm now, and

quiet, staring back at him with big blue eyes. "Robbie, my friend. Uncle Griff might be a little bit of a hypocrite."

Robbie gave a squeal of approval.

"Right?"

When the baby was clean and dry, Griff carried him upstairs, sat with him in his glider, and gave him his bedtime bottle. Robbie's deep pulls on the bottle slowed. His eyes fell closed. He gave a sigh and relaxed fully into Griff's arms.

Griff set him down in the crib and stood looking down at him.

"Babies, man," he said. "You guys are the smartest people I know."

47

"Are you saying you don't have any massage therapists on call?" the woman with the shiny brown hair demanded.

"I *am* saying that," Becca said patiently. "We don't have enough demand for walk-ins to be able to provide that service. But I am happy to make an appointment for you to see one of our massage therapists for the next available opening, which I think is tomorrow morning at nine. Do you want me to look?"

"That's not going to help me sleep tonight," the woman said. "My shoulders are very tight."

"I'm so sorry," Becca said, meaning it. "I wish there was something I could do—"

"If you can't help me, I'm going to go to Balm for the Soul Day Spa. It's just a few blocks from here."

Becca said, "Oh! That's a great idea, actually. I know they have someone in on Thursdays."

The woman crossed her arms. "You won't get my business back if I do."

"I'm certainly sorry to hear that," Becca said. "We'll still be here, though, if you change your mind."

The woman huffed out, and Becca slumped in her seat. Phew. That was done, and best of all, she'd kept her cool.

Her phone chimed. It was Nate.

Are you busy?

She looked at her watch. It was twenty to four. *Working. But there's no one in here right now. Should be quiet for at least ten minutes till the next round of clients start showing up.*

I've got someone here who wants to talk to you.

For a moment her heart went wild, and then her practical self took over. If Griff had wanted to talk to her, he knew where to find her. He didn't have to send an advance guard.

Someone where?

At KidsUp.

Jed.

A FaceTime request chimed through on her phone from Nate and she accepted it. His face flashed by, canted at an angle as he passed the phone, and then the screen filled with Jed's face.

"I got a B on my paper." A small, pleased half-smile tugged at one corner of his mouth. "The one you helped me write."

A buoyant feeling rushed through her chest.

"He came in just to tell you," Nate said in the background. "I told him you weren't here but that you'd want to know."

"I do want to know." She nodded to Jed. "That's amazing. I'm—" she hesitated, thinking about whether she had the right to say what was on the tip of her tongue. "I'm proud of you," she said finally, because it was the truth and worth saying.

The wariness hadn't left his face—she guessed it almost never did—but he smiled. Then he frowned. "I have to write another one. About something I did that changed my life. I wanted to know if you'd help. I thought if you did, maybe I could get a B-plus this time."

Becca looked around her at the shop. The lobby where she sat was elegant, with shelves full of expensive beauty products that she earned a sizeable commission by selling. She was making more money here than she'd made at Julia's or at R&R, but—

"I told him you're in Seattle now," Nate said, but his face held a question.

She *was* in Seattle.

She was in Seattle and not in Tierney Bay. Even though pretty much everything she cared about other than Jenina was in Tierney Bay.

Jenina had been right. New Becca had been so busy trying not to get hurt that she'd run away from the things that were making her happy for the first time in her adult life.

For the first time, I know I'm good enough, and I'm going to treat myself like I deserve the best, she had told Griff. *And in this case? It means I won't set myself up for failure.*

It had felt so true that night.

But now she saw it differently.

She'd pushed Griff away. She'd put several hundred miles of geography between them because it had felt like she would always be living in the shadow of the woman he truly loved and could never forget. She didn't give herself enough credit for being someone Griff could feel that way about, even though Griff was constantly reminding her not to sell herself short.

She'd been so scared of being told—in actions, if not words—that she wasn't *enough* that she'd completely forgotten how hard it would be for a man who'd been hurt as badly as Griff to try again.

Of course he'd gotten angry at her. He had crossed a chasm a mile wide and she'd rewarded him by kicking him in the nuts.

On her phone screen, Jed still waited patiently. He'd been scared to write his English paper but he'd written it anyway, and he'd come back to tell her he'd done it.

Becca knew that the reason Jed had warmed to her was that she had made herself vulnerable to him. And she had had the courage to do it in large part because Griff had made himself vulnerable to her.

It was a small, sweet, human miracle every time one person coaxed another out of their armor, the way she and Griff had managed to do with each other. And the thing was, if you had to get hurt sometimes doing it, well, fuck it—that was the price of making miracles.

She drew a deep breath and smiled at Jed. "When's it due?"

"Next Friday."

"Like a week from tomorrow?"

Jed nodded.

"Can you come back in to KidsUp tomorrow?"

He looked up, presumably to where Nate was standing off screen, then back at her. "Yeah."

Becca nodded. "Okay. I'll be there."

Jed's fist appeared on her screen and grew enormous. She put hers out and bumped back. Then he was gone, and Nate came back on, his voice edged with worry. "Are you sure you can get the time off? You just started this new job."

She smiled at him, her big brother and protector. He and Alia, they'd shield her from every possible danger of being alive, if she let them.

She had no intention of letting them.

"Don't worry about me, dude. I know what I have to do."

48

"What are you doing here?" Alia demanded, flinging the door wide open and throwing her arms around Becca, squishing Robbie—who squeaked in protest—between them. "You *knew!*" she accused Nate over Becca's shoulder. "You knew she was coming and you didn't tell me!"

"Yup," Nate said, self-satisfied.

"I had something to do at KidsUp," Becca said. "And then figured I'd surprise you guys with a Friday Night Dinner appearance."

Robbie was flailing his limbs wildly in excited greeting, and the rest of the guests spilled out of the dining room, hugging Becca and Nate. All the kids were here, too. Mira and Jake's son Sam, and Sam's girlfriend Cora, and Trina and Hunter's girls, Phoebe and Clara—it was a lot of hugging. Only, the one person whose embrace she longed for didn't seem to be in the mix.

"Where's Griff?" she demanded.

She'd been half expecting him to amble out of the dining

room, all casual, making a big scene out of being unexcited by her presence . . . but he hadn't. She peeked around Clara, but the dining room was empty.

Glances flitted around the room between her friends, and Becca got a sinking feeling in the pit of her stomach.

"Do you want to tell her?" Jake asked Alia.

They were going to tell her he'd gone back to Marina. That she'd broken off her engagement and they'd moved in together and Marina was pregnant with twins—

She wasn't sure where that last bit had come from, or why that particular idea figured into her nightmare fantasy, it just *did*. Anyway, the point was, she *knew* she'd been an idiot to think he actually wanted her. She wasn't the kind of person who—

"You tell her," Alia said, and Becca took a deep breath and steeled herself against the worst of the worst news.

"He's on his way to Seattle," Jake said, shaking his head darkly. "He's on his way to Seattle to see you. He said he owed you a big apology, some groveling, and if he got really lucky, makeup sex." He looked around the kitchen, winced, and said, "Shit. Sorry kids."

"Language," Mira said sharply, at the same time Phoebe said, "We're not *babies*. We read *books* where people have makeup sex."

It was taking a minute for Jake's words to sink in to Becca's brain and make sense. "Oh, *shit*," she said, but she didn't mean it at all. In fact, her innards were doing a tap dance of sheer joy. Griff had gone to get her. He had crossed hundreds of miles to tell her that he wanted *her*—*her*! She couldn't help the enormous smile that spread across her face.

Then she considered the implications—he was now hundreds of miles away from her—and frowned. "Poor Griff!"

"You didn't think maybe you should have mentioned something to me about Griff going to Seattle?" Nate demanded of Alia. "I could have kept this from happening."

"That's *right*," Becca said grumpily. "I'd have worked this all out by now if it weren't for *you meddling kids*. Didn't we talk about this the *last time you messed around with my life*?"

Nate and Alia both had the good manners to look ashamed.

"I didn't want to interrupt you at work," Alia said sheepishly. "And why would I think you'd just be dropping by for a casual visit? *Normal sisters* tell their sisters when they're driving in from five hours away."

"I wanted to surprise you," Becca said.

"Text Griff!" Phoebe said. "Quick! Tell him you're here and not there and that he should come back."

Becca did a quick visual survey of her friends. They were all nodding.

She pulled out her phone and did as commanded.

I came to Friday Night Dinner, but you are not here. They say you're on your way to Seattle to find me. Come back!

Three dots hovered on her screen.

You came to FND? Why?

"What did he *say*?" Phoebe demanded.

"He wants to know why I'm here."

"Tell him!" Clara said. "Tell him you're here to see him!"

To see you, she texted to Griff. *To say some things that I should have said a lot sooner. About how I feel about you. Most of which are better said in person. Naked if possible.*

She wasn't sure if she'd gone too far or not said enough,

but she didn't want the first time she told him how she felt about him to be in a text. She wanted to see his face when she finally told him the truth.

*I love the sound of that. *Turns truck around.**

She did a secret internal fist pump. *Not literally, I hope.*

No. Literally, I am sitting in the Toutle River rest area off I-5, feeling like I just won the lottery, said no one EVER before me.

She laughed.

"What?" Alia and Clara demanded at the same time. "What did he say?"

"He said he's turning around."

There was a chorus of cheers. Everyone except Mira, who was looking sheepish.

"What?" Becca demanded.

"Ha!" Jake said to Mira. "Haaa! I won this time! *I* won. I *knew* it! I told you!"

"You were right, dear," Mira said, but she didn't sound at all grudging. She sounded happy.

"What are you talking about?" Becca asked.

"So, I don't know if you know this, but Mira and I bet on Alia and Nate. She thought they'd get together and I said they wouldn't, and, well—well, you know how that worked out. And then we bet on Hunter and Trina, too. And she flipping won again."

"So this time, I put my money on things working out," Jake said. "I just *knew*. Because of the way you guys were at Friday Night Dinners, like an old married couple pretending they'd never met so they could role play picking each other up at a bar."

Becca laughed at that. She liked it, the old-and-new of it. "You *guys*," she said.

Mira crossed her arms. "I actually thought you'd get together, too, but I let him choose the winning position because I thought his ego needed it." She smirked in Jake's direction and he rolled his eyes at her. "Okay, okay," she said. "I might have expressed some concern that Griff was too damn stubborn to ever fall in love again. But I'm really, really glad he did. And we can all see that you were way happier together than apart, even those of us who were dumb enough to bet against you the first time around." Mira's eyes were warm, and Becca threw her arms around her, and then around each of her other friends for good measure because she was stupidly happy.

When she'd finished the hugging, she did a fast Google Maps search and discovered the Toutle River rest area was exactly two hours away.

I'll save dessert for you.

Is there something wrong with me that that totally turned me on?

"You're blushing, Becca," Alia purred.

"Shut up, Alia," Becca shot back.

That was my intention.

On my way.

Drive fast.

She sat with her friends and ate Alia's breaded chicken breasts stuffed full of prosciutto, mozzarella, and basil. But she couldn't actually *taste* it. She also couldn't pay attention to anything anyone was saying. Trina told a story about something fabulous that Phoebe had done, Sam and Cora told a story about a pilgrimage they'd made to Powell's Books in Portland, Hunter and Nate got into a fight about whether the Mariners were having a rebuilding year or if their GM was just an incompetent bastard. But the only thing in Becca's head was Griff's words: *I am sitting in the Toutle River rest area off I-5, feeling like I just won the lottery.*

They were the longest two hours of her life. But the man she wanted most was well worth holding out for.

49

He rang the doorbell at Nate and Alia's and it opened slowly, revealing Becca wearing jeans and a scoop neck pink T-shirt that bared a delicious helping of curves.

Not that he noticed.

"Hey," Becca said. "Eyes up. Groveling before ogling."

She was grinning at him. A full-on Becca smile. It was impossible not to smile back.

He peered behind her. "It's awfully quiet back there."

"Robbie, Phoebe, and Clara are in bed. Everyone else went out to Bottoms Up. I don't think any of them actually wanted to be around when you showed up." She smirked. "Alia may have hinted about how traumatized she was by what she witnessed the last time...."

He made a chagrined face. "Yeah. The couch is off-limits." He smiled at her. "But hopefully that doesn't mean you're off-lim—?" he began, but she grabbed the back of his head and yanked him down. Her mouth was soft and warm, and she opened to the slightest tease of his tongue. And moaned. Which made him instantly hard.

"What if we just skip all the talking and I take you back to my room?" he whispered against the sensitive curl of her ear, and she shivered.

"Mmm," she murmured. She turned her head to capture his mouth again, twining her tongue against his in a way that made him think about other things he was going to do to her as soon as possible, preferably right now.

Then she drew back abruptly. "Wait, no. I don't need you to grovel, but I have things I need to say."

He chuckled, because she looked so fierce. "Shoot."

She drew a deep breath. "There are lots of things I should probably say, but I was thinking about it and the only one that actually matters is that I love you."

He couldn't keep the startled expression from showing on his face. She flinched, but to her credit, she straightened her shoulders and said, "I *do*. I love you, and I hope that you love me, but if you don't, that's okay, too. And for what it's worth, you were right. I looked at you and Marina and I saw what I've always seen in the past, which is that I'm not *enough*, not good enough or smart enough or pretty enough or worth sticking around for. And I can't promise I'll never make that mistake again because it's difficult to unlearn bad habits, but I'm working really hard on it. Because you make me want to be better all the time in all the ways."

"If it helps at all," Griff said, "I don't actually want you to be better. I want you to be exactly the way you are. And I love you. So much."

That made her laugh and cry at the same time, which

made him kiss her again. Until they had to break apart to breathe.

When she'd caught her breath, she said, "I also want to say that you don't *ever* have to worry that I will pull a Marina on you because I cannot fathom how any woman who had you for her happily ever after could possibly throw it away."

"Oh," he said, because she'd struck him speechless.

I cannot fathom how any woman who had you for her happily ever after could possibly throw it away.

"Becca," he said.

She looked terrified. She'd said a lot of things, and he knew better than anyone how hard that must be. She was a woman who'd been shown more than once that she wasn't "worth" the trouble, and he'd almost done what Nate had made him promise he wouldn't and reinforced that message. Still, she'd put everything on the line to tell him she loved him, and—

"I meant what I said about not wanting you to change. I never should have said that thing about you needing to grow up."

No," she said. "You were right. And like most of the things you say to me, it made me realize I had some things I needed to work out. It led to an overdue conversation with Alia about my needing a little more mental space."

"Right or wrong, it was cruel. I was angry and scared and I lashed out."

"I know," she said. "I forgot—I did the worst thing and blindsided you."

He shook his head. "You were just trying to make sense out of the Marina thing. I handled that so badly. That must have been confusing and awful—and then I didn't say the right things at all. I should have said that I had been an idiot for leaving my shit at her house for so long but that I was completely over her because you had blown her out of my head and my heart and there was only room for you. And I should have said that in the beginning I thought we were just playing but every time I was with you, I learned more about you and fell harder for you."

He ducked his head and kissed her, licking into her mouth until she clutched his head and whimpered. He released her, and she protested, but he had important things to say.

"One more thing," Griff said, drawing back even though it pained him. "I know I asked this before, but then I blew it. So I'm going to try again. How would you feel about coming back to Tierney Bay, and we could get a place together?"

Her mouth fell open.

"You don't have to answer that right away. But I thought you should know that I want us—both of us—to keep on growing up together. And I want every Friday Night Dinner from now on to be foreplay for what we do when we go home together. I want to wake up every morning and have donuts and coffee with you. I want All. The. Things."

Becca was laughing *and* crying, and he reached out and brushed tears back from both her cheeks, then took her face between his palms and kissed her until she stopped shaking.

"All the things is good," she said, when he let her go.

She reached her hand out and he took it. Her hand in his felt small but strong and warm.

She got a funny look on her face, and his stomach clenched with worry. She wasn't having second thoughts, was she?

"Or would it be *all the things* are *good*? I'd better learn to be grammatically correct if I'm going to be acting like an expert in the tutoring department," she said. The thought made her smile, thousands of lumens of glorious summer daylight, as she tipped her face up for another kiss.

50

Becca's chest felt tight as she rang the doorbell to the little Portland bungalow where her mother was now living. Part of her wished she'd taken Griff up on his offer to accompany her—or Alia, who'd said she and Robbie could serve as reinforcements. But no, this felt like something Becca needed to do on her own.

Footsteps approached the door and it swung open to reveal a woman so stunning in her familiarity that Becca almost took a step back from the impact. Her mother's face was framed with shoulder-length ash-blond hair, streaked with silver, and her face had new lines in it, but she was still the woman Becca remembered. The face moved slowly into a smile—tentative, a little fearful. "Becca," her mother said.

"Hi, Mom," Becca said.

There was an awkward moment where a hug might have happened for other mother-daughter pairs, and then her mother stepped back, revealing the living room behind her. "Do you want to come in?"

No, said something still wary inside Becca, but she ignored that voice and stepped forward. And got walloped by another familiar sight.

The couch was the couch of Becca's childhood, where she and Alia had sat to watch movies on the television—this television. The knickknacks on the mantle and tables were the ones she had played with, broken, repaired. She drew a deep breath, intending to steady herself, but *oh, God,* the room *smelled* like her childhood, as if the house were only a shell, and Becca suddenly, unexpectedly, found herself near tears.

"I'll make some tea," her mother said. She gestured to the couch, and Becca sat, trying not to breathe too deeply because if she did, she was going to start crying in earnest.

Her mother hurried into the kitchen, and Becca heard the hiss of an electric kettle and the clink of spoons on mugs before her mother reappeared with two steaming mugs. She handed one to Becca.

"Thank you for coming," she said, formally.

"I just thought—" Becca began, and stopped. She didn't have a plan. She hadn't rehearsed any words or decided what this visit was about. She'd simply woken one morning and thought that it was probably time. She and Griff had been together a couple of months, and her worries that he'd grow tired of her, or leave, or—she didn't even know what—had dried up and blown away in the face of his love and devotion.

Because Griff was not a man who stopped loving easily. She adored that about him above all else.

"Becca," her mother said, and Becca realized with a start that her mother was crying. "I'm so, so sorry. I wasn't there for you. I was a terrible mother."

Becca's first impulse was anger. She felt trapped by the apology. Because if she accepted it, did it mean her own suffering was swept away? And if she refused it, did it mean she was heartless? Her mother had, after all, done the best she could.

For a moment she hovered there, gobsmacked and miserable, and then her eye fell on a china shepherdess on the mantle. She'd loved that shepherdess, and she'd played with it over and over, until, inevitably, one day, she'd broken it. She'd sat over the pieces, crying, and Alia had found her and gathered her into a hug. And then her sister had dug in the junk drawers in the kitchen and found a tube of Krazy Glue (that Alia had, no doubt, herself purchased at the grocery store). Alia glued the shepherdess back together and said, "Look. Good as new."

Becca had cried more, then, because Little Becca knew there were cracks and she would never be as good as new.

But the newest version of Becca, Becca 3.0, saw things differently. Those cracked places, mended by her sister, were the strongest parts of that shepherdess.

Jenina was right, after all. New Becca's project had been to wall herself off so she couldn't be hurt, but that wasn't the trick. The trick was to love even though you could be hurt, and to trust that the people around you would help put you back together again.

And really, if this house was about anything, it wasn't about the woman sitting across from her, still uncertainly waiting for . . . something. It was about how Alia had made Becca safe and loved when safety and love were in short supply.

Becca was lucky. She had Alia and Nate and Robbie, Jake and Mira, Jenina, Griff—to name just a few of the people she knew would die before they'd let anything bad happen to her.

If you were well loved—and Becca was—then you could afford to be generous with your own love.

"You were hurting," Becca said, and tears rolled down her mother's face. With surprise, Becca realized there were tears on her own cheeks, too. She reached a hand out, touched her mother's knee, and her mother's hand wrapped around hers and held tight. "Do you remember," she said slowly to her mother, "how you used to make pompom caterpillars with us?"

After all, she wasn't a kid anymore. She didn't *need* her mother. But she could still *love* her.

Becca's mother nodded, her damp eyes raking over her daughter hungrily. In times past the needy look on her face would have set up a panicked craving in Becca—*she does love me!*—but now it only stirred the faint memory of a small girl who'd been disappointed too many times. *It's okay, little Becca,* Becca 3.0 told her oldest self. *We're good, no matter what.*

And she believed it.

"You don't by any chance still have any of those supplies lying around, do you?"

GRIFF PICKED her up two hours later. He took one look at her and said, "We're going to Voodoo Donuts."

"Do I look that bad?"

"You look like you need Voodoo Donuts. Anyway, we need to do a comparison with Dundee's."

He didn't ask what had happened with her mother. He talked at her instead, about CJ, who had driven his smoking hot Shelby Mustang to a bar the other night and taken home a leggy brunette. ("I saw him the next day. He was like a different man.")

She was super grateful to Griff for giving her a reprieve from having to talk about her mother. She needed a few minutes to put herself back together.

When they got to Voodoo and Becca saw the cases with all the crazy donuts—some topped with Froot Loops, others frosted in outrageous colors, every one a donut *event*—she said, "There's no comparison!"

Several minutes later, Griff bit into an eight mile cake and frowned. "I don't know," he said. "This is good, sure, but it's—it's distracting, you know? From the essence of donut."

Becca sampled a blueberry cake donut and had to agree. "It's like they're two different things, you know? A successful life would have to have both Voodoo and Dundee's donuts. Dundee's for Sunday mornings and Voodoo for celebrations."

"I think we can manage that."

It wasn't until he'd filled her with donuts that he asked her how it had gone.

"It was—it was really good to see her. I hugged her when I left, and she smelled like my mother, and that was—" Becca's eyes filled with tears. "I didn't *want* to love her, you know? But I think it might turn out to be one of those things I can't help."

"I know the feeling," he said, reaching out and pushing

her hair behind her ear. They smiled at each other. She could not stop feeling joyful that he was *hers*.

"She's finally found meds that work for her, and she's dating this guy, Chaz—"

"Chaz?"

"Your name is Griff," Becca pointed out. "You can't judge."

"Griff is a respectable nickname for Griffin. Chaz is a total corruption of Charles."

"Anyway, she's doing well, and she's happy. For now," Becca said. "And I told her about you—"

"What did you tell her?"

"Well," Becca said, "I said you were very good-looking. And very supportive. And that you'd taken my V-card and ruined me for every other guy in the universe—"

"You did *not*!"

"No," she admitted. "I didn't tell her that. But it's true."

Griff looked very pleased with himself, which had a funny effect on Becca's southerly geography.

Griff set down his donut and cocked his head. "Do you want to know what I was doing while you were with your mother?"

"I thought you were checking out Powell's."

"Nah. Not much of a reader," he admitted. "I was checking out Portland's downtown hotel scene. And I think I figured out where we're spending the night. I found a whirlpool suite for us. Hot tub in room. Haven't had sex in a hot tub yet, have you?" He smirked at her.

She grinned at him. "You would know."

"Hurry up and finish that donut," he said. "Wait. You have a sprinkle on your upper lip." He grabbed her hand, tugged her forward, and kissed it off. Becca bit back a groan.

She set her donut down.

"Let's go," she said.

Griff's mouth fell open. "Wait a second. You're leaving *mid-donut*?"

"Some things are better than food."

EPILOGUE

Becca flounced through the door and threw herself down on the couch in her and Griff's rental cottage with a dramatic flourish. She tossed her phone aside with the text from her mother still illuminated on the screen.

"That good?" he asked her, with a smile.

"Who knew that my own mother would turn out to be the biggest bridezilla in three counties?" she asked. Her mother and Chaz were tying the knot, and Becca was helping her mother plan the wedding.

"And how does that make you *feel*?" Griff teased. "Tell Dr. Griff everything. I bet he can make it all better."

She rolled her eyes at him, but she was smiling now. He'd already made it better. He made it better by just existing. And she was so damn proud of him. He'd continued leading the support groups. He still had flashbacks, because that trauma was part of him, lodged deep where it would take years—or a lifetime—to purge the poison, but now he went to his own therapist and learned the best techniques for wrestling PTSD to the mat. He was finishing his bachelor's degree online, and his long-term plan was to get a counseling degree and become a therapist himself.

He was also happier than she'd ever seen him, despite the stress of being privy to some of people's hardest moments. He worried about his peers, he suffered with them—but he also lived their successes, small and big, the moments when they walked again, worked again, got their GEDs, spoke their toughest truths. When they told him they felt whole and that he'd helped them heal.

"Tell Dr. Griff about your day," he suggested.

"Work was good. I came up with a new system for dealing with the VA paperwork."

"Of course you did," he said fondly. "The VA will probably be using your system by next week."

"I spent a couple of hours at KidsUp. Jed let me talk him into entering a writing contest about dealing with academic challenge. If he wins, he'll get a $2,000 scholarship."

"He's still letting you talk to him about going to college?"

"He made me a deal," Becca said. "He'll consider it if I agree to think about it too. He wants me to get a teaching degree."

A few months into their working together, Jed had asked Becca why she wasn't a teacher, and Becca had had to admit that she'd never gone to college. Since then, he'd been steadily harassing her, as stern with her as she'd ever been with him. But now she had the best possible reason to give in—because she wanted Jed to go to college more than she feared going herself.

Griff grinned at her. "Tough kid."

"The best," she said.

"Second best," he said, inclining his eyes towards the

photo on his desk, of Robbie. "Soon to be *third* best," he added, because Alia was several months pregnant with a sister for Robbie. "And speaking of . . . Alia and Nate are making grilled pork chops in adobo with applesauce."

"Ohhh," Becca moaned.

Griff made a sound that was halfway between a grunt and a growl.

"How does *that* make you feel?" Becca teased. She was well versed now in how her appetites stoked Griff's.

Griff rose from his seat and stalked towards the couch.

"If you're troubled, Dr. Griff can help," said Becca, struggling to suppress her laughter. Then Griff was kneeling over her, lowering his mouth to hers, and her giggles were swallowed by his warm mouth and swept away by the bliss of his tongue stroking hers. He broke the kiss and rocked back on his heels. "God, Becca."

He slid a palm down her belly and eased his hand under the waistband of her pants. His fingers parted her curls and found her clit.

"Uh—" she said. Words were giving her trouble. "Griff. We'll be late."

"Fuck being on time," he said, but he withdrew his hand from her pants, reaching into his own pants to reposition himself. Not that it helped. His jeans were broadcasting his state loud and clear.

"You said you wanted Friday Night Dinner to be foreplay for the rest of our lives," she said helpfully.

"I did say that, didn't I?" he growled. He scooped her up. "I was full of shit. Friday Night Dinner will be the palate-cleanser between sex beforehand and sex afterward."

He carried her down the hall and set her on her feet in the bathroom.

Their place was a small rental on one of Tierney Bay's adorable side streets. They could walk down to the ocean and have their donuts and coffee there. Plus, they could be louder than they'd ever felt comfortable being in Griff's tiny room. They were saving to buy their own place and would be able to afford something later this year.

Meanwhile, they had discovered some great features of the rental. Like the fact that the detachable nozzle in the shower could make Becca come in under thirty seconds. Which made shower quickies especially fantastic. And especially efficient, since Becca's pleasure pulled Griff's trigger like nothing else.

A few minutes later they were clean, damp-haired, and seated in Griff's truck on the way to Alia and Nate's house.

"If she tries to start talking about my mom's wedding," Becca said, "You need to suggest a game of Taboo. I can't take any more."

Griff laughed. "Will do."

All their friends and family members had long since gotten over their hang-ups about Griff and Becca dating, and now it was just the way things were. In general, Nate and Alia had backed way off on their overprotectiveness of Becca, but she knew from time to time she'd have to remind her sister that she was a big girl.

But she didn't mind. Alia needed to be needed and probably always would, and until she had five or six kids crowding up the house and demanding a hundred percent of her attention, Becca would always be on her radar screen.

"I always like playing Taboo with you, anyway," Griff said.

"Reminds me of the night when you asked me to be your personal Jondalar."

"You did a very good job," she murmured.

"It was not a hardship," he murmured back.

"Stop or we will not make it to Friday Night Dinner."

He was quiet for a stretch, then said, "Becca."

"Mmm?"

"I still think of myself as your personal Jondalar."

"You do *not*."

"I do."

"It's the Wonder Schlong thing, right?" she teased.

"Well, there's that," he said, modestly.

She blew a raspberry at him.

"Seriously, though, baby. You know what it is?"

His voice had gotten, suddenly, much more serious.

"What?" she asked.

"Every time, Becca. Every time with you, it's like the first time. And the best part is? I know it always will be."

ACKNOWLEDGMENTS

This book is the first one I have written "on my own" since first becoming traditionally published in 2012, but I never, ever felt alone.

My family has been unfalteringly supportive of me, even (or, especially) when I ruin dinner because I'm writing or making teaser graphics. My husband is basically a saint. In addition to loving and supporting me in everything I've ever done writing-wise, he has been lending his skills overtime in his tech support and business analyst roles. And my kiddos are so full of faith in me—may you both be rewarded with your loved ones' faith, in turn. I love you guys.

I have had the pleasure of working, for the first time since *To Have and to Hold* was published in 2016, with the fabulous Sarah Murphy, an incredibly talented developmental editor. She has the rare talent for seeing what a book is *trying* to be before it's there, and the even rarer talent of communicating to the frazzled author what that is. Sarah, I love you, and I couldn't have done this without you.

One of the great joys of this project has been meeting new

experts, including my copyeditor, Jaime Green, whose keen eye and wry wit made the final stages of editing this book a delight. Also, Jaime shares my affection for Jean Auel's *The Valley of Horses*, and any fan of Jondalar is a friend of mine ...

The very best professionals are experts at both hands-on and hands-off, and Emily Sylvan Kim, my beloved agent, has been a superhero of both in the time we've worked together. Thank you, Emily, for supporting me on this project—it means so, so much to me.

Once again, Jessica Scott contributed insight into army matters—in this case, invaluable perspective. Any factual errors in the book are strictly my own.

I want to particularly thank Melissa McCulloch for her wisdom on design issues—she was abundantly generous with her time and knowledge, and I learned so much from her. Plus, I had a blast doing it—Melissa, I adore you.

Because this book is part of my indie launch of this series, I also have quite a few additional people to thank, people who have been instrumental in helping me find the courage and learn the resources necessary to get this whole series back out in the world: Amber Belldene, Karen Booth, Sarina Bowen, Cheryl Cain, Dylann Crush, Kate Davies, Christine D'Abo (with sugar and post-its on top), Gretchen Douma, Nicole French, Rachel Grant (see, again, my dedication!), Molly Hays, Gwen Hayes, Gwen Hernandez, Sierra Hill, Christy Hovland, Mira Lyn Kelly, Kris Kennedy, Claire Kingsley, Jaycee Lee, Tamara Lush, Kathy McGowan, Alexa Rowan, Reese Ryan, Ellen Schroer, Jessica Scott (again), Lauren Seilnacht, Sierra Simone, Darya Swingle, Skye Warren, the attendees of Seattle Unconference 2018, the members of The Corner of Smart and Sexy, the members of Emerald City

Author Chicks, the members of Living the Dream Master-mind, the members of LS Author Coup, and about a bajillion other people. I hope I'm not forgetting anyone, but I might be, because there are so, so many generous authors out there willing to buoy each other up, and everyone I turned to during this process gave their time and support generously.

ALSO BY SERENA BELL

Returning Home

Hold On Tight

Can't Hold Back

To Have and to Hold

Holding Out

Tierney Bay

So Close

So True

So Good (2021)

So Right (2022)

Sexy Single Dads

Do Over

Head Over Heels

Sleepover

New York Glitz

Still So Hot!

Hot & Bothered

Standalone

Turn Up the Heat

ABOUT THE AUTHOR

USA Today bestselling author Serena Bell writes richly emotional stories about big-hearted characters with real troubles and the people who are strong and generous enough to love them. A former journalist, Serena has always believed that everyone has an amazing story to tell if you listen carefully, and she adores scribbling in her tiny garret office, mainlining chocolate and bringing to life the tales in her head.

Serena's books have earned many honors, including an RT Reviewers' Choice Award, Apple Books Best Book of the Month, and Amazon Best Book of the Year for Romance.

When not writing, Serena loves to spend time with her college-sweetheart husband and two hilarious kiddos—all of whom are incredibly tolerant not just of Serena's imaginary friends but also her enormous collection of constantly changing and passionately embraced hobbies, ranging from needlepoint to board games to meditation.